# CARTEL

THE JASON KING FILES BOOK ONE

MATT ROGERS

## BOOKS BY MATT ROGERS

### THE JASON KING SERIES

Isolated (Book 1)

Imprisoned (Book 2)

Reloaded (Book 3)

Betrayed (Book 4)

Corrupted (Book 5)

Hunted (Book 6)

### THE JASON KING FILES

Cartel (Book 1)

*"Welcome to Tijuana...*
*Where life is worth a lot*
*And death is a business"*

— Roberto Castillo

# 1

*Tijuana, Mexico*
*June 23, 2007*

Joaquín Ramos shifted his grip on the steel baton.

A fat droplet of blood fell from the tip of the weapon and splashed onto the dirty concrete floor. In the sudden quiet of the humid warehouse basement, the impact made a distinctive *plink*. He glanced down at the crimson ball and spat in its direction.

The man across from him whimpered from his seated position, hunched over in defeat. The chair he rested on had been carried down from the derelict interior above their heads — its frame was still coated in dust and muck. No-one had used this place in years. What was once a thriving *maquiladora* factory that imported foreign parts and assembled them for future export now lay dormant.

Ramos touched the steel club to the man's bloody forehead and pushed him gently into an upright position.

'What were you doing on my property?' he said for the third time.

'Come on, Joaquín,' the man whimpered. 'We grew up together, cabrón...'

Ramos cocked his head. It was true — he had spent many years working terrible jobs alongside the whimpering mess sitting across from him. Which meant he understood the informal use of the word "*cabrón*". Such a term could be misconstrued in other parts of the Spanish-speaking world.

He took the tip of the baton off the man's sweaty forehead and jabbed it into the ball of his throat, pinning him uncomfortably against the chair back. 'You will talk to me like a businessman, not a friend. That's what this discussion is.'

'Okay...'

'What were you doing on my property?'

Ramos had found the man snooping around the unkempt perimeter of one of his processing facilities. He had spent many painstaking months setting up the site in total secrecy, and given the man's rumoured ties to one of the rival cartels in Tijuana, Ramos was taking no chances. He knew the man's name due to their past shared experiences — yet he refused to think it or speak it. It was better to treat him as a soulless piece of meat, given what might have to transpire if certain unpleasant details were uncovered over the course of the interrogation.

A thick glob of saliva and blood dripped from the corner of the man's lips. It splattered across the seat between his legs. Ramos grimaced and rolled up the sleeves of his sweat-soaked shirt — revealing meaty forearms covered in weather-beaten brown skin.

His riches had not come without a certain level of elbow grease.

'You going to answer me?' he whispered.

The man in front of him shivered. He would know that

as Ramos' tone decreased in volume, his infuriation heightened. The man had been in the presence of such instances many times before.

Never on the receiving end, though.

'Please...'

'Why don't you want to talk?' Ramos said. He caught three droplets of sweat from his grimy forehead before they ran into his eyes and used the liquid to slick strands of unkempt hair back off his forehead. Interrogations were unsanitary. He had learnt that long ago. 'You're worried I'll see straight through your lies.'

The man lifted his head and snivelled. Tears had formed in his eyes. 'If I tell you anything, my fate is sealed.'

'It's sealed now.'

The man bowed his head. 'We were like brothers.'

'*Were,*' Ramos snarled. 'This is business. Business is ruthless.'

'This isn't you. The old you was different.'

'The old me was *nothing*. The old me worked for less than minimum wage in a box factory. The old me couldn't afford shit. You know that better than anyone.'

Silence.

Maybe the man across from him was recalling Ramos' distress as his mother wilted away, riddled with cancer and unable to afford treatment. Ramos had certainly not forgotten. Hence his ruthless pursuit of expansion. Hence his determination to never have to want for money again.

'What were you doing on my property?'

The fifth time he had asked the question.

There would not be a sixth.

'I will fry you like I did to many of the men you work for,' Ramos said, low and cruel. Both a threat, and a subtle acknowledgement that he knew the true nature of the man's presence on the site's perimeter.

*The Draco cartel.*

'Then do it,' the man said.

'It doesn't have to be like this.'

The man lifted his head. 'Like I said before — if I say a word, they will only do worse.'

'So you admit they recruited you?'

A pause, then a nod. 'I wouldn't lie to you.'

'What are they planning?' Ramos said, his pulse rising. 'Why are they interfering with my business?'

The man scoffed. 'Really, Joaquín? You are interfering with theirs. That much is clear. They've had this city on lockdown for a decade.'

'I'm the new breed.'

'They don't appreciate that.'

'I never expected them to.'

'Then let me go,' the man said. 'I swear, Joaquín, I'll get the fuck out of Tijuana and never come back. I'll never speak of you or anyone in this godforsaken city again. Please...'

Ramos listened to the spiel, then crouched down on the dusty basement floor. He was close enough to smell the sweat leaking from the man's pores, hear the sharp intake of breath as he rapidly pumped oxygen into his lungs in an attempt to stifle the terror.

'And what example would that set, my friend?' Ramos said.

The finality of the rhetorical question set in.

The man whimpered softly — then he exploded off the chair in one swift motion. The sound of his feet scuffling on the concrete floor echoed off the walls. He made a beeline for the stairs leading up to the ground floor.

Ramos caught him by the throat in a vice-like grip and threw him to the floor. The man landed on his back, knocking the breath out of his lungs in a burst of exhalation. Then his head followed, snapping back against the concrete loud enough to twist even the most hardened stomachs.

When his skull bounced off the floor, it met the length of Ramos' baton. He swung the club with lethal intentions. The blow ruptured the soft tissue of the man's face.

If it didn't kill him, the next four strikes did.

Ramos turned away from the disfigured body and shrugged off a chill. Despite the stifling heat of the basement and the sweat coating him from head to toe, a wave of sudden cold washed over him. It was a foreign sensation that came from within — unpleasant as all hell.

Ramos knew what it was.

Discomfort.

But that's what this business was about. If he wanted to remain in his comfort zone, he never would have made a single dollar as the head of a new cartel. Every day he had to push himself to do the unpleasant but necessary tasks that a figure of power was required to carry out.

Including killing old friends.

He had to maintain his aura of invincibility and unhinged menace, his reputation for reckless forward motion. His reputation as a man who never backed away from a challenge. That's how he had wormed his way into this position — and it's how he would climb his way to the top.

Through ruthlessness.

Through devastation of all competition.

He had heard stories of — and sometimes been inadvertently involved in — the cartel wars of the past. Now, as he made for the stairs that would lead out of his hellhole, he realised he was the first in a new generation.

Those who didn't begrudgingly accept their place in society.

No-one resisted the Draco cartel because no-one knew any better. They enforced their hold on Tijuana through extortion and a reign of terror. Ramos considered himself a man of the people. He would destroy the Draco cartel piece by piece without them ever knowing it was him, and then he would appeal to the masses who had been oppressed by the group.

His cartel was low on numbers, but rapidly expanding.

And he had momentum on his side.

As he reached the doorway and planted a dusty trainer on the first step, a sharp electronic beep rang through the basement.

He froze.

'What the...' he whispered.

He turned back to the grisly remains of the man he'd beaten to death and noticed a dull artificial light blinking in the lip of his pant pocket. When the man had fallen to the ground, the device must have become dislodged from the bottom lining of his pocket. That's why Ramos hadn't come across it on his initial search.

He crossed back to the corpse and tugged the small black rectangle free from the displaced lining, tearing strands of fabric in the process. He scrutinised it. It was some kind of panic button — used to call upon reinforcements in the event that the man found himself in trouble.

Ramos had no doubt that the man had activated it at some point during the interrogation.

'You slimy fuck,' he muttered.

Above his head, the distinctive sound of an approaching

car engine made him freeze. Tyres squealed, and doors slammed.

Ramos hadn't brought any help. He was alone, and trapped. He cursed himself for his inexperience. Errors in judgment seemed to present themselves on a consistent basis these days, largely due to the brash nature of his cartel's rapid expansion.

He'd backed himself into a corner.

Once again.

There was a cluster of broken furniture hoarded into one corner of the rundown space. The only illumination down here came from a flickering bulb fixed into the ceiling in the centre of the room, which plunged each of the corners into shadow. Ramos slid a semi-automatic Glock pistol from his waistband — smuggled across the border after being plucked out of unnoticed U.S. Army surplus by a bribed serviceman — and tucked himself into the darkness behind a rotting desk.

He waited with a pounding heart.

It wasn't the Draco cartel. A man and a woman came tearing down the stairs at a tactically dangerous pace, probably worried that their contact had met an untimely demise. They were attempting to compensate for such a delayed response. They both wore black khakis and baggy black polyester jackets, despite the Mexican heat. Both swept standard-issue U.S. firearms over the room. Both were white.

Law enforcement.

*Traitorous bastard,* Ramos thought of the dead man.

He kept himself pressed to the filthy floor. Sweat leaked out of his hair — he ignored it.

The pair noticed the corpse in the centre of the room. Their eyes boggled at the grotesque nature of his injuries and they lowered their weapons, all their attention seized by the body.

*Amateurs.*

'My God,' the man said, and his accent confirmed Ramos' worst suspicions.

*They're American.*

He looked at the corpse occupying the pair's attention.

*What the fuck were you doing talking to Americans, my friend?*

'Do we know who it was?' the man said.

'Whoever owns that facility,' the woman said softly, as if hesitant to disturb the dead.

'Five years,' the man said, staring into space. 'Five fucking years we've used this guy. We're back to square one.'

'This needs to go to D.O.D. It's beyond us.'

Ramos rose into view when the perfect opportunity presented itself. The Americans had spent the entire conversation fixated on the corpse at their feet, still slightly aware of their surroundings. They thought they were well and truly alone — but when their eyes met upon the mention of the Department of Defence, their guard dropped away entirely.

Ramos stood up and shot them both twice each in the stomach, targeting the liver and other juicy internal organs with expert precision. The gunshots were like bombs dropping in the contained room. They roared and cracked off the walls.

Both of them dropped in ungainly fashion, their faces paling in an instant, the sidearms in their hands cascading to the dusty floor and scattering away. All important motor functions were temporarily impaired as the overwhelming agony took hold.

Ramos smiled and stepped out from behind the desk.

'You two have not been in the field long, have you?' he said, speaking English for the first time that day.

The woman was mortally wounded, already slipping into unconsciousness, and the man wasn't far behind. Ramos crossed to where he lay on his back and wrenched open his jacket, yanking an identification badge out of his inside pocket. He regarded the insignia with a mounting fury.

'DEA?' he said incredulously. 'You're *DEA?!*'

Neither responded. The woman's eyes closed — either dead, or close to it. The man flapped his lips like a dying fish. It seemed he was trying to form a sentence, yet the massive internal bleeding prevented a single syllable from leaving his mouth.

'What the fuck is the Drug Enforcement Agency doing over the border?' Ramos said.

He squatted down, so his face was mere inches from the American man.

'Should have stuck to your jurisdiction, my friend,' he whispered.

He followed it up with a fifth bullet, sending it through the man's forehead. The exit wound splattered gore across the concrete underneath his head.

Ramos got to his feet, tucked the gun back into his waistband, and made for the stairs again.

*An interesting development.*

He'd roll with it. The United States could keep sending their agents, for all he cared.

He'd send them back in bodybags for as long as he drew a waking breath.

# 2

*The Pentagon, Washington D.C.*
*June 24, 2007*

Lars Crawford had never held much interest in official military procedures.

He shuffled through the high-ceilinged hallways of the Pentagon with intent in his stride. The tie that usually adorned his uniform had been left in the car. Whenever something captured his attention so completely, structure and demeanour went out the window.

He was cerebral in that regard.

Which was likely half the reason he had received the call this morning to report to the Pentagon as soon as humanly possible.

His dream had finally been approved.

Soon, he would be accomplishing great things.

He could barely contain his excitement.

He moved from the open public corridors of the Pentagon to the smaller, tighter maze of interlocked passageways that led to all manner of backrooms and private quarters. He had been told to report to a certain office — one he had never set foot in before. Nevertheless, he knew the Pentagon like the back of his hand — a feat few could boast about — and he had little trouble finding the right door. A photographic memory had certain advantages.

It was an indiscriminate wood-panelled thing, set into the wall with no plate signifying what lay beyond. Lars twisted the handle and pushed it open and strode purposefully into the sweeping carpeted office.

He came face to face with the General of the Army himself.

'Oh, shit,' Lars muttered, before composing himself and offering a brief salute. The General extended a hand, and Lars shook it firmly.

There were three other men in the room. Lars didn't recognise any of them — despite his savant-level memory he wasted little time on becoming familiar with the upper echelon of the military — but the medals and ribbons adorning their uniforms said it all.

They were important.

'Is this about my request, sir?' he said, unable to contain his hope.

The General gestured to an empty chair. 'Sit.'

Lars sat.

The General skirted around to the other side of the broad oak desk and took a seat. He was flanked by the other commissioned officers — two to the left and one on the right. He drummed his fingertips on the desk and stared at Lars with noticeable uneasiness flashing in his eyes.

'We've only spoken over the phone,' the General said.

Lars nodded. 'It's an honour to finally meet you in the flesh, sir.'

'You too. I had a look over your files. You've done excellent work so far. That's half the reason you're here.'

Lars stifled a beam of joy. It was true — he had accomplished a lot during his years working for the Defence Advanced Research Projects Agency, more commonly known as DARPA. Much like the men in the division he was looking to create, he had been accelerated through the ranks of his organisation at an astonishing rate. He didn't shy away from the promotions — they allowed him greater responsibility, and he appreciated the generous salary packages as a bonus.

'I wish it didn't have to come to this, to be frank,' the General said. 'Initially, I dismissed your proposal.'

'Oh...?'

'We have a rapidly escalating situation in Tijuana. Tensions are reaching a boiling point. I think the division you're looking to form would be uniquely applicable to what's going on.'

'Mexico?'

'Yes.'

'What are we doing in Mexico?'

'We *were* keeping tabs on a radical new cartel that sprang to life in the area. They're aggravating both the existing drug empire and local law enforcement alike. Muscling their way into the game by any means necessary. It seems to be working — despite the risk involved with their rapid growth.'

'Is that our concern, sir?'

'Not particularly. But ultimately most of the product ends up here. The coca's grown in Colombia, and converted into cocaine in jungle labs in Guatemala and Honduras. It's packaged and sent through to Mexico, and smuggled across the border at any number of crossings. It makes the border towns violent as all hell. You control the crossings, you control the game. We've always kept tabs on certain hotspots — places with the highest threat of descending into all-out war. It seems like things have kicked off in Tijuana. I gave the order to passively watch this newly-emerging cartel — to see if anything comes of it. I'm sure you can understand that we weren't supposed to be anywhere near it.'

'I understand.'

'The two DEA agents we had on the ground in Tijuana are dead. Shot mercilessly in the basement of an abandoned factory. They responded to a distress call from our informant. He's dead too. Killed by blunt force trauma, according to local authorities.'

'Shit.'

'Precisely my thoughts,' the General said.

'Wait...' Lars said. 'Does this mean—?'

The General nodded. 'I'm reluctant to green-light your project, but something in the dossiers you sent over grabbed me. These circumstances presented themselves, and I'm relenting. You get a trial run.'

'Is any of this official?'

'Not a word. This is black operations. Nothing's on the books, and nothing will be acknowledged by our country. Understood?'

'Of course. I've spent months on this, sir.'

'You get one shot. If this fails, it'll be even more expensive than usual. You know how much it costs to keep a Navy SEAL in the field?'

'Roughly a million dollars a year,' Lars said.

He knew that much.

'Precisely. It takes half that to get them there in the first place, once you add close to a year of training. Underwater demolition, advanced skills, redeployment — not to mention all the basic Navy training. The elite of the elite are goddamn expensive.'

'I thought black operations had access to all kinds of funds.'

'They certainly do,' the General said. 'That doesn't mean I want to waste them. You have a blank cheque, but what you do with it is of the utmost importance. Understood?'

'Of course.'

One of the officers — a surly fifty-something man with greying hair and hard lines creased into his forehead — piped up. 'I don't like this.'

Lars hesitated. 'I don't think this kind of thing transpires from perfect situations, sir. It's uncomfortable, but necessary.'

'Bullshit,' the man said. 'I've read the dossiers. All your papers on reflexes, and all that other shit. None of it matters in the field. Solo operations don't work.'

'I think they can,' Lars said. 'With the right men. My vision for this project involves only a handful of soldiers. Selected from DEVGRU, SEALs — whoever has the best. Vetted, tested, their mental data recorded in ways that are only just developing.'

'I've read it,' the man said, interrupting. 'Spare me. Sounds like a fairytale.'

'Some men work better alone,' Lars said.

'I disagree.'

'Prove us wrong,' the General said. 'I certainly want you to. I don't want a team heading into Tijuana. This is close to the most sensitive operation I've approved in years. Use your screening process — see if it works. Select whoever you want from our ranks. If they accept, we'll send them into Mexico. We need to come down hard on anyone who puts a finger on U.S. officials. There was an unspoken rule not to touch us, at risk of severe consequences. At least, I thought there was. The existing cartel in Tijuana have wordlessly followed it for years.'

'Are we on their side?'

'We're on our own side. Cartels are cruel, malicious entities — all of them. It's the nature of the drug trade. But we can't win that war quickly. We can, however, send a message that the DEA — or any U.S. officials — are not to be interfered with, under *any* circumstances.'

Lars nodded.

'Lars,' the General said, boring into him with a fixed gaze. 'My reputation is on the line here. Do not fuck this up.'

'Understood, sir.'

'You're green-lit. Get to work.'

Lars reached a hand across the table, struggling to prevent his fingers from trembling with anticipation. The General locked it once again in a vice-like grip. 'I'm going to fly out to the facility you set up. If this pays off, it might just be the greatest development in the history of secret operations.'

'I agree,' Lars said. 'That's why I proposed it.'

'You're sending a man to his death,' the surly officer said. 'You'll be wasting a prodigy. The SEALs focus on co-operation for a reason.'

'Because they've been set in their ways,' Lars said. 'I'm looking for the new breed. Lone warriors.'

'Like I said, fairytale bullshit.'

The General said, 'Do you have anyone in mind so far?'

Lars paused. 'Have you heard of Jason King?'

# 3

*Curt Gowdy State Park, Wyoming*
*June 26, 2007*

In a rundown log cabin on the edge of a vast field of green, Jason King jolted awake, torn from unconsciousness by the distant howling of a siren.

It was his third day in the isolation camp, and the experience so far had been close to hell.

He rolled off the mattress — thin as shit and barely able to provide a shred of comfort — and tugged a thin, long-sleeved cotton shirt over his frame. Three strands of thick brown hair drooped over his eyes. He tucked them behind his ears and swept the rest of his hair back off his forehead.

Even though the two had never met, King had similarly little regard for official military uniform as Lars Crawford.

Delta Force operatives seldom did.

He had come to learn that many of the rigorous disciplines and practices instilled in him from an accelerated SEAL training course were disregarded when one reached this level of the game. Delta operatives grew their hair and beards as they liked. They wore what they liked.

They armed themselves with what they liked.

During his two-year stint in the unit, he had also come to learn that youth was seen as an irreconcilable black mark in the Delta Force.

He was twenty-two years old. Through either sheer dumb luck or actual talent, he had made it into Operational Detachment-D — someone had told him he was the youngest recruit in the organisation's history. He had six months of basic Navy training and a year and a half of SEAL training under his belt. For reasons unbeknownst to him, he had been thrust from division to division with little patience, accelerated to greater heights with each passing month.

He chalked it up to a mixture of a strong build, natural athleticism, a sharp mind, and unwavering self-discipline that had provided him with the results he'd achieved.

There was movement in the bunk above his head, and a moment later a man dropped onto the wood-panelled floor of the cabin. This man also took full advantage of the allowances Delta operatives were offered — his hair was dreadlocked, tied back in a thick ponytail at all times.

His name was Dirk Wiggins.

He was King's only friend in the unit.

'How'd you sleep?' King said, still bleary-eyed and half-asleep.

'Could have been better,' Dirk said. 'But at least we're not in the barracks.'

King nodded understandingly.

Dirk was twenty-nine, and one of the youngest men in the Force apart from King. The pair had been separated from the rest of the unit for the extent of this isolation camp after tensions had risen the previous evening.

Truth was, King lived in an almost perpetual state of stress.

He'd done so since he was first invited to join the ranks of Operational Detachment-D.

Special Forces soldiers were often touted as a brotherhood in all the media King had ever seen on the subject. It couldn't have felt further from the truth. It was a result of the age barrier — King was separated from the rest of the squadron by at least ten years. They were collectively older, more experienced, hardened to the stoic nature of an operative's life. They functioned as a collective hive-mind, in tune with each other and able to effortlessly co-ordinate as a tight-knit unit.

King never let his weakness and inexperience show — but that didn't matter.

Whether they intended to create it or not, a noticeable barrier had formed, preventing acceptance into the ranks.

An event that spelled disaster in the upper echelon of the Special Forces.

King wondered how long it would take before they kicked him out.

Frankly, he wondered why that decision hadn't been made already.

Subconsciously, he knew why.

None of them could touch him in a fight. He posted the most consistent results in the rigorous firearms testing. Maybe that was why they shunned him — whether they liked to admit it or not, he was damn good at his job. At twenty-two, that was likely to infuriate plenty of them — especially since it was easy to ascribe King's results to God-given ability and natural talent rather than sheer hard work.

They rarely let their disgruntlement show.

There was no room for petty competition at this level of the game.

But they shut him out all the same.

The alarm petered out, replaced by an eerie silence. The piercing shrill had scared off the flocks of birds that usually milled around the woods. They stayed quiet in the aftermath of the racket. King listened to the wood cabin softly creaking all around him as he stepped into heavy-duty combat boots and shuffled out into the morning fog.

It was barely light.

He looked out over the clearing, tucked into an off-limits section of Curt Gowdy State Park. Francis E. Warren Air Force Base lay twenty miles to the east, but the thick woodland provided more seclusion than the dry, roiling plains of Cheyenne. Delta Force operatives were trained separately to ordinary soldiers, for obvious reasons.

The isolation camp had been designed to test their physical and mental limits, but despite the gruelling exercise and training that came along with such a program, King found solace in the actions. His squad had returned from the Middle-East three weeks previously, and he wanted to put everything that had happened behind him.

As if reading his thoughts, Dirk piped up next to him. 'Has anyone questioned you about Ramadi yet?'

*Ramadi, Iran.*

A city he would love to tuck away in the deepest, darkest hole of his memory. He was still conflicted about what had unfolded.

'No,' King said.

'You think they will?'

'I assume so. I broke protocol.'

'Not really...'

'You were there, Dirk.'

The man nodded. 'You think they'll chew you out?'

'We'll see.'

The pair made their way across the grassy field, their boots crunching through dew and flakes of ice. Winter in Wyoming was ruthless in its chill. King exhaled, watching as a thick cloud wafted out in front of his face. He bowed his head and made for the soft beacon of light coming from the other side of the clearing.

Exterior lights along the front of a long lodge-style building flickered into life, piercing through the gloom of dawn. King entered the building first, shoving a set of double doors inwards and stepping through into a rudimentary mess hall. Seven burly men spread across a handful of rickety trestle tables looked up from their chow.

All eyes on King.

He shrugged off their piercing glares and snatched up a plate to heap with chicken and rice and beans. They were taken care of in the culinary department. Their diets during the isolation camp had been set at four thousand calories a day in order to compensate for the unforgiving intensity of the training. King took care to always eat a little more. He had the frame for it.

As he crossed to an empty table, the hostility was palpable in the air.

'Bit late, brother,' David shot from across the room.

King looked up from his plate. The man was thirty-three. He'd been a Delta Force operative for five years. He used the same colloquialisms with King as he did the rest of the unit, but they felt oddly hollow when addressed to the young pup of the group.

King didn't imagine the man really thought of him as a brother.

'Sorry,' King said, and kept eating.

Long ago, he'd found that ignoring the subtle digs fared easier than reacting to them. He knew that the mental walls he'd erected weren't healthy, especially given the nature of his occupation. But he didn't care. He was sick of catering to the wit of the other operatives, deciding to replace his attempts to fit in with reserved silence.

He was drawing into himself, and he didn't know how to reverse it.

Especially after Iran.

He thought his actions might have brought the squad closer together, but in hindsight the only result that could have come from such a brash decision was disapproval.

Dirk dropped onto the bench next to him and tucked into his meal, ducking his head and employing full concentration on the food before him. King did the same. He'd come to appreciate the silence. It meant no-one was grilling him. It meant momentary calm.

From outside, the sharp barking of a pissed-off instructor tore through the reserved quiet of the mess hall. All nine of them abandoned their plates and dropped them back off at the kitchen counter, receiving curt nods from the chef as they returned their dishes. They shuffled out the door wordlessly, King and Dirk hanging back to allow the seven older members to pass through first.

Just another nuance that King had grown aware of.

Anything to make the day flow smoother.

The source of the harsh commands that had separated them from their breakfast was a five-foot-six drill instructor with a receding hairline and a horrible temper. Ironic, given that his specialty was yoga.

King had been through the routine for close to two years now. He knew the *vinyasas* and the sun salutations and the warrior poses off by heart, to the point where he took himself through the sixty-minute session on autopilot. It didn't take long to warm up. At first the icy grass underneath his palms chilled him to the core, but as the positions grew more difficult the sweat began to leech from his pores, materialising in unison with the piercing Wyoming sun.

By the time they finished the session, King guessed that he had shed close to a pound in bodyweight. When he'd first been promoted to Delta Force, he'd found the concept of yoga just as ridiculous as the other members had when they first joined. It posed a humorous sight to any onlookers — nine of the toughest, meanest men on the planet carrying themselves through a routine ordinarily reserved for middle-aged women in hot *bikram* studios.

But the benefits were astounding. After two years of relentless consistency in the practice, King had first-hand experience in its advantages — his muscles recovered faster, he could move in ways he'd never imagined, his dexterity had heightened considerably...

Operatives of their calibre had to be obscenely athletic.

This kept them that way.

King wiped a chain of sweat droplets off his forehead and flicked them to the grass below his boots. His heart thudded in his chest, and he felt the endorphins of physical exercise snaking their way through his system. He felt loose, like the tightness of sleep had been uncoiled by the workout.

It would have to be. He knew what lay ahead.

That was a warm-up for the fourth day of the isolation camp.

As he squinted in the sudden glare of the sun rising over the distant treetops, the low growl of an engine resonated across the clearing. The sound came from the same direction as the sun, making it hard to ascertain exactly who the new arrivals were.

When King pressed a hand to his eyebrows to shield his vision, the breath caught in his throat.

'Ah, shit...' he muttered.

Dirk mimicked his actions and followed his gaze. 'Think they're here about Iran?'

'Looks that way,' King said. 'We're not supposed to have visitors.'

A khaki-coloured open-topped jeep trawled across the empty field, churning the grass under its thick off-road tyres. There were four occupants — all men, all decked out in green service uniform indicating their importance. The passenger and the two men in the back seat looked to be in their fifties, with greying hair and wrinkled brows. The driver was younger — King guessed he was close to thirty — and seemed out of place amongst the old-school regality of his three comrades. He wore the same uniform, but it didn't seem to fit right. Like he had no interest in official procedure.

The jeep slowed in front of the cluster of nine sweat-soaked Delta Force operatives, and its occupants got out. The parties exchanged pleasantries in the form of salutes, before the drill instructor stepped forward.

'I have them for the day,' he said to the new arrivals. 'I wasn't expecting anyone. What's this about?'

The driver of the jeep turned to the instructor. 'I'm Lars Crawford — I'm with DARPA.'

'Okay.'

'These men,' Lars said, gesturing to the trio behind him, 'have come to verify the proceedings. You should have received word a few hours ago...'

'There's a lack of communication out here,' David said,

shoving his way to the front of the group. He kept his shoulders straight and his chin held high. Demanding attention. 'It's an isolation camp, after all.'

Lars stared at the man for less than a second before turning his attention to the other members of the party.

King watched the piercing gaze wander from face to face, analysing and dismissing each member in the blink of an eye. Finally, Lars' gaze came to rest on him.

'Jason King?' Lars said.

Informally, without a shred of diplomatic authority.

Like greeting an old friend.

'That's me,' King said.

*Here comes the interrogation,* he thought.

Several of the other operatives shifted uneasily, probably deep in thought as to what purpose King could serve to the mystery man before them.

'Get in the jeep,' Lars said. 'We've got places to be.'

# 4

The suspension underneath King's rear shuddered as the jeep diverted off the main trail, darting onto a narrow dirt track that could only allow one vehicle in each direction at a time.

He sat in the middle rear seat, flanked by a stern military official on either side. Lars drove, twisting the wheel from left to right in an effort to battle the loose dirt under the truck.

No-one said a word — not that they could if they wanted to. The lack of a frame meant that the wind was deafening, slicing at their faces and numbing their cheeks. King stared down at the rear footwell to shield his eyes from the icy bombardment.

Cold sweat dotted his brow. He chalked it up to the aftermath of the intense yoga workout, but deep down he knew the truth. He had made a serious error of judgment in Iran, and had been anticipating a response to his actions ever since he stepped foot back on U.S. soil. Briefly, he wondered if the rate at which he'd been yanked out of the isolation camp spelled grave consequences.

Maybe they were carting him off to a CIA black prison.

He'd heard rumours of those...

He quickly sized up the appropriate response if they moved to detain him. Elbow to the throat of the man on the left, headbutt to the right, scything front kick into the back of the driver's head. The front passenger was in no position to mount any kind of resistance.

Out the door before anyone was the wiser.

Disappear into the woods.

Start a new life...

He shook it off. Such thoughts were ridiculous — he didn't have it in himself to mount any kind of attack against military personnel. Call it code of conduct, call it morality. But it didn't stop his imagination from running wild as the jeep pulled up to a large steel warehouse buried in the backwoods of the state park.

The building lay in the centre of a dirt clearing, surrounded on all sides by thick forest. It appeared new. King guessed it had been constructed within the last two years.

'What's this?' he said as Lars killed the engine and thrust the driver's door outwards.

'New facility we built a few years ago. Hasn't been assigned a purpose yet. That's what we're here for — hopefully.'

'Are we still on military ground?'

Lars nodded. 'The very edge of our territory. There's some things even the Delta Force shouldn't know about.'

King gulped back apprehension. 'Should I be concerned?'

Lars twisted in his seat and flashed a glance back at King. 'No. Why would you be concerned?'

King hesitated. Either the man was an excellent actor and the question was a front, or he genuinely wasn't here about Ramadi. King had no choice either way. He had enlisted into the service of the United States Armed Forces, and he would begrudgingly comply with whatever they decided to do with him.

Even if that meant military prison.

With reserved caution, he followed the group out of the jeep and made his way over to the ominous structure. Up close, the warehouse dwarfed him, spearing into the sky like a giant artificial cube. It couldn't have looked more out of place amongst the otherwise-untouched flora surrounding them.

Lars led the pack, moving to a padlocked set of towering garage doors that led inside the corrugated iron building. He slipped a key into the lock and twisted, yanking the chain out of its slot a second later. He wrapped a hand around each handle and heaved the doors apart. They slid on their tracks with a horrendous groan, sending a nearby flock of birds careering away into the morning sky.

Lars gestured into the darkened space between the two roller doors. 'After you.'

King said nothing. He stifled a chill and stepped forward, heading straight through into the warehouse. He was steadfastly determined not to show hesitation or weakness of any kind. He had no idea what to expect.

The interior proved to consist of a single cavernous space, with a ceiling shrouded in shadow and a dusty concrete floor almost entirely devoid of furniture. Along the far wall, a thin wooden partition led through to a cluster of offices, which King guessed could be converted into living quarters if given the attention.

He shrugged off the unease as the emptiness of the warehouse revealed itself. This was no secret torture laboratory — it was an abandoned structure dropped into the shadows of the state park, not yet ascribed a purpose. Just as Lars had stated.

Some of the fear melted away.

Maybe they really did intend merely to ask questions.

Lars strode past him, heading for the only object currently in the warehouse — a fold-out plastic table with five chairs scattered around its perimeter. King glanced at a mass of documents sprawled across its surface.

'This all looks pretty informal,' he noted.

Lars nodded without turning back. 'We're running on a tight schedule here. Sit.'

His voice rang off the walls, sinister in its volume. King followed the man over to the set of chairs and dropped into one of them. The weak metal groaned under his two-hundred-and-twenty pounds of bodyweight. The trio of seemingly-mute officials who had accompanied them into the space followed suit, surrounding Lars on the other side of the table.

King noted the panel-like composition of the chairs.

The four officials on one side, their eyes scrutinising him, boring into him.

King on the other.

As if he were being prepared for a job interview.

He wondered what for.

Lars let the scrapes of chair legs against concrete fade into silence, until sheer quiet enveloped the inside of the warehouse. There was little natural light — that which spilled in through the high-set barred windows only served to accentuate the shadows. He crossed his fingers together, interlocking his hands, and leant forward across the table.

'Sorry for the abruptness of all this,' he said. 'I haven't had much time to prepare.'

'That's okay,' King said.

'We're going to have a conversation, and I'm going to make you an offer. If you choose to refuse, nothing that was discussed here will ever see the light of day. You'll return to your camp and pretend you never left. You'll erase all of this from your memory and carry on with your job. Understood?'

King nodded. 'Got it.'

'How's the Delta Force?'

'I'm sorry?'

'Tell me about your experience transitioning from basic Navy training, to the SEALs, to the Delta Force. It's somewhat unprecedented.'

'Is this a counselling session?'

'I'm simply asking you to tell me about it.'

'It's fine, I guess. I don't have time to think about it.'

'You don't shy away from embracing how your career has escalated? Twenty-two is a young age to be dealing with this shit.'

King shrugged. 'Like I said, I don't think about it. I just do it.'

'Do you enjoy it?'

'It's my job. There's not a lot to enjoy. I tolerate it.'

'But you haven't considered quitting? Even when the workload increases dramatically?'

'That's not my style.'

'Quite stoic,' Lars noted.

'I'm good at my job,' King said, deciding to voice just a touch of what had come to the forefront of his mind. 'I don't have to be cocky to understand that. I seem to have a unique talent for this sort of thing. It'd be selfish of me to quit. Right?'

Lars nodded. 'That's what I was thinking. Let's talk about—'

'Iran?'

A pause. 'No. I want to know about your fellow operatives. What do you think of them?'

'They're fine.'

'You get along with them?'

'We're in a volatile field. There's not much time for buddy-buddy talk.'

'There's a brotherhood, though,' Lars said. 'It's one of the most important aspects of the SEALs, and Delta embrace it too. You feel connected to your team?'

'Not really.'

Lars nodded, like he had already made a wide range of conclusions and was simply running them by King personally. 'You work better alone?'

'I've never worked alone.'

'Would you want to?'

'I don't know. I've never tried it.'

'If I were to offer you a position in a division specialising in black operations, how would you react?'

'I'd have questions.'

'And we'd be happy to answer all of them.'

'Is this a new venture?'

'It is.'

'Off the books?'

'Of course.'

'Did you come to me based on my performance results?'

'That was one aspect of it. I'm more interested in your tendency to branch away from the pack. It's a unique and largely untested aspect of your personality. The lone wolf approach. I'm under the impression that great things can be done with a man like you. I'm giving you the chance to test it.'

'Okay.'

'Okay — what?' Lars said.

'Sign me up.'

'What about your old unit? Do you want the chance to say goodbye?'

'It really doesn't bother me one way or the other.'

'I can see that. You hold no connection to them?'

'They shut me out. Because I'm so young. I guess I've been secretly hoping for the opportunity to participate in something like this. I always thought this secret world was a work of fiction.'

'This particular venture currently is,' Lars said. 'Hence our surroundings.'

'You didn't have time to set things up?'

'We were approved two days ago. Due to unforeseen circumstances. Something's presented itself that greatly interests the people in charge of this division. I'm firing on all cylinders here. If you're onboard, we have a week.'

'Until what?'

Lars shook his head. 'That comes later.'

'I want to know what I'm getting myself into.'

'You can't. Jason, I want you to weigh this decision very carefully. If the nature of the tasks you'll be elected to carry out bothers you, then I suggest you bid me goodbye and head back to the camp. Your personality's cerebral, but you need to think hard about this. You'll effectively adopt the role of a one-man-army, carrying out operations that a SEAL team would be encumbered by. Operations where a single man can slip through the cracks. Unimpeded by fellow squad members.'

'An assassin, you mean?'

'No. Anything the government deems appropriate. Personally I see the greatest benefit in hostage extraction, but time will tell. It's all just theories right now. Smoke and mirrors. If you're happy to proceed, we'll make it a reality.'

'Why me?'

'Like I said, a number of reasons. You're aware of your reaction speed, I'm sure.'

'What?'

'Your reflexes.'

'I don't really pay attention to all the testing they put us through. They don't share the results with us. I just do my job.'

'You're off the charts.'

'Nice to know.'

'Here's my standpoint,' Lars said, leaning forward. 'This is all just speculation, but here goes. I think a team restricts you. I think your personality suits solitude, making decisions on the fly, not having to rely on your fellow operatives to form a collective agreement. Subconsciously, you want all the control, because you know you're faster than everyone else. You don't like to admit that you're gifted, but deep down you know that you would prefer to be solely responsible for the operations you're tasked with completing. You put up with the other soldiers in an attempt to fit into a predetermined hierarchy of supposed "brothers." But really, you want nothing more than to handle everything yourself. If any of this is accurate, I invite you to test it out in the field. The United States of America is offering you the opportunity to do your own thing. What do you say?'

King shifted in his seat, weighing every syllable that had left Lars' mouth. The murky cloud of suppression that had been draped over the thoughts plaguing him for the last couple of years began to lift.

He nodded slowly, looking down at the documents and contracts adorning the table before him. 'Tell me where to sign.'

# 5

*Mexico*

Beyond the limits of Tijuana's official city grid, a battered Toyota pick-up truck trawled through potholed streets, surrounded on either side by dense rows of shanty town dwellings. It was close to mid-morning, and the air hung thick. The heat was palpable, soaking through the driver's flimsy shirt. He wiped a handful of perspiration beads off his thick eyebrows and gripped the wheel a little tighter to mask his sweaty palms.

Despite his occupation and his imposing reputation, Joaquín Ramos cared to spend as little time as possible in these parts. He had business to attend to, but once that was taken care of he would be gone. He sliced in and out of the poorer slums with precision, never lingering, never wasting a second.

The violent tendencies of the population out here created unpredictability.

He hated not having control.

Further within the city limits, the civilians were more

susceptible to fear. He had learnt that from experience, using a combination of manipulation and terror to coax them into following his demands. Out here, anything could happen. It was cheaper to do business, but at the cost of safety.

No-one was scared to gun down a drug lord in these streets.

They had nothing to lose either way.

Trash blew past on either side of the dirt road as he mounted an incline and gunned the pick-up truck up a steep hill. The dwellings seemed unimpeded by the slope of the land. Ramos guessed that they were only temporary, built shoddily to house those who would otherwise be homeless. He'd snatched one up for half the asking price a few months earlier, paying cash.

That was where he was headed.

He found the low tin building he was looking for and turned into its driveway, almost bursting one of the front tyres as he dropped into a particularly nasty pothole. He yanked the handbrake into position and killed the engine, letting the faint whoops and hollers of illegal migrants trawling the district fill his ears. They unnerved him. He had flourished in his newfound position by consistently acting like a reckless madman, taking risks and making leaps in business that no-one else dared to stomach.

In the shanty towns, he was just as mad as everyone else. Half the people out here had no access to decent sewage and water.

Frontier life was built on shaky foundations.

Ramos stepped out of the truck's cabin, breathing in the scent of cheap fast food. There was a border brothel somewhere nearby. He heard the muffled shrieks and moans of satisfied customers and poorly-acting whores. Checking left and right for any signs of an ambush, he tucked his head to his chest and hustled up the driveway to the dilapidated front porch.

The screen door swung outwards before he made it up onto the rotting wood. A wide-eyed man in an oversized white T-shirt and a pair of grey tracksuit pants gestured for him to step inside. The guy seemed three times as nervous as Ramos.

Ramos didn't blame him.

In certain areas, it was a death wish to be seen with him.

His reputation had spread fast.

'You crazy coming alone,' the man muttered in disjointed English as Ramos brushed past him.

He stepped into a dark living room that smelt of musty body odour and sugary energy drinks. All the blinds had been shut, and instead of artificially illuminating the small house, its occupants had opted to work in the lowlight. The only glare came from the white lights of their computer screens, which were arrayed in a tight circle in the centre of the room. Besides the desks upon which the monitors sat and the chairs upon which the fatasses sat, all other furniture had been cleared out.

It was a workspace. Nothing more, nothing less.

As Ramos nodded to the other three men in the room — all overweight and in their early twenties like the man who had answered the door — he realised he didn't care about the conditions they decided to operate in. Their work was good, and he would continue to pay them handsomely if they kept up the results.

'Any trouble?' he said to the guy who'd answered the door.

His name was Carlos, and Ramos had plucked him out of the unemployment line after noticing his credentials. He didn't know the names of the other three. He didn't need to. Carlos vouched for them, and Carlos was single-handedly responsible for ensuring that everything went smoothly. Ramos had given him free reign. If Carlos trusted them, they would be brought in.

But if the man's judgment was ever wrong...

Ramos had explicitly detailed the consequences, pulling no punches. Often, the threat of violence was the only way for him to enforce order in his ranks.

So far, it seemed to be working.

'No trouble,' Carlos said. 'We don't leave often. Too many crazy motherfuckers out there.'

'Anyone onto you?'

'No,' Carlos said. 'It's a cesspool of migrants looking to cross the fuckin' border. Looking for their one lucky break. They don't care about us, as long as we avoid them. They're more than happy to fight each other.'

Ramos nodded satisfactorily. 'Walk me through the set-up. I haven't seen it in action.'

'You think you'll follow along? Bit complicated for you, man.'

Ramos smirked. 'You think I'm just a no-brained street thug?'

Carlos raised an eyebrow, clearly aware that he may have worded his playful banter wrong. 'Of course not...'

'Take me through it. One last time. I like to keep a tight ship. You know that. Don't like being in the dark.'

Carlos gestured to the bank of computers. 'The site we're running is only accessible through the TOR browser. Means that no-one's going to accidentally stumble across it. The rumours you spread are working. Traffic is rising every single day. Orders are pouring in.'

'In bulk?'

Carlos nodded, seemingly still surprised by that development. 'Lots of dealers, man. You realise what you've done, right?'

Ramos shrugged, as if he had no idea. 'Enlighten me.'

'You're cutting out the middleman, hombre,' Carlos said in a low voice. 'The Draco cartel, they don't work like this, man. They don't know what they're doing. You made the smartest goddamn move in the world bringing me on board, man. We're selling direct to dealers themselves. Shipping packages out anonymously. All online. You're a fuckin' genius...'

'That was always the plan. You're saying it's catching on?'

'Five-hundred-and-fifty thousand revenue this week, man.'

'You're one-hundred percent certain that everything's secure?'

'That's what the PGP encryption is for,' Carlos said. 'We spent weeks implementing it, but it's foolproof. All the personal information these dudes give us is a jumbled mess to anyone other than us. But ... I wasn't expecting this.'

'I had a hunch all this time,' Ramos said. 'The old way of doing things is outdated. I see these Draco drug-runners working the streets, losing supply and skimming profits and getting jumped. Look what a little bit of innovation has done for us.'

'It's unreal, man. If I were you, I'd lay low. You don't need to seize their attention. We can do this shit from the shadows.'

Ramos shook his head. 'Only up to a certain point. The drugs need to be imported and packaged and shipped from somewhere, and the Draco cartel owns the physical space. They have for years. That's why I need to stand my ground. We need to carve out a portion of the market for ourselves, and let everyone know not to fuck with us and what we're doing. There's only one way to do that around here.'

'It's risky,' Carlos said. He spoke with the hesitation of a man who spent all his time cooped up indoors, slaving away in a virtual world. Ramos understood.

The man had his areas of expertise, and so far he had been executing them flawlessly. He would do good to change nothing.

'Keep doing what you're doing,' Ramos said. 'Leave everything else to me and my men. As long as this ship keeps sailing smoothly, you'll all make enough money to last you the rest of your lives.'

The three tech guys sitting around the array of monitors smiled in unison, exposing yellowing teeth. Ramos shook his head. Early twenties, and already losing their health. They would work themselves into an early grave at this rate, slowly decaying in their seats as the days passed.

Then again, he wasn't one to comment...

He checked his watch. 'I have somewhere to be.'

Carlos cocked his head. 'Got something to do with what we just discussed?'

'Certainly does.'

Ramos shook the man's hand and left the low-ceilinged room, stepping back out into the scorching sunlight. A gunshot in a neighbouring street made him flinch, but he recovered his wits and made for the Toyota. Not all the violence in Tijuana was directed at him.

Sometimes, it felt like it was.

Nothing he hadn't called upon himself, though.

He backed out of the driveway and rolled the driver's side window down, letting the passing breeze circulate through the humid cabin. It stopped the sweat dripping off his forehead momentarily. A temporary relief, but a welcome one.

He made for the westernmost district of the city.

Playas de Tijuana.

A visit to the beach.

There was a message that needed to be sent.

Ramos glanced at the faded passenger seat, occupied solely by the tool that he would use to deliver it.

A black-market Colt AR-15 semi-automatic rifle.

# 6

Playas de Tijuana seemed a world away from the shanty town which Ramos had come from. It was a tourist hotspot, close enough to the U.S. border to be deemed safe for frivolities. Towering hotels scattered the shoreline. Tourists and locals alike participated in water activities like surfing and kayaking, then made their way up to the Plaza Coronado for authentic Mexican cuisine and shopping.

Ramos hated when an area was considered safe.

He wanted everyone in the country to fear his operation at all times. Terror created apprehension, and apprehension created all manner of business opportunities offered up on a silver platter due to the lack of competition.

It was a fortunate coincidence that the inside information he'd received meant that his business today landed in Playas.

He guided the Toyota through narrow streets, these smoothly paved and bordered by thriving shops and hotels.

Hopefully, his business here would unfold quickly and efficiently.

Problems had arisen when word had spread of the two DEA agents he had murdered in the abandoned maquiladora factory's basement last week. Despite the violent and oppressive tendencies of the pre-existing Draco cartel, it seemed that their presence in Tijuana was largely ignored if they obliged by the unspoken rule: do not lay a finger on the U.S. authorities.

Ramos was new to this game.

He was still learning.

He hadn't quite figured out the do's and don't's.

He imagined that, even if he did seize a knowledgeable grasp on the unspoken rules, he would more than likely end up breaking them anyway.

*Fuck the old school.*

The media had spread the fresh developments like wildfire. The Draco cartel had distanced themselves from the killings, placing the blame squarely on the shoulders of the mysterious new entity snaking its way into Tijuana's darkest corners. Ramos had found himself shocked by the rate at which the news had spread.

Flabbergasted, even.

Somehow, the Draco cartel had ins with the journalists, resulting in a smear campaign of the highest intensity. Judging by word on the street that his men had relayed to him, Ramos' organisation had become public enemy number one.

Ordinarily, he wouldn't have cared one bit. He wanted nothing more than to impose a tyrannical rule over Tijuana, crushing all their faces into the dirt if they so much as dared to speak a word of protest. But the media blitz had achieved something he couldn't stand — it had raised the profile of the Draco cartel to new heights, painting them in a near-angelic light.

They were the heroes of Tijuana, standing up against Ramos and his band of devils in order to protect the sanctity of the city.

Ramos knew the truth.

He knew the blood that was spilt every single day in order for the Draco cartel to impose their hold on Tijuana. He knew they were just as evil as he was.

Today, he would seek to prove that.

Or nothing good would come of it, and it would only create a handful of dead bodies.

*Whatever.*

He'd take that outcome too.

Any chaos he could create would be good for business.

He found the destination he was looking for after a long five minutes of cruising up and down the traffic-clogged streets. A café with floor-to-ceiling glass windows and a posh interior decor rested at a corner junction of the district's largest intersection. Just a street away, Ramos stared through the gap between two residential buildings to see the early afternoon sun twinkle off the Pacific Ocean. A serene setting, in all respects.

Soon to be shattered by soul-chilling violence.

Just his specialty.

He parked illegally out the front of the café and flashed a second glance at the AR-15 to ensure everything was in order. Satisfied with his preparation, he searched for his targets through the clear glass. The intel his man had provided him with spelled out the time and the meeting point — and nothing else.

It didn't take long to find them.

They weren't hiding.

There were two men sitting at a corner booth in the café, visible to passers-by at a certain angle. Thankfully, Ramos had parked in a location where he could see the backs of their heads, but they couldn't see him. He recognised them immediately. Adrenalin flooded his veins, threatening to set his hands shaking. He suppressed the sensation and reached over to snatch up the AR-15.

One of the men was Miguel Torres, a lowly employee of the National Institute for the Combat of Drugs. He had been swayed by the dollar signs, evidently, and was in the process of meeting the other man to discuss staging a crackdown on Ramos' cartel exclusively. Ramos didn't know the name of the man with whom Torres was meeting, but he knew of his reputation as a powerful figure within the Draco cartel.

Garcia, possibly.

That rang a bell.

Ramos shrugged it off.

His name would mean nothing once he was dead.

All in all, a clear-cut sign of corruption. Two men resting on opposite sides of the moral spectrum, putting their differences aside to unite against a common enemy for the benefit of a hard-earned dollar.

Ramos had nothing against that.

He just needed to send a message.

Money talked, and bullets talked.

He let the adrenalin take over his motor senses, flooding his brain and draping a tunnel vision over his conscious state. He slipped a finger inside the trigger guard of the AR-15 and threw the driver's side door open.

Plenty of passers-by saw him wielding the high-powered rifle. They opted to stay silent and stare at the ground, electing to distance themselves from whatever business Ramos had.

Better to stay quiet and live to see another day than speak up and catch a bullet for your troubles.

He burst into the café, much to the horror of its occupants. All eyes turned to him — he felt the weight of the abject terror in the air pressing down on him.

*Good.*

He wanted them scared.

He wanted them to remember.

He sized up the corner booth in an instant — both Torres and the man from Draco had decided to leave their firearms in plain view, as a vainglorious method of showing off their power. Torres had his standard-issue sidearm resting on the corner of the tabletop, and the other guy had his fearsome-looking pistol out of its holster, propping it up barrel-to-grip in a rudimentary pyramid shape.

Neither of them were ready to respond. They were fixated on their stature, smug and confident that no-one would dare interfere with them. Two hard-working individuals keen to unite for financial gain.

It would cost them.

Despite the panicked whimpers of surrounding customers and the tense nature of the situation, Ramos calmly lifted up the A1 adjustable sight and pressed the stock to his shoulder. He lined up his aim in one, smooth motion and pumped the trigger twice. The gunshots were blisteringly loud in the otherwise-ambient café, tearing through the silence in vicious fashion.

Civilians screamed and leapt for cover.

Torres made no move to react, because the two NATO rounds destroyed the top of his head. His scalp blasted apart, caught by a glancing shot. The other bullet sunk deep into his skull, killing him instantly. His limbs stiffened and he toppled further into the booth in a pool of his own blood.

The Draco henchman fumbled with his pistol. Ramos sent a deafening third shot through the man's larynx, freezing him in his tracks as blood fountained from the soft tissue of his throat. If he wasn't already dead, he would be in seconds.

Ramos watched the pistol cascade out of the guy's fingers. He twisted away from the scene, recognising the lack of danger. Café dwellers were sprinting for the double doors, bursting out onto the busy intersection and taking off across the road.

For good measure, Ramos gunned down a woman in her thirties dressed in corporate attire, sending her sprawling across the tiled floor. She had almost made it to the exit. To safety.

*Shame,* he thought.

If killing civilians bothered him, he never would have got into the drug trade. The grisly death of an innocent would ensure that the incident received full coverage. Everyone would see what would result from complying with the Draco cartel.

Their reign would come to a sudden and devastating end.

He was sure of it.

He would tear them apart piece by piece.

He stepped over the body of the woman he had killed, taking care not to slip on the pool of arterial blood underneath her. He lowered the barrel of the AR-15, satisfied that his work was complete, and hurried for the Toyota he'd left idling by the sidewalk.

He slipped into the driver's seat and stamped on the gas, roaring away from the scene just as quickly as he'd arrived.

Another day.

Another dollar.

# 7

King had never sweat so much in his life.

It had been a whirlwind of a week. It turned out that accepting a position as the United States' most secret operative came with all kinds of baggage. He had been effectively required to sign his life away — nothing he wasn't already used to. Lars' took care to handle the majority of paperwork and simply pass contracts and documents over to King at the end of the day's training to be signed and returned at the earliest available convenience.

Most of the time, he didn't bother to read them.

It had only taken three days of living at the complex to realise that he felt right at home. He had no fellow soldiers to experience the journey alongside — it was nothing but himself and the horde of trainers that had been amassed to sculpt him into top physical condition.

And it was exactly what he preferred.

Lars kept most of the technicalities to himself, only sharing with King what was absolutely necessary. King thanked him for that — he himself was a foot soldier. His business didn't lie in the bureaucracy of the upper echelon. He was simply told what to do, and he did it.

He trusted the judgment of his superiors.

Over the last seven days, he'd got the distinct sense that there was something in the pipeline, an event that had triggered the creation of the division without any kind of prior planning. So far, nothing had been shared with him. He got up before the sun rose and spent the entire day working one-on-one with a wide variety of coaches, ranging from weapons training to mixed martial arts to reactive conditioning. His skills were already top-notch, but the individual attention allowed them to be honed by experts from across the country. He had the work ethic and the natural athleticism to keep up with the gruelling schedule, and so far it had paid dividends.

A week in, he felt clearer and more composed than ever.

According to Lars, his old Delta comrades had been informed that King had been selected for other work. They were to pretend he never existed, and carry on with their duties.

King didn't think they would mind.

He felt bad that he hadn't had the chance to explain himself to Dirk, but he was sure the man would understand. Dirk knew how miserable King had been in Operational Detachment-D. He would likely be happy that his friend had found a different path.

King didn't know where this path would lead him.

But he was committed to it.

'*One-two-two*,' Randall yelled. 'Last minute ... come on.'

Randall was a kickboxing instructor from one of the mega-gyms out in Florida, where hundreds of professional mixed martial artists trained in the intense humidity for their upcoming bouts. He had been flown out by the U.S.

government, all expenses paid, to hone King's skills for an upcoming, yet-to-be-announced operation.

Randall had embraced his new role with determination and discipline.

He had put King through the meat grinder for seven consecutive days.

King felt the sweat dripping off his frame in fat droplets, splattering across the damp canvas underneath his feet. He was bare-foot and bare-chested, dressed only in Muay Thai shorts with the traditional split down the sides to provide maximum range of motion. His muscles rippled underneath the dim warehouse light, accentuated by the downward-facing glare.

A result of shedding away what little body fat he'd already been carrying.

His hands were taped up in traditional boxing wraps, covered by four-ounce gloves that were common in MMA.

Randall stood opposite him, just as sweaty, holding out two pads at shoulder-height that he used to absorb the power of King's blows. A timer on the far wall slowly ticked down, currently at "*0:58*."

The pair flowed smoothly around the boxing ring. The only audible sounds were King's vicious exhales and the distinct *thwack-thwack-thwack* of his punches ricocheting off the leather. As the round reached its final ten seconds, he unleashed a volley of straight shots that detonated off the pads at an unbelievable rate, pushing through the lactic acid that had built up in his arms from the intense workout.

Two punches per second, then three.

King clenched his teeth, stomached the pain, and continued to deliver staggering blows to the pads.

Randall relented, taking a step back as the momentum thrust him away from King.

Finally, the timer shrieked, signalling an end to the five consecutive rounds of live sparring.

King sucked in air and dropped his hands to his hips, wincing in order to ride out the sheer physical depletion that had descended over him. The day's training had come to an end, and he had begun to think that he needed a day off. Overtraining was a serious risk, and threatened to render him useless if he needed to be deployed at short-notice.

He yanked the four-ounce gloves off his hands and dropped them to the sweat-stained canvas beneath his feet. Randall stepped through the ropes and returned with a pair of steel scissors, which he used to hack through the hand wraps that King had bound tight between his fingers. They prevented any broken bones, which would spell disaster given the nature of his line of work.

It seemed that — for now — he was the division's sole operative.

Randall retrieved a gallon jug from the side of the ring, full to the brim with pale-blue liquid. It had been King's go-to beverage after every hard sparring session — a concoction of Randall's that had been approved by King's superiors before he was allowed to consume it.

He didn't ask what was in it.

For all he knew, Randall had assembled a cocktail of designer drugs that aided in the recovery of elite athletes. He had no qualms with the steroids, if that's what they truly were feeding him. He recognised that without artificial assistance, his body would have worn down days ago, simply breaking apart under the sheer stress it had been subjected to. He was here to do good, and serve his country. He wouldn't object to a little help, if that's what his superiors decided was necessary.

Steroids were met with abject disdain in professional sports, for good reason. In King's world, it meant that he had a slightly greater chance of survival.

He gulped down half the gallon, feeling the cool taste of the beverage on his lips. Then he dumped the half-empty jug at his feet and stepped out of the ring, leaning against the side of the canvas floor to recover.

Across the warehouse, the entrance door slid open and Lars strode inside.

He came and went as he pleased. King imagined that the man's life was chaotic — at least for this turbulent period in which the division was being created. King hadn't had much time to get to know Lars, given his frequent trips to God-knows-where. The fact that King was training out of a rundown warehouse in the backwoods of Wyoming signified that everything had not been painstakingly prepared.

They were reacting to something.

'How long are you here for?' King said as Lars dropped a leather bag filled with documents and a laptop onto the table in front of him.

'A few days,' Lars said.

'That's an eternity.'

'Compared to what I've been doing lately — yes, it is.'

'Things are sorted?'

'Somewhat. The foundations have been laid. We can almost stop and take a breath. Almost.'

'I still have no idea why we're rushing.'

'We're still deciding the extent to which we want to act,' Lars said. 'Black ops are muddled. I'm sure you can understand.'

'I'm calm in the chaos,' King said.

Lars smirked. 'Poignant.'

Outside, King heard the sharp mechanical beeping of a

truck reversing up to the double doors. Behind it, another large vehicle rumbled into the clearing, visible through the slight crack in the doors that Lars had entered through.

'New training gear?' he said.

Lars nodded. 'That's what I've been working on acquiring. A lot of my work at DARPA was based in the field of reflexes. It's something of my specialty, and it's why I was so excited to form a new division. Basically, I believe that reflexively-gifted individuals are hindered by working in groups. If you can react at the speed of light, then why would you want a team weighing you down?'

'You think I'm that gifted individual?'

'Everything I've seen so far seems to indicate as much. But we'll find out exactly how gifted you are shortly. That's what the new equipment is for. King, tell me about Iran.'

The statement threw him off completely. King had dropped his guard, sinking deeper into the conversation and relaxing as the talking progressed. He hadn't been expecting the sudden change in topic — and it was a subject he would much rather not discuss.

'Uh…' he said.

'You don't need to be nervous,' Lars said. 'Don't think of me as a military official. I'm simply asking as a friend.'

'I barely know you.'

'And I barely know you either. But what happened in Ramadi was not normal. I've been told that it caused something of a rift between you and your fellow Delta Force operatives.'

'You know what happened,' King said. 'It would have been detailed in the mission report.'

'I want to hear it from you.'

King paused. He thought back to the hot, dusty streets of Ramadi, to the chaos and confusion that had unfolded. It was the first time he had ever branched away from official orders, and he was still surprised that he had lived to tell the tale.

'It happened in December last year,' Lars said, prodding further.

Attempting to facilitate conversation.

'It did,' King said.

'What were you there to do?'

'Clearing houses that we believed were home to insurgents. Delta had been called in to ensure everything unfolded with minimal civilian casualties.'

'Insurgents?'

'There were groups believed to be training Iraqi insurgents and importing weapons for use against the coalition forces. We targeted hotspots that we believed were home to clusters of these radicals.'

'What happened on the day in question?'

'We raided a two-storey house on the outskirts of Ramadi.'

'Standard procedure?'

'Standard procedure.'

'How did it go?'

'Disastrously,' King said.

'What happened?'

'The man in front of me — Brad — got shot in the face.'

'Died instantly?'

'Yeah. And gruesomely. The bullet destroyed his nose and went through into his brain. He was one of the kindest people in the Force. One of my few friends.'

'What should you have done?'

'Fallen back to regroup with the rest of my unit, who were still on their way into the property.'

'What did you do instead?'

'Charged into the house, abandoned all procedure, and killed the four insurgents who were firing on me.'

'That's what I'm interested in, in case you didn't realise. Tell me about it.'

King found that the breath had caught in his throat. He had barely spoken of the incident since it had unfolded. He had disobeyed all orders and taken matters into his own hands, in what could only be described as a vigilante act instead of a measured effort in co-operation with his fellow operatives.

He was still surprised he hadn't been dishonourably discharged from the military for such reckless actions.

'I saw Brad drop. His blood coated me — from the exit wound. I don't know how to describe it, but I felt this sudden clarity. Like whoever was in the house had just given me permission to kill them. It was like everything was happening in slow-motion. I sized up exactly who was armed — all of them. I charged straight in, used one of them as a human shield, shot two of them through the head, then beat the other man into unconsciousness and killed both him and the human shield with rounds to the head.'

'I know the details,' Lars said. 'Like you said, that was in the mission report. I want to know how you felt in the moment that you made the decision to act.'

'Like I was unstoppable,' King said.

'Oh?'

'It didn't feel real. Everything felt so ... simple. I saw what I needed to do, and I did it. I've never been in a situation like that before, so I can't really relate it to anything else.'

'Did you think about your fellow operatives?'

'No. They weren't in the line of fire.'

'You didn't think of relying on them for help?'

'Not one bit.'

'You shut everything out, basically?'

'Exactly.'

'I think you entered a different state, a more reactionary state. I've done a lot of research into this. I think your normal consciousness shrank away and was replaced by something else. Like the performance-enhancing chemicals that flood your brain in a life or death situation seized hold of your senses and went into autopilot. An instinct to survive, which can be lethal when combined with a skill-set such as yours. I think you're one of the fastest-reacting operatives on the planet when you enter that kind of state — like an unstoppable force who ignores everything else. And I don't think it correlates with working in a team.'

'Possibly,' King admitted.

'If you don't mind,' Lars said, gesturing to the two trucks that had come to a halt outside the warehouse, 'I'd like to see just what this state looks like in your brain.'

# 8

The house was modern, with smooth edges and sweeping glass windows looking out over a stunning infinity pool. Ramos had purchased it — with cash, just how he had bought almost everything he owned — under a false name three months ago. That was the first sign he'd received that what he was doing was working. Before then, it had all been a pipe dream — an online drug empire bringing in hundreds of thousands of dollars a week in cold, hard profit.

When he'd handed over eight hundred thousand USD in freshly-printed bills for a property in one of Tijuana's most prestigious neighbourhoods, it had demonstrated that hard work had its rewards.

He still used the same Toyota pick-up truck in his day-to-day business dealings. A man as hated as he was required a certain level of discretion when conducting his duties. He had a Lamborghini Aventador Coupè, but reserved it exclusively for tearing through the arid foothills of the neighbouring mountains on warm summer nights.

Everything else required acting like a regular citizen.

Now he sat poolside, dressed in swimming trunks, stretched out on a sun lounge next to a gorgeous Spanish brunette lying in the nude on an identical chair. She charged a sizeable fee, but it was worth every peso. A month ago, he'd been informed by one of his men that she was an international model, and would be happy to offer her services to Ramos for a price.

He'd complied.

Sitting up, he slapped her on the rear and made his way inside the mansion. It was cooler indoors, and despite the scene straight out of a magazine cover, his nerves were set on edge.

They had been ever since he'd killed the two men in the café one week prior.

He hadn't anticipated such a response. The Draco cartel had hit back with unbridled fury, targeting anyone who was rumoured to be involved with Ramos' dealings. Eight of his men had been killed in shootouts since, along with nearly a dozen members of Draco and a handful of innocent bystanders too. The skirmishes were threatening to break out into all-out war, and Ramos was determined to ensure that didn't happen.

In terms of sheer manpower, the Draco cartel outnumbered his own forces ten to one.

He preferred to operate with clinical precision.

Destroy the high command of the rival cartel, and they'll implode.

He had triggered a nerve with the slaughter of the two men in the café, but now he was plotting to hit them where it really hurt.

He slid a Motorola Razr flip phone out of his pocket and pressed a single key, activating speed dial.

The call was answered immediately.

A good sign.

'You intercepted them?' he said.

'Yes,' the voice on the other end of the line replied. 'Eight Draco thugs, split between two trucks. They'd come from Guatemala, just as you said. How'd you know?'

'That's where one of our production facilities is,' Ramos said. 'I figured Draco were using the same area. The Usumacinta region is chaos with all the cartels vying for territory. Anyway, how much supply did you get?'

'There's at least two hundred kilograms of cocaine here,' the man said.

'They're all dead?'

'Of course.'

'Did we take any casualties?'

'Two.'

Ramos shrugged. He would take those results.

'What do we do with the supply?' the man said.

'Destroy it.'

'We're not going to use it?'

'We don't need it. I don't know what the hell it's tainted with. For all I know, Draco anticipated that we would hit them on their supply chain, and poisoned half the stash. I don't want anything ruining our reputation. The online trade relies on it.'

'You sure? This is a lot of coke, boss.'

'Destroy it,' Ramos repeated. 'We have more than enough.'

He ended the call.

The ensuing silence set him on edge. He wasn't sure what it was — either the water gently lapping at the edge of the infinity pool outside, or the sheer emptiness of the high-ceilinged kitchen in which he stood. It was quiet.

Too quiet.

As if on cue, the phone in his hand shrieked, signifying an incoming call. He checked the display and noted the "No Caller ID" plastered across the top of the screen. Tentatively, he swiped across the lower half to answer the call. He didn't usually take unsolicited inquiries, but something about this one told him it would be worth his while.

Something about this one told him he needed to answer.

There had been all too much calm in the aftermath of his attack on the Draco henchman.

It was about time shit hit the fan.

He pressed the receiver to his ear and a voice exploded into life, speaking in thickly-accented English. Perhaps they knew where Ramos was, but not what language he primarily spoke.

'Did you think you could hide forever?' the voice boomed.

Male.

Likely in his fifties or sixties.

Someone who possessed a distinct air of superiority.

Ramos smirked. 'I haven't been hiding. Where are your men? I've been waiting for weeks.'

'You think you are safe?'

'Nothing about this business is safe. Come on, old man. Where are your forces? I've been waiting patiently.'

Ramos flashed a glance to the AR-15 resting on the marble kitchen countertop — the same weapon he'd used for his murderous spree in the Playas café. It was fully loaded. The safety was off. He had never been more ready to use it.

He thrived in the chaos.

Sooner or later, Draco would break.

He was sure of it.

'I know what you want,' the old man said. 'You want this to become a dogfight, eh? You want us to come charging in through your front door.'

'All I hear is talk,' Ramos said. 'I'm ready for anything.'

'I doubt that.'

'I'll keep up this madness until you back off.'

'How can you keep up anything when you have no system to sell your product? It amuses me that you thought you could hide your little tech-house forever.'

An artificial beep signalled that the man on the other end of the line had killed the call. Ramos stood poised in the centre of the kitchen, frozen in time. The cool touch of the phone stayed pressed firmly against his ear. He didn't want to move. If he did, it might be confirmed that this was reality.

He did his best to suppress a wave of panic that rolled over him in concentrated bursts of horror. All the potential consequences slammed their way into the forefront of his mind, causing him to break out in an uncontrollable sweat. If the Draco member hadn't been bluffing, then it was entirely possible that the framework of his operation had just been torn out from underneath him.

With all the ramifications still pressing down on him like a thousand-pound deadweight, he tucked the phone into his back pocket, snatched up the AR-15, and ran for the front door.

He didn't consider the fact that there might be scouts lying in wait.

He didn't consider anything past taking action.

He had made it this far on cerebral reaction alone, taking situations one step at a time. He would do the same here.

The street was quiet — a wide, well-paved stretch of asphalt twisting through a neighbourhood of similarly lavish houses. There was no sign of anyone staking out his residence. If Ramos noticed anything out of the ordinary, he would have ducked back into the house.

The coast seemed clear.

He unlocked the Toyota and dived in. Briefly, he touched a hand to the left side of his chest, worried at the rate at which his heart was pounding. Copious amounts of caffeine and the nootropic Modafinil had enabled him to work fourteen, fifteen, sixteen hour days building a drug empire. Now, the same cognitive enhancers threatened to put him into cardiac arrest. He focused on his breathing as he reversed out of the driveway at breakneck speed and surged for the shanty towns to the east.

The drive took nine minutes.

Ramos almost caused a head-on collision three separate times, each one spiking his heart rate even higher. It was the longest, most agonising nine minutes of his life. He considered what he might find at the safe house, what disaster that might spell. Along the way, he came to realise the extent of the responsibility he had placed on a select few individuals. He should have known that if certain members of his inner circle — like Carlos — were affected, it would tear the rug out from underneath his entire operation.

When he squealed into the shanty town's limits and pulled to a halt outside the tech team's shoddily-constructed tin building, he cursed his own foolishness. He should have been more careful. He should have had his men stationed outside the property twenty-four hours a day, brandishing the highest-calibre weaponry they could get their hands on.

He should have personally protected the most crucial node in his empire's system.

The front door hung wide open, its accompanying mesh screen torn off its hinges. Ramos stepped out of the Toyota's cabin with the AR-15's barrel raised, pointed straight at the darkened doorway. He stomached a stabbing bolt of tension and pressed forward.

Instantly, his suspicions were confirmed.

Arterial blood had been used as paint to adorn the front wall of the building with a large insignia, almost the same size as Ramos himself. It depicted two fangs intersecting. The crimson smear was still fresh.

The Draco cartel's symbol.

It was unmistakable.

Ramos suppressed the fury coursing through his blood and headed straight into the building. He didn't care if Draco thugs were still on the premises.

In fact, he hoped they were.

He would make them pay.

It took a few seconds for his eyes to adjust to the lowlight. The blinds on the opposite wall were still drawn — only faint slivers of daylight filtered through the cracks. They illuminated four silhouettes, strung from the ceiling by crude lengths of rope, dangling limply by their necks.

Ramos took one look at what had been done to their faces.

He'd seen everything that he needed to see.

The trestle tables in the centre of the room were gone, as well as all the technology atop it. The Draco cartel had seized it all.

The blow would be debilitating to their day-to-day operations. Maybe even crippling. There was a sizeable chance that Ramos wouldn't be able to come back from this. He would need to take risks, and act quickly and decisively.

Thankfully, he had lived half his life that way.

He stepped out of the foul-smelling building with one concept consuming his thoughts.

*Revenge.*

# 9

It took two hours for the room to be constructed.

By the time it was ready, King had wound down from the day's training. He'd soaked for twenty minutes in an ice bath, foam-rolled the tight knots out of his muscles, and finally dressed in casual clothing for the final portion of the day. He wasn't sure exactly what Lars had in store, but he knew it had something to do with his brain. The man's area of expertise seemed to revolve largely around an untested area of combat.

King was intrigued to find out what the results would show.

As the sun disappeared below the horizon and the woods of Curt Gowdy State Park were plunged into darkness, Lars emerged from the warehouse's adjoining offices, wiping sweat off his forehead.

King sat at a makeshift dining table, shovelling a plate of chicken and rice into his mouth. He peered across the room as Lars made his way over, dropping into the chair opposite with an emphatic sigh.

'We're ready,' Lars said.

'What's ready, exactly?'

'I'd rather just take you through the exercise, instead of explaining it to you in detail. It's preferable if you're unprepared for what might happen.'

'You've got me worried.'

'Don't be. You good to go?'

'Let me finish this.'

King scraped the last forkfuls of the meal off his plate and gulped them down with a tall glass of water. Satisfied, he skidded his chair back across the dusty concrete floor and followed Lars into the previously-abandoned offices.

He hadn't spent much time in this section of the warehouse. The rooms were empty, cleared out by the last occupants — or never furnished in the first place. Like most of the warehouse, it was cold and empty.

Not anymore.

Lars gestured for him to step into one of the rooms, squeezing through a narrow doorway that hadn't been designed to handle King's bulk. He entered a wood-panelled space, far cosier than the rest of the complex. A projector screen had been stretched across one wall, facing a plain office chair that seemed to be the only furniture pointed in the screen's direction. Behind the chair, a tight semicircle of high-tech gadgetry was set up. There were two other people in the room — a young, stern-looking woman with brunette hair pinned up in a tight bun, and an elderly balding man adjusting a dial on the side of one of the machines.

'What the hell is this?' King muttered. It looked like something out of a bad science-fiction movie.

'Nothing as sinister as you might think,' Lars said. 'King, this is Anne and Raymond from the Defence Sciences Office at DARPA. They're here to see what your brain does when placed in a live situation. You'll be hooked up to an EEG monitor for the duration of the test. I assume you're okay with that.'

'Sounds like my idea of a fun Sunday evening,' King said.

Anne and Raymond smiled simultaneously. They both stepped forward and introduced themselves with pleasant handshakes. King greeted them both in turn, then sat himself down in the chair while Anne prepared to attach the receptors to his face and scalp.

'Been here long?' she said quietly as she pressed a cool silicon node to the upper portion of his cheek.

'Not long,' he said. 'I'm probably just as confused as you are.'

She smiled, exposing a row of pearly white teeth. King flashed a subtle glance at how the official military uniform rested against her frame. She evidently kept in shape, judging by her curves. He couldn't suppress his attraction — it had been far too long since he'd been romantically involved with anyone.

*Wonder how brief her visit is...*

'I want you to watch the video in front of you,' Lars said, tearing King's train of thought back to the present. 'Just let it flood your senses. Don't resist it. Don't think of this as an experiment, or anything of the sort. Just sit back and let your natural instincts take over.'

King nodded. Another ten or fifteen receptors were pressed onto his head, ranging from the back of his skull to the space just below his eyes. He sat completely still, unnerved by the quietness of the room. He was used to sweat and exertion. Hard training had consumed his life for the past year. He had come to resent anything that involved sitting around unnecessarily.

After a few more beats of waiting, he shifted uncomfortably in his seat.

Then the projector screen burst into life and everything changed.

In an instant, he recognised what he was looking at. The grainy footage had been recorded from the under-barrel of a combat rifle, wielded by some sort of high-level operative. King guessed DEVGRU. The footage blurred as the weapon began to bounce up and down, indicating that the man behind the camera was sprinting toward an unknown destination. King glimpsed a shoddy dirt trail and an overgrown front garden.

The man behind the camera took cover momentarily — King tuned into the sounds of shuffling footsteps behind him. It seemed that he was the leader of the unit. His barrel stayed trained on the ground while he mouthed near-silent commands to his fellow soldiers. King tuned into the small details — the rasping of his voice, the scuffing of boots on gravel, the sheer silence of the neighbourhood.

It brought back memories of Ramadi.

'What is this?' he muttered.

No-one responded.

Lars, Anne, and Raymond had all stepped out of his peripheral vision. Briefly, King felt like turning his head to make eye contact with them, but he couldn't resist keeping his eyes locked on the screen. The images filled his vision — he realised that speakers had been installed in the walls around him, providing unparalleled surround sound.

King fell quiet and concentrated on the feed.

For all he knew, he could be witnessing a live operation. Very little information had been fed to him regarding the video footage. His heart skipped a beat as the barrel lifted to aim at a rundown two-storey residence surrounded by overgrown vegetation.

The soldier moved in. King heard the man's attempts to mask his laboured breathing. He heard every intricacy of the noises. His own heart rate quickened in turn. The set-up of the video feed had been expertly crafted. It felt like he had stepped into a war zone himself, despite full knowledge that he sat in a makeshift theatre room in a warehouse in Wyoming.

The operative on the projector screen approached the front door of the residence. He paused on one side of the flimsy wood, waiting for a comrade to take up position on the opposite side. The man filling the camera's view looked to be in his thirties, with a thick frame and a bushy beard. His face had been coated in dark khaki paint.

*Definitely DEVGRU*, King thought.

The man across from the camera's feed nodded imperceptibly. There was a brief pause — like the calm before the storm — before the guy dropped his boot into the centre of the door. It crashed inwards, loud enough for King to jolt in his seat.

The scene descended into madness.

Sharp screaming — half in Arabic, half in English — flooded the speakers, rolling over King's senses in waves that were intense enough to cause a panic attack. He struggled to suppress the sensations — Lars and the two DARPA scientists had deliberately organised the video to be as immersive as possible.

The shaky footage stabilised for a brief second, and King got a proper look at the interior of the house. A man with his face covered by a bandanna had a Kalashnikov AK-47 pressed to the side of a screaming woman's head. There were two more insurgents on the stairs, barking harsh orders and shaking identical firearms in the camera's direction.

The yelling reached a crescendo — which culminated in the bandanna-clad man wrenching the trigger of his rifle. Blood sprayed from the side of the civilian's head and she dropped, all the tension slackening from her limbs simultaneously.

King barely noticed the footage coming to an end. He registered the cracking of unsuppressed gunfire and honed in on the hostiles, sizing up the distance between the camera and each of the three armed men in the frame.

The footage abruptly cut off as vicious swathes of assault rifle ammunition tore across the interior of the house.

The overwhelming sound died out.

# 10

Lars stepped into King's view and nodded with satisfaction.

King stared up at him. 'That's it?'

'That's all we needed.'

'Seems like a lot of set-up for a brief test.'

'We wanted to see how your brain would react in a volatile situation. I'm interested in exactly what goes on in there.'

'Uh-huh.'

'You're still in that state, aren't you?'

King couldn't deny it. His heart rate had shot through the roof, and it took enormous effort just to make conversation with Lars. He felt wired, like a shaking adrenalin-junkie experiencing a massive dose of thrills. 'That sound system and projector combination is goddamn effective.'

'It's quite remarkable, really,' Anne said. 'Your norepinephrine and dopamine levels have skyrocketed.'

'Sure feels that way,' King said.

'Could I ask you to bring those down — if you're able to?'

King nodded, recognising the dissolution of the perceived threat and attempting to react accordingly. He felt the narrow tunnel of concentration shrink away, replaced by a zen-like calm. It only took a few seconds.

'Holy shit,' Raymond breathed, staring at the monitor in front of him.

'He can control it?' Lars said. 'Turn it up and down?'

'It seems so.'

'You always been able to do that?' Lars said.

King shrugged. 'As long as I can remember.'

'The times you've found yourself in live combat situations — you've used that to your advantage?'

King shrugged again. 'Never really thought about it. I just keep myself in that zone until the job is done.'

'I think this might just work.'

As Anne began the process of removing the EEG receptors from the sides of King's head, he stomached a certain sense of annoyance at the situation.

Lars seemed to notice.

'Everything okay?' he asked as King finally came free of the sticky nodes and got to his feet.

'How much longer are you going to keep me cooped up in this warehouse, running tests and leaving me in the dark?'

'You don't like it?'

'The wait doesn't bother me. The secrecy does. I want to know why this division was hurried into existence, and why I'm being tested in this room instead of at DARPA itself. What are we still doing in Wyoming?'

'You were already here,' Lars said. 'We thought we'd come to you. At first, I was told I had two weeks to get you ready. That's changed.'

'Get me ready for what?' King said. 'I'm not going to keep asking for much longer...'

'There was an incident in Tijuana nearly a week ago,' Lars said. 'Two DEA agents were murdered.'

'Drug cartel?'

'Drug cartel.'

'I've got no experience with the war on drugs,' King said. 'And, frankly, I've got my own opinions about how you guys are handling it. If that was what this was all about, you should have told me at the start because I would have refused.'

'You're right,' Lars said. 'What we're doing certainly isn't working. That's why this project was green-lit. You and I have the chance to pioneer an unconventional method of doing things.'

'Like a secret agent? James Bond shit?'

'Not exactly. But I do want you to tear this new cartel apart from the inside.'

'I'm going to need a lot more information than that.'

'I was planning to drip-feed it to you over the next week. But you're flying out tomorrow morning.'

'What changed?'

Lars paused and grimaced slightly. 'There was another incident this morning.'

'What happened?'

'It's late. I'll brief you tomorrow. Come for a morning run with me.'

'Alright.'

Anne and Raymond had silently observed the conversation from the back of the room. King imagined they had full clearance, or Lars wouldn't have breathed a word about military proceedings around them. The four of them left the room, making their way back out into the warehouse itself.

Raymond and Lars pulled ahead, discussing the specific results of the test in low tones. They seemed entirely preoccupied with their conversation, ignoring King.

It gave him the chance to talk to Anne.

'How long are you out here for?' he said.

She smirked. 'Is this you trying to chat me up?'

King paused. 'Sorry. Are you married?'

'No. Single.'

'Oh.'

'I study the brain,' she said. 'It's pretty clear when a guy is keen. Even one as macho as you.'

He sensed the underlying sarcasm and hesitated. 'I didn't mean...'

'I'm just playing with you,' she said, punching him lightly in the shoulder. 'Sorry — I'm not great at small talk either. Spend ninety percent of my life at work.'

'I can relate,' King muttered.

'You're off tomorrow, I hear?'

'Apparently so. This is all a bit of a whirlwind at the moment.'

'I can see that.'

'Are you two leaving tonight?'

'I drove myself,' Anne said. 'I can hang around ... I guess.'

'Your choice.'

'Could be a nice release.'

'I'd say so.'

She eyed him up and down, all too obvious in her intentions. King guessed that she had abandoned subtlety after the barriers of small-talk had come down. He decided to do the same.

'My room's out back,' he said. 'I won't say it's a nice joint, because it's not. Like I said — this has been a whirlwind.'

'I'm sure I won't mind.'

There was a moment of hesitation, with both of them unsure how to proceed. Anne shook her head in disbelief. 'This was an awfully quick decision.'

King shrugged. 'I've had my mind and body wrapped up in this craziness for the last year, almost. I think I'm pretty desperate for a release, to be honest. I hope I wasn't too forward.'

She shrugged back. 'I'm feeling the same. Let me go talk to Raymond — let him know that I'm too tired for the drive to the airport and that I'm crashing here. He'll understand.'

'I'm sure he will.'

'Just a quick fling?'

'Sounds good to me,' King said. 'I can't say that I have time for anything else.'

'Me neither. This feels ... cold. Like a business decision.'

'Like I said, it's up to you.'

'Don't worry,' she said. 'You're not bad on the eyes.'

King smiled and watched as she headed for the other side of the warehouse. Lars and Raymond had disappeared through the towering sliding doors, trudging into the darkness beyond. Maybe they had recognised the underlying tension between him and Anne.

King turned on his heel and headed past the partition of offices, ducking through a side door that led into his temporary living quarters. He muttered a silent thanks for his timing — the washing basket that had previously been piled high with sweaty workout gear had been emptied that morning. Otherwise, the room was spotless, containing nothing but a plain double bed and a narrow desk on the opposite wall.

King sat down on the bed and waited for Anne to arrive.

There was a knock at the door less than a minute later,

three rapid taps filled with nervous excitement. He let her in and they pounced on each other, two spirits consumed by work and in desperate need of a release. He peeled his shirt off and felt her hands running along his chest, down his stomach, lower...

He kissed her ravenously, breathing her scent. She reached for his belt and he picked her up off the floor, carrying her to the bed. He put her down, and they took it slow, appreciating the privacy they would have until the following morning.

Hours later, when they finally grew tired of lovemaking and Anne dropped into a quiet doze, King draped an arm around her naked frame and leant back against the pillow.

Before he dropped off, he wondered just what the hell had happened in Tijuana that had provoked such a rapid response.

He had a feeling he would need all the rest he could get.

# 11

*Mexico*
*Twelve hours earlier...*

Joaquín Ramos had his back against the wall.

He wouldn't have preferred it any other way.

It seemed like he was in his element in this position. He had made the most progress career-wise months ago, without a single dollar to his name. Back then, the only way to achieve anything had been massive, relentless action.

Now, he felt like he'd been thrust back to his old roots.

The Draco cartel would regret testing him.

Ramos pulled his beat-up Toyota to a halt outside the building he'd been scouting for the last few days. It looked exactly how it had in the surveillance photos — one-storey, unremarkable, stretching a couple of hundred feet back into the block of land. There were no clear markings on the building's exterior to signify its purpose.

Ramos imagined that was intentional.

It was one of the headquarters' of the National Institute

for the Combat of Drugs. For as long as he could remember, the organisation had been under the rule of the Draco cartel. Key officials had been bribed, others threatened with their life or the lives of their families.

Ramos held no emotional weight over the way in which the Draco cartel had brutally seized control of their empire.

If he had been in their position years ago, he would have done the same — if not worse.

But the power that Draco possessed regarding the National Institute posed significant problems for his own rise. Chiefly, the authorities were seriously concerned by what Ramos was doing in Tijuana. They were applying pressure to his operation in a variety of ways, many of which had been exacerbated by the slaughter of his four tech-gurus.

Lately, they had teamed up with certain members of the U.S. government in a public display of co-operation, intent on suppressing the sudden wave of violence that had seized the city in the wake of Ramos' power-grab. Ramos had seen the hordes of American tourists that flooded the Avenida Revolución in the warmest days. All of them came to this city for cheap thrills and hidden pleasures, for things they couldn't find back in their own territory. He knew that the violence between his cartel and the Draco cartel threatened the lives of innocents.

Hell, he had gunned down his fair share of civilians along the way.

It was a part of life around here.

But after what had happened to the DEA agents in the basement of the abandoned maquiladora factory, it seemed the attention on Tijuana's dark side from across the border had amplified.

Ramos was here to achieve two things.

Demonstrate the consequences if key regulators continued to be wooed by the Draco cartel.

Send a message to the United States that they had no business in this town.

The usual response to added sensitivity would be to shrink away from the DEA investigations, to cover up his dealings and prevent anyone from interfering.

He never did things the usual way.

He would continue the reign of terror until all his enemies determined that it was not worth their while to mess with him.

The AR-15 had been reloaded.

It was ready for use.

He waited for a lull in pedestrian activity to make his move. He'd killed the engine a few minutes ago, and the heat started to permeate through the interior, soaking his shirt once again. It seemed that no matter how many times he changed his attire, the Mexican heat turned it to filth within the hour.

It didn't matter.

He loved when things got dirty.

He thrived in this kind of environment.

When the stretch of sidewalk in front of the National Institute's headquarters cleared of passers-by, Ramos snatched up the AR-15 and slung the leather strap over one shoulder. He stepped out of the Toyota, sweat dripping off the sides of his jaw in rivulets, and strode purposefully for the tinted set of double doors leading into the facility.

He had no idea what he might find.

His only intention was to cause chaos.

He thundered a sneaker into the left-hand door, hard enough to splinter the sheet of darkened glass as it swung into the corridor within. He strode through, meeting the wide-eyed gaze of a pair of American agents leaning against the reception desk.

A man and a woman, just like the pair who had swarmed his position in the basement a week earlier.

Ramos recognised their uniform — they were special agents working for U.S. Immigration and Customs Enforcement. Probably here for a meeting with those in power, to discuss the violent grip Ramos had seized on the city.

He killed them with a pair of perfectly-placed head-shots, sending a thick round through the centre of each of their foreheads. The roar of the semi-automatic rifle and the gory results of the exit wounds were shocking enough to send the young receptionist into an uncontrollable bout of screaming. Ramos silenced her with a third shot, less accurate due to his aim at a moving target. She had almost made it off her swivelling office chair before the bullet blew through one half of her face, dropping her unceremoniously to the thick carpet behind the desk.

He pressed into the offices, marching down hallways that were entirely devoid of life. It seemed that the employees of the National Institute had opted to hide from the armed lunatic patrolling its corridors. He found himself angered by their hypocrisy. They had no qualms taking blood money from the existing cartel in exchange for turning a blind eye to their dealings. But when the drug war made it into their offices themselves, they wanted nothing to do with it.

Cowards.

Ramos found the door he was looking for and shouldered through the lock with the type of strength that only came from a massive dose of adrenalin. He found the man he was looking for seated behind a broad oak desk, shoulders hunched and head bowed, frozen by hesitation.

'Hey, Hernández,' Ramos said, his hearing still impaired from the unsuppressed AR-15 gunfire he'd unleashed moments earlier. 'Great to finally meet you in the flesh.'

'Who the fuck are you?' the man cursed.

Hernández was ex-Army. For years, he had acted as the National Institute's poster boy, glamourising their escapades in television interviews and media days. His face and voice were spread across all the major television networks and radio stations, promoting his division's effectiveness on the war on drugs.

All the while receiving hefty bonuses under the table for allowing the Draco cartel to maintain its hold on the packaging and processing facilities they operated in Tijuana's working district.

'Hopefully this stirs the pot,' Ramos muttered to himself.

Before Hernández could respond to the rapidly escalating situation, Ramos shot him dead. He unloaded an entirely unnecessary amount of bullets into the man's unprotected chest. Blood fountained across the desk, soaking through the various documents that Hernández had been transfixed on before Ramos' surprise entrance.

When the crimson aftermath had reached unbelievably gory heights, Ramos turned and left the building, moving fast. He passed the three corpses in the reception area, taking a glance at the two dead U.S. officials.

Briefly, he wondered if his actions had truly been necessary this time.

He had little experience with the Americans.

He wasn't sure how strongly they would react.

His only goal had been to kill Hernández — the deaths along the way were only collateral, events used to hammer home his point. It wasn't often that a cartel attempted to enact a takeover on the existing regime — when attempts were made, they usually ended in bloodshed. The Draco cartel always came out on top.

Not this time.

Ramos had slaughtered the most important figurehead of the National Institute for the Combat of Drugs, a man revered by society and promoted in the media. It would serve as an announcement to anyone thinking of aiding the Draco cartel that there would be serious consequences.

As far as Ramos was concerned, anyone protecting the Draco cartel — whether that be through accepting bribes or caving to intimidation — was fair game. He was willing to do whatever it took to ensure that every individual in Tijuana distanced themselves from the Draco cartel.

That way, they could be crushed.

That way, Ramos could enact the equivalent of a corporate takeover.

He peeled his eyes away from the three dead bodies in the reception area and hurried back to his Toyota. Already, sirens howled in the distance. He had three armed men on call, just in case the local police decided to enter a shootout with him. He wouldn't put it past them — Draco had them on the payroll too.

However, it seemed he'd be long gone by the time they arrived.

He threw the AR-15 through the open driver's window, ignoring the screams of fleeing civilians in the distance. Anyone within the vicinity of the National Institute's headquarters had fled for their lives, for good reason.

Ramos fired up the engine and tore away from the sidewalk, passing a police cruiser with flashing lights only a few moments after leaving. They didn't give chase — if they did, he would have gunned them down in the street.

He couldn't shrug the feeling that things had reached a tipping point.

He had left too many bodies in his wake.

He had crossed the line from an annoying grievance to an out-of-control tyrant.

It was all or nothing.

The takeover had begun. Seeds had been planted. Roadblocks had been met. He already had a three-man team of tech prodigies hurrying down from San Francisco. Men swayed enough by large dollar signs to abandon their promising careers in Silicon Valley for a riskier venture, but a higher payday. They would get the back-end in order. The three of them were due to arrive tomorrow.

Until then, he had to bunker down.

After the killings he'd dealt out over the last few days, it was clear that he'd started a war.

And he would finish it, too.

He twisted the wheel hard to the left, screeching around a corner, and rocketed back to his mansion with power on his mind.

# 12

At 0600 the sun had yet to rise, but the sky had shifted from a murky dark blue to a paler pre-dawn light. It was a cloudless day — King could see the breath steaming in front of his face even before the sun had risen. He pounded along the steep mountain trail, breathing deep as the blood circulated through his system and his limbs warmed up.

Lars led the way, hurrying to the mountain's summit before the sun rose. He'd told King that he saw it as something of a personal challenge. He wanted to witness the sunrise with his own eyes.

So did King.

Something about today felt different.

It started with the familiar sensation of pre-operation jitters — the difference today was that he still had no idea what he would be heading into. He knew enough about Mexico and the drug business to understand just how ruthless the industry was. The glamourised tales of drug kingpins sweeping the entertainment industry were a cruel ruse. He was aware that cartels were monstrous entities, devoid of any morality and willing to kill and torture and dismember over and over again to get what they wanted.

Now, the sheer detachment from his previous comrades became obvious. He *loved* the solitude of training alone, but field work threatened to be an entirely different beast.

What if he found himself in an unprecedented situation with no reinforcements or contacts to rely on whatsoever?

He would have to trust his intuition.

They reached a small gravel clearing at the top of the mountain trail just as the first fingers of sunlight began to crawl over the horizon. King caught his breath, resting his hands on his hips. It only took a few seconds. He had never been in better shape — the added agility and martial arts training had honed his senses beyond his wildest dreams. He was poised.

Ready for war.

'I'm guessing this is where you tell me what the hell I'm here for,' he said.

He cocked his head. His voice sounded strange surrounded by nature.

Like he was destroying the peace.

*That's what you're here for,* he reminded himself.

'What do you know about Tijuana?' Lars said, sitting down on a fallen log that had been set up as a resting place for hikers to admire the view.

King dropped down alongside him. 'It's hot. And the drinks are cheap.'

'It's a border town,' Lars said. 'Which means it's a goddamn hotspot for cartel activity, as you can imagine.'

'Frontier life,' King mused.

'Frontier life indeed.'

'What are you expecting me to do about it?'

Lars paused. 'I want you to kill the leader of a new cartel — and any other of its senior members that you can find.'

'That sounds like it would be highly frowned upon in official circles.'

'It would. What do you think this division exists for?'

'I'm going to need more details than that.'

'Obviously.'

'So shoot.'

'Joaquín Ramos,' Lars said.

'That's a little less information than I was looking for.'

'He's your man.'

'Who is he?'

'We know very little about him. He hides himself well. Pays for everything in cash. Uses a maze of false names and trust companies to hide his assets. No-one knows his exact whereabouts at any time. What we do know is that he's the head of a radical new cartel, and he's currently in the process of attempting a full-scale takeover of Tijuana's drug trade.'

'You think it's going to work?'

'Oh, it's working,' Lars said. 'Whether through sheer dumb luck or actual talent, he's managed to send the previous cartel's ranks into meltdown. He's one of the more reckless individuals I've ever had the chance to follow. He's almost single-handedly responsible for the murder rate in Tijuana quadrupling over the last year.'

'Surely people have attempted this before.'

'Not like this.'

'What's he doing differently?'

'We're still in the dark about a lot of Ramos' operation,' Lars said. 'But it's quite unique. As far as we can tell, he has no street-level dealers to speak of. His business is almost entirely online. The Department of Defence has been attempting to track his online activity, but it's near-impossible. He's got the entire system hidden in the Dark Web.'

'I'm not a computer guy,' King said.

'It's a section of the Internet that can't be accessed by standard search browsers. Everything's encrypted beyond measure. We managed to find a private cryptocurrency wallet that we believe is storing Ramos' funds. It disappeared under a layer of encryption as soon as we came across it, but it contains almost fifty million USD. More than likely his personal profits from his business endeavours. He's slowly building a drug empire using methods we've never seen before. The way it's set up means that there's no single point with which to track them, and everything's encrypted. He's cutting massive operating costs and maximising profits. That's how he's giving the Draco cartel a run for their money.'

'The Draco cartel?' King said. 'They're the power players in Tijuana?'

'Yes.'

'What are we doing to stop them?'

'If we wanted to try and take down every node of the global drug trade, the government would laugh us out. The system does $300 billion in revenue every single year. We don't have a chance at making a dent in Draco's empire. Not yet. You're heading into Tijuana to send a message to every cartel in the country. U.S. personnel are not to be touched. Under any circumstances.'

'What happened?'

'A week ago, two DEA agents were murdered in a basement in Tijuana. We were preparing to begin a campaign of arrests. Cracking down harshly to try and reimpose the unspoken law that we're not to be touched. Then shit hit the fan.'

'Today?'

'Yesterday morning,' Lars said. 'Two of our Customs Enforcement agents were gunned down in the lobby of a Mexican government building. A senior member of their National Institute for the Combat of Drugs was killed too. We think it was Ramos — no-one else is that insane to try and provoke us further. Not even Draco.'

'So you need me.'

'We need someone. I'd been arguing for the forging of a division like this for quite some time, but it kept getting shot down. Finally, this situation presented itself. Using SEALs or DEVGRU wouldn't cut it. They'd be identified in a heartbeat if they headed into Tijuana's slums as a pack. This is the opportunity for a single man — a lone wolf — to enter the city and take out the men who are antagonising us.'

'So an emphasis on stealth?' King said. 'You want no-one to know that I'm affiliated with the government?'

'Exactly. No uniform. No official mission. Just approval from the highest powers in the government for a single man to do what's necessary.'

'So I assume...' King started.

Lars clearly recognised where the conversation was headed. 'You'll need to accept the risk. We won't be able to come to your rescue in the event that you need it. If something goes wrong and you find yourself imprisoned by one of the cartels, or Mexican officials ... there's nothing we can do. You don't belong to us. You don't belong to anyone. You'll have to accept that before you decide to go through with this.'

'I always assumed as much.'

'It doesn't bother you?'

'Of course it bothers me. But that's always the way it was going to be.'

'This is a lot for your first task,' Lars admitted. 'I'd rather you test the waters as a solo operative with something a little safer.'

'I can handle myself,' King said. 'Throw me in the deep end — I couldn't care less. Just gives me a chance to prove myself to whoever's watching.'

'You really want to do this?' Lars said.

He spoke with an incredulous inflection to his tone. Like he had been expecting a mountain of resistance to have to push through to get King on board.

'Operating alone excites me,' King said. 'But it's really been decided that I'm the best solution to this problem?'

'There's no easy fix,' Lars said. 'But we need to restore order. This is a new breed of criminal. Tijuana's reached a boiling point, and our agents and officers are at risk. Not to mention all our tourists that head to the city for cheap thrills. Civilian casualties are at an all-time high. Collateral from the drug war.'

'And you think that if I kill Ramos and all his men that problem will magically resolve itself?'

'I think nothing of the sort,' Lars said. 'But it's a fact that a single organisation is responsible for the massive spike in murders. Executions, mass graves, shootouts in tourist hotspots. Bodies are turning up every single day. Before Ramos came onto the scene, there was relative calm. Draco had full control over the city. It's easier for us to address the larger problem of the Draco cartel when this new blood-thirsty entity is out of the way.'

'Got it. And how do you propose I do that?'

'In what sense?'

'If Ramos is so hard to find, how am I supposed to do it? I'm not a detective.'

Lars smiled and nodded. 'You sure aren't. Thankfully, we

had the lucky break of a lifetime. That's why we have to rush you into the field. Today, if possible.'

'What happened?'

'We caught a guy trying to cross the border. His story didn't add up, and by the time the border officials contacted us, we were certain we had our man.'

'Who is he?'

'A tech guy. From Silicon Valley. Heading across the border for a supposed vacation after quitting a high-six-figure position at one of the Internet giants. His story fell apart after minor interrogation. He didn't exactly excel at social interaction. Apparently he was sweating bullets and shaking just trying to cross the border. That's how the officials were alerted in the first place.'

'Ramos hired him?'

'We're almost certain. He admitted to accepting an anonymous offer for the position of a lifetime. He knew it was illegal. No-one else is offering that sort of money in Tijuana. It has to be Ramos.'

'And if it's not?'

'Then we regroup, and try again later. But this is the golden opportunity. If you're willing to go through with it, we'll act now.'

'Hang on,' King said. 'You want me to pretend to be this guy?'

'For as long as you need to.'

'That's a stretch.'

'I know it is.'

'I couldn't answer a single question about computers.'

'So you put a bullet in Ramos' head before he gets the chance to ask you anything.'

'What if I only meet face-to-face with the men in his ranks?'

'Then you trace them back to Ramos and kill him.'

'I don't know...'

'You don't have to accept this. But the makeshift training camp we've got down in the woods will be shut down. You'll be integrated back into Delta ... or maybe something more bland. We're on thin ice here already.'

King sighed. 'Okay. Send me in.'

'You sure?'

'Not at all. But if it's your superiors asking, then you tell them that I'm one-hundred percent certain.'

Lars stood up and stretched in the dawn light. 'Let's get back down there. We've got a lot to take care of.'

King got to his feet in turn. Together, they set off down the mountain trail, clouds of breath still forming in front of their faces.

'Fucking Mexico,' King muttered under his breath, wondering just how smoothly this operation would unfold.

# 13

*San Diego, USA*
*1 mile north of the border...*

The chartered military plane touched down at Brown Field Municipal Airport early in the afternoon that same day.

King sat in the cold metal fuselage, his rear resting against the cold metal seat, his back leaning against the cold metal wall. He was the sole passenger of the aircraft, strapped into a military safety harness while the body of the plane rattled around him as it begun its descent.

The morning had been a whirlwind of confusion. What seemed like half the U.S. government had shown up in Wyoming upon confirmation that King had accepted the mission. He had been thrust from contract to contract, signing his life away every ten minutes. He had accepted full responsibility for the outcome of the operation, and been informed time and time again that he would not be extracted or acknowledged in the event that he was captured.

Then it had been a short drive to Cheyenne Regional Airport, followed by a flight direct to the Otay Mesa neighbourhood in San Diego, California.

When he landed, it would be boots-to-asses.

He'd been informed that there was little time for stalling, or Ramos would grow wary of a change in schedule and disappear forever.

If King was to infiltrate their ranks, he would have to act now.

React intuitively.

Just how he liked it.

The nerves began to set in. It started with a slight tremor in his hand, which he quickly suppressed just in case either of the pilots flashed a glance back into the fuselage. He didn't want any reports of nervousness making their way through the upper ranks of the government. He wanted them convinced that their operation rested in good hands.

In reality, the fear threatened to overwhelm him.

He'd expected to roll with whatever came his way, but the idea of failure and excruciating torture at the hands of a livid drug cartel sent shivers down his spine. The stakes were impossibly high — if he slipped up or allowed himself to be captured, there would be no-one coming to his rescue. If he wasn't killed quickly, it would spell a horrific demise at the hands of whoever he had antagonised.

But he was ready.

He had spent half his life training for something like this. He had one opportunity to make a first impression upon whoever was in charge of this division, and he convinced himself that he would make it count. The idea of a career as a solo operative enticed him, providing him with an excitement that he hadn't previously felt.

The military plane slammed down onto the runway,

jolting King in his seat. He rode out the rattling and shaking until the brakes kicked in and they coasted to a halt somewhere near the terminal. There were no windows in the fuselage, and King had no idea what lay outside.

The co-pilot stuck his head around the corner. 'There's a car waiting for you. Apparently you have everything you need otherwise.'

King glanced down at the black duffel bag resting on the seat beside him, and shrugged. 'I guess so.'

'Good luck out there.'

With the artificial hiss of hydraulics, the rear ramp of the plane descended toward the tarmac outside. Slivers of daylight punched through the darkened cabin, until the ramp hit the ground and sunlight flooded into the large metal tube. King unclipped his seatbelt and slung the duffel bag over one shoulder. He strode down the ramp, his scuffed boots ringing off the steel.

Just as the co-pilot had said, in the time it had taken the plane to power down a car had been sent from the terminal to collect him. It was a second-hand Chevy Buick with scuff marks above all four wheels and a stern-looking man in the driver's seat. King opened the passenger door and dropped inside, escaping from the scorching San Diego heat.

He reached across the centre console to shake the hand of what he presumed was a rental-car official. Instead, the man — complete with greying hair and a permanently furrowed brow — flashed a military-grade identification badge at him.

King took a look at the ID.

Department of Defence.

'Oh,' he said. 'Hey.'

'Hello, sir,' the man said formally.

'This isn't a rental car?'

'This is James Bennett's car.'

'Who the hell is James Bennett?'

'You.'

Everything clicked. If King was to be impersonating the tech-guru from San Francisco, he would have to ensure that everything matched. If Ramos got the slightest hint that his contractor had been compromised, he would high-tail it out of Tijuana to avoid arrest.

'Sorry,' King said. 'Things are moving pretty fast. I've got a narrow window to capitalise on this situation.'

The DOD official shrugged, like he couldn't care less about the details. 'I've been told to transport you outside the airport's limits and then leave you with the car. Then it's all yours.'

King paused. 'Are you in the dark about all this?'

'I certainly am.'

'Is that normal?'

'Not normal for me.'

King nodded. 'Thanks for the help, then.'

He settled in as the driver set off across the runway, following a pre-determined path to avoid interfering with any air traffic. As they sat in silence, he stomached a gut punch of nerves. They were only a mile from the border. As soon as they left the airport behind, King would be left to his own devices. It would be his first official day in the field as a solo operative.

He couldn't shrug off how disorganised the mission felt. It seemed like only an hour ago he had been unconcerned with live operations, focused on his training alone, preparing for a date far in the distance when he would first be deployed on his own.

That day had raced up on him in the blink of an eye.

The Chevy trawled through a guard checkpoint built

into the airport's perimeter fence, allowed through after the driver had a brief conversation with the guard manning the booth. They came out onto a wide dusty road surrounded by sweeping plains of dead grass. In the distance, King spotted the traffic congesting as the line to one of the border checkpoints began to form.

There wasn't much distance between the two.

'Well, I'm heading back in,' the driver said, coasting the Chevy to the side of the road and deploying the handbrake. 'Best of luck with whatever it is you do.'

'Thank you,' King said, opting to otherwise keep his mouth shut. If the man didn't have clearance, he didn't want to accidentally share any information that might get him into trouble in future. Despite the haphazard nature of the operation, King still felt the need to employ some sense of professionalism.

The pair exited the car simultaneously. King slammed the door shut behind him and crossed over to the driver's side, watching as the driver himself waved farewell and set off back for the airport gate behind them. King slid into the driver's seat, closed the door, and placed both hands on the wheel.

The interior of the vehicle descended into silence.

He took a deep breath and let the calm wash over him. There was no passing traffic to jolt him out of the state. He had exited the airport into a section of no-man's-land, the strange scattering of unpopulated roads near the border that signified a change in territory.

Before he set off for the border checkpoint, he rummaged through the duffel bag on the passenger seat and came out with a military-grade satellite phone Lars had given him for a check-in.

He dialled the only contact number that had been entered into the phone and waited for Lars to answer.

It only took a couple of seconds.

'Made it safe and sound?' the man said.

'I'm out of the airport,' King said. 'Guessing you told them in advance.'

'Of course. The border officials have been instructed to let you through without a second look, too. Your photo's in their system.'

'You sure that's a good idea?'

'What do you mean?'

'What if Ramos has bought them off?'

'Ramos hasn't bought anyone off,' Lars said. 'Not yet. Everything's still under Draco's control. Ramos is still making a name for himself.'

'If you say so.'

'Just let me do my thing. You focus on getting into Tijuana.'

'Where am I headed?'

'The address has been entered into the Chevy's GPS. We had to pry the meeting point out of Bennett, seeing that the original message that Ramos sent to him was blocked by TOR encryption, then deleted. His memory is the only thing keeping this operation alive.'

'Where is Bennett?'

'Still in custody.'

'What's going to happen to him?'

'Depends. He was about to help expand a mass-murdering psychopath's drug cartel. That carries serious consequences.'

'Fair enough.'

'I can't stress the importance of this operation,' Lars said. 'The two of us haven't had much of a chance to comprehend what's about to happen, but it'll spell the future of this division if you succeed. You need to succeed.'

'Of course I need to succeed,' King said. 'I'll be kidnapped and cut up into a million pieces if I don't. That's enough incentive.'

'You understand that you're not affiliated with the U.S. government, right? You're James Bennett.'

'Of course. And I have full discretion?'

'You can do whatever the hell you want,' Lars said. 'You're not operating within the boundaries of the law. Just don't get caught.'

'I won't.'

'Stay in touch.'

'I'll do my best.'

That was all that needed to be said. King ended the call and threw the phone into the footwell. If Lars had been truthful and he really had no risk of being apprehended at the border, he could dispose of the device once he had entered Mexico.

He peeled away from the stretch of gravel on the side of the road and set off for the long line of traffic heading into Tijuana. He cast his gaze down the length of the sixty-mile stretch of San Diego border county, where it trailed into the distance before disappearing from sight between the rolling hills.

He entered the line of traffic and wiped sweat from his palms.

It had begun.

# 14

The crossing took forever.

By the time King reached the front of the line in the old Chevy, the digital clock on the dashboard signalled that almost an hour had passed. The sun beat down outside, beginning its descent toward the opposite horizon as the early afternoon set in. At one point, he rolled down the window to gauge the heat. It was oppressively warm, powerful enough to draw the sweat from his pores within moments. He rolled the window back up and savoured the air-conditioned interior.

It might be the only reprieve from the heat he would get for some time.

The uncertainty began to take hold. Sitting in banked-up traffic for close to an hour gave him ample time to think about the lack of a coherent plan, the isolation he would experience in Tijuana, and the danger he would face in loosely impersonating a guy from San Francisco who he had never met. There were forged identification documents in the duffel bag, but they would only hold up at a glance. Bennett's photo had been replaced with a mugshot of King's face, but the gig would only last so long.

It was simply a thinly-veiled ruse to get Ramos into a vulnerable position. Everything from that point onwards would be entrusted to King's intuition. He recognised this operation for what it was — a raw test.

How could he handle making decisions on the fly?

How would he react to adversity?

Questions that would soon be answered.

He recognised that he had truly been thrown to the wolves.

He coasted the Chevy to a halt alongside the nearest booth after what felt like an eternity waiting to reach the border. He handed the forged ID over to the blank-faced official behind the window and waited patiently as the man ran it through the system.

Crystal-clear realisation spread across the man's face as he brought up a window on the monitor in front of him. He double-checked the ID, glanced out at King, then nodded satisfactorily.

'Good to go, sir,' he said. 'Enjoy your stay.'

Lars hadn't been bluffing. King had been approved within seconds, the border officials clearly informed earlier that day that he would be coming. He nodded back to the guard and let the Chevy coast through the checkpoint.

The air seemed to palpably shift as he entered Mexico. It wasn't anything physical — more a sense of foreboding taking hold. The familiar territory of the States shrank away, replaced by the mystery of Tijuana. He didn't know what was waiting for him in the shadows. Maybe Ramos had already wised up to the fact that Bennett was taking too long. Maybe he was waiting to receive King at gunpoint, at which point he would apprehend him and interrogate him for the next month before finally bringing his miserable life to an end.

There was a Beretta M9 in King's duffel bag, along with a handful of spare magazines. If Lars hadn't allowed him exclusive access across the border, he would have been arrested by the officials back at the checkpoint. King didn't know what to do with the weapon — if he took it into his meeting with Ramos or his men, he would have to act instantly in the event of a frisk search.

Maybe he should leave it in the car when he reached his destination.

Play it safe.

The uncertainty amplified.

He coasted into the city, unsure whether the evil that he sensed was just a placebo conjured up by the tales Lars had spun, or something tangible. The streets were unnaturally quiet, like the residents of Tijuana were opting to stay indoors instead of venture out into the lawless war zone created by the drug war. Lars had told him that the border states had the highest murder rates in Mexico, but the recent developments in Tijuana had speared it ahead of the pack.

The address Bennett had been provided with rested in the shanty towns on the other side of the city. To get there, King would have to drive through the centre of Tijuana itself. He imagined the central districts were safer than the outskirts, but he couldn't be sure. Following the modified electronic GPS that had been installed in the centre of the Chevy's dashboard, he realised just how little he knew about the city.

It had been the sparsest mission briefing he had ever received.

Maybe that had been deliberate.

He had effectively been given free reign to do as he pleased. Maybe they were assessing just how well he could improvise.

He entered a district that seemed a little more open and airy than the rest of Tijuana. The streets were wide and smoothly paved, and broad tourist-riddled hotels speared into the sky on either side of his vehicle. The foot traffic increased the further he headed into Tijuana's centre, but he still got the distinct sense that everyone was hesitant. News of the constant murders must have spread rapidly through the city.

People were scared.

He caught a glimpse of the mountains in the distance, broad and sweeping and dotted with clusters of cheap housing. The GPS told him that the shanty town rested between the city centre and the mountains beyond. King imagined certain sections of Tijuana were effectively lawless.

He had been here many years ago, taking a short vacation between deployments in the SEALs. Back then, every street corner had bustled, packed with vendors selling anything from Mexican cuisine to trinkets to flyswatters and fans. Now, the city was a shell of its former self.

The crossover into the shanty town couldn't have been more visually obvious. The open, pleasant streets of the tourist district morphed into car wrecking yards and rusting tin buildings. Everything seemed like it had been thrown together in a day, like no-one intended to reside here permanently. Lars had explained that most of the population of these shanty towns consisted of illegal migrants and the poorer working class. They were searching for other opportunities, clearly in the process of finding any other available options.

*It's the perfect location for Ramos to conduct his business dealings*, King realised.

He turned down a street far narrower than the rest, following the instructions of the artificial monotone voice seeping out of the GPS. According to the electronic display, his destination was at the very end of the street, a building tucked into a small semi-circular courtyard.

The road was a dead end.

King's heart rate started to quicken as he recognised the volatility of the situation. He could easily be cornered and outgunned in this street. He had a Beretta M9 in a duffel bag and nothing else. There were three pedestrians ambling along the dusty, unpaved sidewalks. All three of them were young Mexican men, skinny, dressed in loose-fitting singlets and shorts that stretched well past their knees. King made out the noticeable bulge of firearms poking out of the rear of their waistbands. They turned towards the source of the noise as King turned the Chevy onto the trail.

He found himself in a staredown with the trio. He had no doubts that he could effortlessly handle the three of them, but the last thing he wanted to do was cause commotion. He was supposed to be an inexperienced tech prodigy from California, not an easily-triggered thug intent on starting a fight with anyone who looked at him funny.

He kept the tinted windows of his Chevy up and stared straight ahead, slowly crawling past the three thugs in an attempt to appear unimposing.

It seemed to work.

Barely.

They hurled insults at him in Spanish as he passed by. One of them yanked the black-market pistol out of his oversized shorts and tapped the barrel against the passenger's side window, yelling obscenities through the thin glass. King ignored them completely, adopting an expression of unease. He didn't want to seem too tough for his own good. If they thought he was intimidated by them, they might be satisfied and avoid taking things further.

One of the thugs snatched at the passenger door handle. King touched his foot lightly to the accelerator, quickening the Chevy's pace for an instant. The guy came up short. King glanced in the side mirror and watched as the trio regarded the Chevy for another moment longer.

Then it passed them by, and they turned their attention to something else.

King breathed a sigh of relief.

Not because they scared him.

But because if Ramos was watching, he had flawlessly played the part of an uncomfortable software engineer far out of his depth in these parts.

He reached the courtyard at the end of the road and coasted to a stop outside a small block of rundown apartments, three storeys high and rotting away before his eyes.

On the second floor balcony, two mean-looking thugs stared down at his car.

King peered up through the tinted windshield and made eye contact with him.

They beckoned him up.

He killed the engine and stepped out into the arid heat.

# 15

In the brief seconds of contemplation he had before the thugs on the landing above grew suspicious, King decided not to bring the Beretta. If he chose to arm himself, it would make it unavoidable to use the weapon when they opted to frisk search him. He wasn't entirely convinced that Ramos was on the premises, and a couple of dead henchmen would leave him no closer to tearing the cartel apart, like Lars had instructed him to do.

He had enough confidence in his ability to fight at close-quarters to head in unarmed.

The move spiked his adrenalin as he left the Chevy. He had never found himself in a situation as precarious as this. He had never impersonated another man, let alone attempted to integrate himself with a highly dangerous drug cartel. It took all the willpower in his body to calm himself.

Then again, the nerves would help convince the cartel of his persona — a terrified office worker taking a risk. He decided to let them show. In fact, he amplified them.

*What if they've seen a photo of Bennett?* King posited.

He made his way toward the flight of stairs connecting to

the upper levels of the apartment complex, thoughts churning through his head.

He doubted that they would know what the software engineer looked like. All signs pointed towards a rushed decision that had been easily foiled by border officials. Ramos had likely panicked, acting in the aftermath of an unknown situation that made him scramble. He'd reached out to bring in more help behind-the-scenes.

He would have trawled through online resumes, more than likely.

By now, King was in too deep anyway. He had committed to action the moment he left the Chevy. There was no diplomatic resolution to a situation like this. Violent confrontation was a given. It would come down to whether that would occur here, or at a later time.

Whatever the case, someone would die.

He told himself that all the training he had put himself through would ensure it would not be his body carted off to the morgue.

He felt the twin pairs of eyes boring into the top of his skull as he crossed underneath the second-floor balcony and mounted the flimsy flight of stairs. The thugs were watching intently.

This was it.

He made it to their level in a few seconds, taking the stairs three at a time like an eager contractor, excited to get into the dirty business. He smiled greedily at the two thugs as he crossed the space between them, while they scowled disinterestedly back at him. He embraced the persona of an excited software engineer who didn't really know how the world worked outside his cubicle.

Both the thugs were built like tanks and covered in tattoos from head to toe. Their heads were shaved, either to add to their tough-guy demeanour or to hide receding hairlines. They had the same features, with pronounced jawlines, thick lips and beady eyes — King imagined they were related.

Cousins, or brothers. Raised on the streets.

Hard, cruel men.

Perfect for the enforcer roles.

'You are software guy?' the larger of the two said in stunted English, regarding him with an incredulous look.

'That's me,' King said. 'Am I in the right place?'

'I don't know,' the man said. 'You do not look like software guy.'

Briefly, King sized up the space between them and prepared to smash the man's head into the nearest railing, bashing him unconscious before the other, smaller man could make a move.

Then he realised that the guy was referring to his build. They didn't know what James Bennett looked like. They were evidently taken aback by a six-foot-three, two-hundred-and-twenty pound powerhouse showing up. They had clearly been imagining a different stereotype.

'I lift weights sometimes,' King said. 'Good genetics.'

The man simply grunted.

'Arms out, bitch,' the smaller man said. He was still heavyset, probably an inch or two under six-foot. He lacked a visible neck — instead, the trapezius muscles around his shoulders had bunched up to bury it under a mountain of artificially-enhanced sinew. King glanced at the veins running along the man's forearms and guessed that the pair had altered their frames with a cheap cocktail of Mexican designer steroids. Ramos probably had access to a few dealers.

Strength would only get them so far, though.

Despite the hostile demands, King complied. He spread his arms straight and wide, poking them out in either direction. At the same time, he took care to shuffle restlessly on both feet, showing his unease. The shorter enforcer stepped forward and patted King down hard, manhandling him as he searched for weapons underneath his clothing.

Finding nothing, he backed off, satisfied.

King visibly squirmed, unsure of what would come next.

'I was told to meet a guy who would put me to work straight away?' he said, improvising. 'Is that you two?'

The taller of the pair cast a long, laboured gaze down the trail which King had ascended moments earlier. The street was dead quiet. Across the neighbourhood, the faint screams and hollers of gangs and drug dealers wafted through the air.

It seemed that King had come alone.

The guy nodded and ushered King toward a closed door built into the cheap plaster wall running the length of the balcony. One of the apartments in the complex, no doubt snatched up by Ramos to facilitate his online operation. King wondered what had happened to the men that had previously been running the man's business.

*In a ditch somewhere,* he concluded.

King stepped tentatively up to the door. He hesitated, unsure of what to do next. The enforcers stood behind him, one on either side, spaced an equal distance apart in the event that King tried any funny business. He paused, then raised a hand to knock on the thin wood.

A hand seized the back of his shirt.

He restrained himself, deciding not to act. Instead, he raised an eyebrow inquisitively. The taller of the two thugs had yanked him back by the shirt, constricting the air around his throat. King guessed that they felt suddenly threatened. They hadn't expected the software engineer to look more imposing than the enforcers themselves, and they were trying to assert their dominance however they could. King let the shirt material tighten uncomfortably around his neck and looked over his shoulder.

'What is it?' he said.

The taller thug snarled. 'Are you sure he's clean?' he said to the shorter man.

The other guy nodded. 'Yeah, man. No weapons.'

The first man shrugged in satisfaction and let go of King. 'Don't get smart with me, motherfucker.'

King paused, stifling a retort. Instead, he nodded. 'No problem, man. Do I knock?'

'Yes, you knock. What are you — fucking stupid?'

King pursed his lips, as if unsettled by the hostility, and turned back to face the door.

He knocked twice, softly. He didn't want to appear too eager — James Bennett would no doubt be shitting himself at this point in time.

Inwardly, King was too.

The door opened instantly. King came face-to-face with a man dressed in an expensive leather jacket and designer jeans, despite the heat. He was taller than King, but not by much — he guessed six-foot-four. The guy had a wiry yet strong frame, like he didn't work out but was gifted with a natural athleticism. He had long black hair hanging in strands over his forehead, and a cruel, youthful face. King guessed he wasn't far over twenty-five years old.

Joaquín Ramos.

The man who was in the process of razing Tijuana to the ground.

# 16

Ramos offered a hand, extending thin, spindly fingers in King's direction. 'Mr. Bennett?'

'That's me,' King said, shaking Ramos' hand.

The man had a strong grip, which he used to full effect in an attempt to intimidate King. King let the slightest hint of a wince cross his features. He wanted Ramos to feel like he had control.

Ramos stepped aside, gesturing into the small apartment.

King hesitated momentarily, recognising that if he accepted the gesture and stepped into the room, his back would face all three of them. Then he resigned himself to the fact that he was going to have to put himself at risk if he wanted to blend in. James Bennett wouldn't cover his six at all times, so neither would King.

He walked in, brushing past Ramos on the way inside.

The room was dark and musty — he guessed Ramos preferred it that way. The curtains had been drawn across the small set of windows facing out onto the balcony, casting a dark shadow over most of the room. The ceiling light hadn't been turned on — instead, the only illumination came from a desk lamp next to a rudimentary computer set-up, with a handful of monitors connected to a central PC via a nest of tangled wires. King was no tech guru, but he could spot amateur work when he saw it. He realised that whatever happened to Ramos' previous helpers must have thrown him off his game. Ramos was improvising now, coming up with makeshift solutions on the fly. King expected that he hadn't used this place as a headquarters before.

Most of the usual stock-standard furniture that came with an apartment like this had been stripped out, converting it into a utilitarian workspace. A doorway on the far wall led through to what King imagined was a bedroom/bathroom combination — otherwise, the main living area was the only notable feature of the apartment. It couldn't have been more than fifty square feet in total.

King wondered just what conditions James Bennett would have been forced to work in if he had ever made it into Tijuana.

He heard the creak of wood behind him as Ramos and the two enforcers stepped into the apartment and shut the door. King wheeled on the spot as the trio spread out in front of him. All three of them watched him like hawks, assessing him for any sign of confrontation. Maybe his appearance truly had thrown them off.

'Little cramped in here,' King said. 'Nowhere for the four of us to sit.'

'I imagine we won't be here long,' Ramos said. 'You've got plenty of work to do. We'll leave you to it soon.'

'Looking forward to it. For the right price, of course.'

An uncomfortable silence settled over the low-ceilinged space as neither of the three responded. King eyed the bulge in the side of each enforcer's waistband, indicating that they were armed. He didn't let his gaze linger for long. He didn't want them to take his curiosity the wrong way.

'How was the drive over?' Ramos said. 'No problems at the border?'

King shook his head. 'No problems.'

'It was very brave of you to drop everything and come help me,' Ramos said. 'Like we discussed, you'll be compensated heavily if you get everything up and running smoothly.'

'I appreciate that.'

'What did you think of my offer?' Ramos said. 'In my initial message. Did it tantalise you?'

King made sure not to hesitate, but inside his head the gears whirred. As far as he knew, Lars and the D.O.D. hadn't been able to get their hands on the log of messages that Ramos had exchanged with Bennett. He remembered getting told that the messages had been protected by PGP encryption, which made their contents indecipherable for anyone except the receiver.

Apparently, Bennett had destroyed them before leaving his old life behind to cross the border.

King would have to make everything up on the fly.

'It appealed to me,' he said. 'I'd be grateful for anything close to that amount.'

Ramos paused, staring straight through King. 'I lowballed you, though. We discussed that after, remember? I've agreed to double it.'

'Frankly, I'll take all the money I can get,' King said, taking care not to stammer.

'I hear your last job was mid six-figures per year...' Ramos said, obviously confused. 'You got money troubles?'

*Fuck,* King thought.

'I... uh...' he said. Then he got an idea. He could use his hesitation to play the part of a man hiding a secret. 'I have a few issues. Gambling, drugs. You know...'

'Drugs?' Ramos said.

'I'm not looking for supply, don't worry.'

'I wasn't worrying.'

'Okay.'

'So ... what do you need me to do first? I'm familiar with the TOR browser, if you want to start there.'

Ramos paused again. The silence turned deafening. It drew out longer, and longer still. Three seconds, four seconds, five.

'I damn well expect you to know what the TOR browser is...' Ramos said. 'This is amateur stuff. How did you get your last job?'

'I know what I'm doing,' King said, like he was insulted that someone would dare question his capabilities.

'What's the safe word?' Ramos said.

'What?'

'Three seconds.'

'Sorry, I'm tired. It's been a long day. Refresh me.'

'Two seconds.'

'Uh...'

'One second.'

'Do you understand what I've just done?' King said, grasping at straws. 'I'm not in a great mental state at the moment. I just dropped everything to seize this opportunity. It meant leaving everything behind. All my friends, my family. I don't even know if I'll head back in one piece, given the nature of this business. Spare me at least a single courtesy and remind me what the hell we're talking about.'

The spiel did little to affect Ramos' expression. It

remained steely, his eyes wide, his gaze fixed on King like a snake watching its prey.

Finally, he relented.

'In my initial email,' he said. 'The word I sent you to ensure that you didn't get intercepted at the border. The word that would confirm that it's you standing in front of me, instead of someone simply impersonating you.'

King couldn't afford to pause for even a single breath. He stomached a sharp inhale of mounting tension as it dawned on him that Ramos had employed a safety measure. The PGP encryption meant that James Bennett — sitting in a cell at the San Diego-Mexico border — was the only one who knew the safe word. He hadn't bothered to share it with the authorities.

In doing so, he had abandoned King in the deep end.

King didn't know the word.

He couldn't respond.

The two enforcers sensed his sudden hesitation and panic. They reached for their guns.

# 17

King recognised the approaching combat, and his vision narrowed.

The atmosphere shifted, the mounting tension palpable. He saw realisation spread across Ramos' face as the man's worst suspicions came to life.

King bull-rushed Ramos, switching from stationary and placid to a charging, explosive battering ram in the blink of an eye.

He dropped his shoulder low and drove it straight into the centre of Ramos' chest, taking the man by surprise. He focused on pushing through with his legs, adding momentum to the tackle. Ramos was taken off his feet, entirely unprepared for the blunt trauma punching its way through his frame.

He toppled back into the enforcer behind him — the smaller of the two. Together, the pair cascaded to the floor in a tangle of limbs, bruising skin and straining muscles. The tiled floor underneath them offered no protection from the fall.

King carried straight on, barely slowing down. He

vaulted over the two scrambling bodies and intercepted the larger thug just as the man slid a compact semi-automatic pistol out of his waistband. The guy fumbled with the trigger guard. King realised that he carried the firearm more for intimidation than anything else.

He clearly had no idea how to use it.

Years of non-stop training kicked in and King went through the motions, reacting reflexively. He clamped two hands down on the thug's wrist and locked his arm in a vice-like grip, preventing the guy from swinging the barrel in his direction and squeezing off a lucky shot. Then he used the strength that came from a rigorous powerlifting routine and an added dose of life-or-death adrenalin to smash the back of the guy's hand against the nearest wall.

The man released his grip on the pistol at the same time that his hand tore straight through the flimsy plaster, caving a decent-sized hole out of the wall.

The thug winced in agony. The mean-mug expression vanished off his face, replaced by pain and a hint of fear. He had felt King's raw power. It had certainly shocked him.

King used the slight pause in action to line up a bullet-like uppercut, treating the underside of the thug's chin as a sparring pad. He envisioned Randall in front of him, instructing him to twist his body into the motion and use every ounce of explosive power in his mid-section to add weight to the shot.

He swung through, preparing for impact. It came with the audible crack of breaking bone as the thug's jaw crunched into his top row of teeth, snapped up by the punch. His head jerked back, stiffening his neck as the force resonated through his skull.

His legs caved before King's eyes.

King realised that he had knocked the man unconscious

with a single, staggering punch. The guy dropped like a deadweight, folding in on himself as the lights went off upstairs. The tough-guy demeanour vanished along with his consciousness and he careered back against the plaster wall, whiplashing his head against it on the way down.

King noted the dissolution of the threat and spun to dive on Ramos and the smaller thug. The pair were still making their way to their feet, scrambling on the slick tiled flooring. King analysed the different threats — first and foremost, the smaller thug had a finger inside the trigger guard of his weapon. All he had to do was raise the barrel and blast King's face to shreds. It was a precarious situation — one that needed to be resolved within the next second if King wanted a chance of seeing another sunrise.

Ramos appeared unarmed.

His mind was made up.

He dropped low and wrapped a powerful arm around the enforcer's waist, heaving him off the ground. The vertigo kicked in and the guy slackened momentarily, shocked by his lack of control. In a fight to the death, where animalistic instinct often took over, a fifty-pound bodyweight difference meant everything. King felt the ease with which he could manhandle the smaller thug, and it gave him a boost of confidence.

He took off in a full-blown sprint across the room, using the momentum of his wild charge to hurry toward the bank of computer monitors on the far wall. The thug dangled uselessly over King's shoulder, swinging wild, unhinged punches into King's upper back.

They achieved nothing.

King knew exactly how to cause a world of neurological damage if needed. The years of relentless martial arts training had its advantages. Punching him in the back would cause bruises, but nothing that couldn't be healed by some ice and rest.

What came next for the thug on his shoulder would take a little longer to recover from.

King changed his momentum mid-stride, ducking forward and wrenching the guy's legs down. He effectively threw the man like a rag doll into the collection of trestle tables, sending him crashing head-first through the field of electronics. Glass shattered and wires disconnected as the table legs gave out. The entire setup came crashing to the floor of the apartment, with the smaller thug landing in the midst of the destruction in a dazed heap. The impact had stunned him, causing him to falter.

In King's heightened state of awareness, a single moment's hesitation felt like an eternity.

He had the upper hand.

He scrambled for the firearm the man had dropped, recognising it as a FN Five-seven semi-automatic pistol. A reliable weapon, likely smuggled into Mexico and purchased for a hefty mark-up on the black market. King snatched up the gun, locking it in his grip in a single motion. He twisted on the spot and brought the barrel up to head-height, searching for Ramos in the cramped apartment.

He froze.

There was no sign of the man.

Ramos had reacted blindingly fast. The door was still swinging on its hinges from where he had made a mad dash out onto the balcony. He must have sensed the tide turning in King's favour all at once, because he had fled from the scene without a moment's hesitation.

King swore under his breath and bolted for the door. He almost lost his footing on the shiny floor underneath his feet, moving too fast as panic took hold. If Ramos got away, the operation would screech to an earth-shattering halt and King would be forced to slink back over the border with his tail between his legs.

His entire future came down to these next few seconds.

# 18

He burst out into the open-air corridor outside the apartments only a few seconds after Ramos. As he exited the apartment, he caught a flash of movement on the edge of his peripheral vision.

Noting that the man could have been in possession of a hidden firearm, King's instinctive training kicked in and he swung the barrel from left to right, assessing the threats.

What he found shocked him.

No sign of Ramos.

*Where the fuck is he?* he thought.

A split second later, he heard a crash emanating up from the ground below. He sprinted over to the railing and glanced down, searching for the source of the noise.

Ramos had leapfrogged the railing, making the one-storey drop out of desperation. He had landed hard on the dusty ground beneath, and was now scrabbling for purchase.

King lifted the Five-seven and squeezed off a cluster of shots. They rang off the nearby walls, causing screams of surprise to drift out of neighbouring apartments.

He missed every shot, because Ramos was no longer there.

By the time he'd brought the barrel over the railing to aim at the ground, Ramos had got his feet underneath him and dived for cover. King watched the man disappear from sight, ducking underneath the second-storey balcony upon which he stood. The bullets sunk harmlessly into the dirt where he'd landed a second earlier.

King threw a glance toward the flight of stairs he'd ascended just a few minutes earlier. They were too far away. If he wanted any hope of catching Ramos, he would have to throw caution to the wind.

He gripped the railing with his free hand, noting its flimsiness. Then he pushed off both feet and launched over the edge. His stomach dropped into his feet as he rocketed towards the ground ten feet below.

Mid-fall, his heart rate leapt.

Ramos had been anticipating the move. As King dropped through the air, he noticed a shadowy figure charging straight at his landing trajectory. He couldn't do anything but watch as Ramos sprinted out from under the balcony to intercept him. He caught a shoulder in his solar plexus — Ramos timed the tackle expertly, slamming into King before his feet had even touched the ground.

The momentum changed drastically.

He kept a desperate hold on the Five-seven as Ramos dropped him unceremoniously into the dirt. Instinctively, his finger tightened around the trigger. As the back of his head smashed into the ground hard enough to disorient him, he felt the gun go off in his palm. The shot went wide, hitting a neighbouring building. In the confusion, he watched Ramos take the opportunity to swing the point of his elbow in King's direction.

King saw the blow coming, but was powerless to stop it.

He caught the elbow directly in the soft tissue of his throat, wrenching all the breath from his lungs. Briefly, he wondered if he'd been permanently damaged by the blow. It was one of the hardest strikes he had ever received, shocking his system into temporary paralysis.

Pain tore through his head and chest, resonating from the point of impact. King froze up, the blood draining from his face as he gasped for breath. He realised that his youth and inexperience in the field had come around to haunt him, shutting his senses down for a few seconds. He lay in the dirt, seized up by the pain of the landing.

In the brief moment that it took him to regain control over his motor functions, Ramos had capitalised.

King quickly realised that he was dealing with a foe more dangerous than he previously anticipated. He had likened Ramos to a foolish new gangster on the block. In truth, the man was cunningly smart, and highly reactive.

Just like King.

He rolled over and pushed himself up to his knees, noting a drop of blood that fell from one of his nostrils as he did so. His vision had blurred, either from the damage done to his throat or the back of his head when he'd landed on the hard earth. In the corner of his gaze, he made out the shaky silhouette of Ramos sprinting at top speed down the road.

Desperate to act, King reared to his feet and aimed with the Five-seven, his hand shaking. He stumbled, righted himself, then fired.

By then, Ramos had ducked into the gap between two low shanty town houses. King's bullets went wide.

Crazed yells tore down the street in his direction, from somewhere off to the side. He jolted in surprise and followed the source of the commotion to see the three thugs he'd passed earlier wrenching their second-hand firearms out of their pants.

They were responding to King's shots.

They thought he was starting a war.

With his senses flooding back to him, King swore in frustration and ran across the bare lot in front of the apartment complex, high-tailing it towards the idle Chevy. He was cruelly exposed in his current position, susceptible to a wave of gunfire if he didn't move immediately.

The trio of gangsters unloaded a handful of rounds in his direction.

Thankfully, they seemingly hadn't fired a gun before in their lives.

The bullets went wide, missing King by several feet each. He hurled open the driver's door of the Chevy and threw himself inside, twisting the key in the ignition before his ass had even touched the seat.

The sedan coughed into life.

A bullet shattered the passenger-side window, spraying glass fragments into the interior. King ducked reflexively away from the horrific blast of noise, stamping on the accelerator at the same time. The back wheels of the Chevy skidded out as the car bit for purchase on the hot ground.

Finally, they found their grip in the dust.

King's stomach fell as the acceleration slammed him back against the seat. He twisted the wheel, fishtailing the Chevy in a tight arc to send it hurtling back down the road. Every second he spent stationary was another opportunity for Ramos to escape.

Based on his estimates, he imagined that Ramos had sprinted through to the next street over. King roared away from the trio of gangsters. They kept firing on him as he sped past. Lead punched through the thin chassis of his vehicle, each impact sending a bolt of fear through his chest. His heart thumped hard against his chest wall, riding out an overwhelming wave of adrenalin.

At the end of the street he swerved left, heading back the way he had come. On the way to the apartment complex he'd glimpsed the street parallel to the one he'd just left. He guessed that was where Ramos was headed.

As he skidded around the next bend and entered the adjacent street, a horrifying scene unfolded before his eyes. He peered out the tinted windscreen to see an overweight civilian sprawling uncontrollably out of her car in the middle of the road ahead, thrown out against her will. He caught a flash of rapid movement as Ramos' gangly frame ducked into the seat she'd just vacated. The man had chosen to hijack an ordinary hatchback, currently the only car in the entire street.

King heard the crack of a gunshot, and saw the elderly woman collapse in a limp heap. At the same time, a muzzle flare flashed out of the open driver's door.

Ramos had killed the woman.

For no good reason.

King rode out a wave of blistering rage and mashed the accelerator into the footwell, chasing after the hatchback with newfound anger in his blood.

# 19

Two minutes into the pursuit, it dawned on King that Ramos knew the streets of Tijuana a hundred times better than he did.

They twisted at breakneck speed through the shanty town, drawing the attention of anyone brave enough to step outside their house. A bald, drug-addled gangster with oversized shorts that stretched down to his ankles waved a fully loaded firearm in King's direction as he tore past. Maybe the guy thought that the speed at which King was travelling was a sign of hostility.

It didn't matter.

What mattered was keeping up with Ramos — or his short-lived career as a solo operative would come crashing to a halt.

As the poorer slums melted away — replaced by the wider avenues and bare fields of land that sat between Tijuana and the arid mountains behind it — King dared to increase his speed. He throttled the Chevy up to ninety miles an hour, gaining ground on Ramos with each passing second.

The hatchback in front of him swerved violently into oncoming traffic. It took King by surprise, and he adjusted his course to try and keep up. Then the hatchback's tyres squealed as Ramos slammed on the brakes. It skidded uncontrollably for a brief second before finding purchase on the asphalt and darting down a narrow side street.

Just in time.

In the space that Ramos' vehicle had preoccupied a moment earlier, a thick line of oncoming traffic flashed past. King realised that the angle didn't add up. He would have to slow his Chevy considerably to make the same turn that Ramos did, allowing the cartel leader to peel away and put distance between them.

Instead, King darted back into his lane and pressed on, electing to try and turn down a similar side street up ahead.

Hopefully, all the narrow alleys led through to the same parallel road.

He waited for a gap in the passing traffic before screaming through to the other side of the road. He twisted the wheel, correcting course just in time. The Chevy ploughed onto a narrow trail curving between two residential apartment buildings, both a little more aesthetically pleasing than the shanty town complex he'd just visited.

The left-side mirror exploded in a shower of sparks as King scraped the car against one of the brick walls. He seized a tighter hold on the wheel and focused as hard as he could on the path ahead.

It was going to be tight.

At the end of the alley, he spotted Ramos' hatchback screaming past. Satisfied that he'd made the right call, he burst through the gap ahead at fifty miles per hour. He clenched his teeth, praying that a pedestrian didn't decide to cross the road as he roared into the next street.

It would be a grisly result, no doubt.

Thankfully, the streets were relatively empty — King wondered how much that had to do with the brutal drug war currently gripping Tijuana.

A war that he was currently contributing to, unless he eliminated Ramos before the day drew to a close.

They left the grid of residential buildings behind, and the land began to incline. King noticed the mountains drawing closer and closer with each passing second. The road they were currently travelling along grew narrower up ahead, twisting and curving as it rose into the hills. He made out the steep hillsides dropping away from the edges of the road and fought down hesitation.

He wasn't the most skilled driver in the world, preferring to utilise sheer speed and recklessness instead of any kind of precision. Deep down, he knew that if the pursuit reached the dangerous off-road trails of the mountains, he would be at a significant disadvantage.

And — worse than that — one wrong move would spell disaster.

He started to doubt his ability to succeed.

Then he shoved all negative thoughts to the back of his mind and accelerated faster.

He remembered the way the elderly woman's body had crumpled in the street just moments previously.

If he didn't do something to make things right, he would never be able to forgive himself.

The hatchback peeled away, as if Ramos could sense his hesitation. They rose further and further above sea level, battling the steep mountain roads. Ramos swerved around slower traffic, and King followed suit. He kept up with the hatchback's lightning-fast pace, regaining confidence with each passing second.

A minute later, they entered a flat stretch of road running along the side of the mountain. To King's right, the land sloped sharply up to the peak. To his left, a long length of thin metal railing separated his vehicle from a vicious fall down a gravel hillside.

There was no traffic ahead.

This was his opportunity.

King gave the Chevy's engine all it had, pushing the car faster. His surroundings on either side began to blur as the speedometer reached close to its maximum speed.

The hatchback ahead couldn't match the pace, its engine a tad less powerful. King watched as its rear bumper edged closer and closer to the hood of his Chevy. He gripped the wheel tight, knuckles white, brow furrowed. He would only have one chance to ram Ramos' car off the road, and he would take full advantage of it.

Then the world went mad.

Several things happened at once.

First, Ramos slammed on the brakes up ahead. King noticed the red lights on the back of the hatchback flaring, and he lunged for his own brake pedal to avoid a collision.

Briefly, he wondered why the hell Ramos had decided to cut the chase off so abruptly. If they both screeched to a halt in the middle of the road, King would have ample opportunity to disable the hatchback's tyres with his Five-seven.

He paused, sizing things up.

Then, a behemoth of a vehicle came steaming into view from an alcove to the right. King hadn't even seen the groove in the mountainside where the enormous tank-on-wheels had been parked. His eyes widened in surprise and he snatched at the wheel...

...but it was too little, too late.

With a churning stomach, he realised that Ramos hadn't led King into the mountains for no good reason.

He had brought him here deliberately.

He'd slammed on the brakes to manoeuvre him into position.

King braced for impact.

There was nothing else he could do.

The collision almost tore the Chevy in half, gouging a massive dent into the entire right-hand-side of the vehicle. Unrelenting sound flooded his senses — the screaming of twisting metal, the screeching of his tyres on the asphalt as the Chevy was thrust to the left.

Then — most shocking of all — the unmistakeable whine of twisting metal as his vehicle tore through the thin railing to the left and dipped off the edge of the hillside.

The truck had near-demolished his car, forcing it off the road without much effort. King's view outside blurred, and before he knew it he realised that the Chevy was starting to rotate...

'Shit,' he muttered, barely audible amidst the carnage.

He clicked his seatbelt into position and held on for dear life as the sedan entered an uncontrollable barrel roll.

# 20

The momentum of the fall whisked shards of glass around the interior of the cabin as all the windows shattered simultaneously.

King closed his eyes to prevent the fragments from slicing them to pieces. He rode through each impact as the Chevy smashed its roof against the ground, then its side, then its undercarriage. The relentless barrage continued for what felt like an hour, but in reality couldn't have been much more than fifteen seconds.

When it finally came to a jarring halt, the sudden change of momentum slammed King against his seat back hard enough to stun him into a lucid state. He sat motionless in the driver's seat, with shock setting into his psyche.

He assessed his injuries. The glass had cut deep lines across his face, wounds that were already starting to leak crimson. He wiped a hand across one cheek and winced as it came away almost entirely red. His foot had been bent to an awkward angle by the crazed vertigo of the barrel roll. Already, it throbbed badly. His sternum ached from the beating it had taken, slammed back and forth between the seatbelt and the seat in jarring fashion.

Otherwise, he seemed okay. Superficial wounds, wounds that would ordinarily land him in hospital if he lived any semblance of a normal life.

In the world he currently operated in, he considered himself unscathed.

A dull ache sprouted to life behind his eyeballs. He grimaced as he considered the ramifications if he ended up with a serious concussion. It would impede everything he did from this point on. He would have to take it one step at a time, and hope that everything remained functioning upstairs.

He still had a job to do.

He stared around at the destroyed wreck of a vehicle that he sat within and shook his head in disbelief. It was hard to comprehend how he had survived. The metal chassis was twisted and crumpled beyond any hope of repair.

King let the uncanny quiet settle over the wreckage before he leant forward and rummaged through the footwell, already littered with broken glass. He fetched the Five-seven pistol out of the mess and checked that its magazine was still slotted into the bottom of the grip.

Satisfied, he shifted position until his feet faced the driver's door. Then he kicked out, hard, sending the mangled door swinging outward. It was the only way to open it after the beating it had endured.

He stepped out into the rocky valley, devoid of all vegetation and completely exposed to the dry air. He kept low, skirting around the edge of the wreckage just in case any of Ramos' thugs felt the need to fire on his location. His head swam and his eyes watered. Briefly, he paused and rested a hand against the side of the crumpled Chevy, steadying himself.

He tried to deny the fact that he was in a bad state, but after pausing to consider his pounding headache, he had to accept that he needed time to recover.

There was no time, though...

He heard the roar of a modified engine and peered up the hillside that he had just violently descended. His heart leapt in his chest as he spotted the gargantuan vehicle that had rammed him off the road. The truck drove through the portion of railing he had torn off and mounted the off-road surface with ease, surging down the mountain toward him.

They were coming to finish him off...

Now that he had a few seconds to comprehend what lay in front of him, he got a better look at the vehicle that had almost killed him. He couldn't believe his eyes.

It was a highly-modified dump truck, more than likely used in a past life for collecting trash around the suburbs of Tijuana. At some point, it had been purchased by Ramos' cartel and converted into an armoured monstrosity.

King stared at the steel shell covering the dump truck, made of thick plates. Its wheels had been upgraded to handle the additional weight, replaced by massive off-road tyres that churned up the gravel as it descended the hillside towards him.

Small portions of the steel had been removed to allow for firing ports, which lined the side of the dump truck. They provided room for assault rifles and other weaponry to be poked out of the sides. King imagined that was how they intended to finish him off. He wondered just how the monstrous vehicle was able to travel through the streets of Tijuana without drawing the attention of the police.

Then he realised that this was Mexico.

Anyone could be bought and paid off.

He guessed that was how they were allowed to operate such an obvious tank-on-wheels without interference.

Or it was a new invention, only recently being put to the test.

Whatever the case, it was descending into the valley at a blistering speed.

King stayed out of sight, thinking hard. He didn't know if the occupants of the monster truck had spotted him leaving the wreckage. If they hadn't, he still had the element of surprise on his side. Maybe they thought there was no chance of the barrel roll being survivable, but they had been instructed by Ramos to head down and confirm his demise in person.

Just to make sure.

If that was the case, they wouldn't expect a firefight.

King pressed his forehead to the twisted metal door of the Chevy, breathing deep. He forced his shaking hands to calm, letting a portion of the adrenalin dissipate. He knew the benefits of the rush of neurochemicals, but the amount of cortisol flooding his system in the aftermath of the deadly tumble had reached disadvantageous heights. He couldn't aim a firearm effectively with this much energy in his system. He calmed himself, then crouched low, planning a strategy of attack.

The options were grim. He was clearly outgunned and outnumbered, up against a *Mad Max*-esque contraption with a possible concussion and a single semi-automatic pistol in his arsenal.

He'd make it work.

Or die trying.

He peeked around the corner of the destroyed Chevy and soaked in the finer details of the approaching tank —

namely, the steel plates covering the windshield to prevent anyone from taking out the driver or passenger. Nevertheless, those two occupants still had to see what lay in front of them, which meant that twin identical portholes had been removed from the steel plates in much the same style as the firing slots running along the side of the chassis.

That gave him a chance.

King opted to act instead of spending too much time stressing over the details. Improvisation was a tool that hadn't let him down in the past. He narrowed in, using the same tunnel vision...

...and stepped out from behind the wreckage.

He was in clear view of the armoured truck. It corrected course slightly as it noticed him stumble into open ground. He played up the extent of his injuries, acting semi-conscious when in reality his senses were recovering as each second went by.

As a result, the driver underestimated him. Instead of safely pulling to a halt and gunning King down from a distance, the truck picked up speed, opting to try and mow him down where he stood, crushing him into paste.

As it grew closer, King lifted the Five-seven pistol into view and narrowed his gaze, utilising the thousands of hours of firing practice he'd put into military ranges all across the United States.

The Five-seven felt like an extension of his own arm.

He methodically lined up the sights and pumped the trigger over and over again, nailing a target area without any room for error whatsoever.

The sheet of glass across the porthole shattered, the bullets tearing it apart. King shook his head at the cartel's foolishness. They had coated every shred of the dump truck's exterior in thick steel plates for added protection, but had failed to make the small porthole windows bulletproof in the process.

A glaring weakness, which King had just exploited to maximum effect.

The monster truck veered wildly as the driver slumped across the steering wheel. King had fired eight shots, plus the three shots back at the apartment complex, which left nine rounds if the Five-seven was fitted with a standard-issue magazine. Only one of them needed to land home, but it seemed that multiple had.

The truck drifted off-course, eliminating the potential for a direct impact on King. Even if it had continued straight forward, he would have dived out of the way. He watched it roar past — the driver must have jerked involuntarily against the accelerator in his death throes. It threw the gunners off their game plan, because no follow-up shots came King's way. The firing slots remained empty.

King ducked low, ready to try and avoid any oncoming fire. When none came his way, he took off at a sprint across the uneven ground, falling into step behind the out-of-control dump truck. He imagined the passenger wrestling for control of the wheel, searching desperately for the brakes.

His suspicions were confirmed.

The brake lights flared and the truck began to slow at the lowest point of the valley. Its fat wheels rumbled against the ground.

King didn't slow down for a second.

He charged at the massive vehicle, gaining ground until its steel hull dwarfed him completely.

Operating on instinct alone.

## 21

Despite his relative inexperience in the field, the following situation suddenly seemed all too familiar to King. He had the opportunity to concentrate on his reflexes, recognising what he would need and what he could discard.

Clarity settled over him. Even though everything about the confrontation spelled disaster, he experienced a palpable shift in his mentality all at once. Like the fog of adrenalin and confusion had cleared.

As he ran full-pelt toward the slowing dump truck, he tightened his grip on the Five-seven in his left hand and exhaled deeply.

It was time to act.

He headed straight for the passenger-side door, anticipating the moves that would unfold a second before they happened. His intuition proved accurate. The door flew outward, kicked open by the man in the passenger seat. King caught a glimpse of a heavy-set combat boot and the glint of an assault rifle's unsuppressed barrel in the afternoon sun.

He took a flying run-up and leapt straight in through the open door.

Chaos reigned. In the cramped cabin, King crushed against the cartel thug who had been in the process of exiting the vehicle. The pair slammed back against the centre console, almost colliding with the bloodied corpse of the driver, still slumped across the wheel.

King used the sudden confusion to bring the barrel of his Five-seven around in a tight arc. He shoved the steel into the upper half of the passenger's forehead, forcing the man's skull back against the headrest.

He pumped the trigger.

The shot rang through the truck's interior. King caught a flash of movement through the gap between the driver and passenger's seats. The cabin's rear wall had been removed during the modification process, allowing easy access to the main body of the tank-on-wheels. Now, King stared through the narrow slit to see two Latino henchmen diving for cover, reacting to the unsuppressed gunshot up front.

They were both armed.

King noted their presence and ducked back outside, dropping into the dirt only a couple of seconds after diving into the cabin. He scurried around the side of the vehicle, listening intently for any sounds of movement from within.

Unfortunately the steel armour coating the vehicle masked all noise coming from inside.

He reached the back of the truck and peered up at the two massive rear doors, both firmly bolted shut. There was no way inside from here. Still firing on all cylinders, he squatted low to minimise his target area and thought of another plan of attack.

He needn't have bothered.

With an audible groan that came from directly above him, he ducked instinctively as both doors swung open. If he'd been standing up straight, the steel would have crushed into the side of his head, likely knocking him unconscious.

Thankfully, he was still crouching. He dropped to his stomach and rolled fast, taking skin off his forearms and elbows in the process. He had perhaps a second before he would come into view of the two henchmen, both of which he imagined were aiming their weapons out the rear of the truck in search of him.

In their haste to act, the two men leapt straight out of the interior.

King made it underneath the truck at the same time as their boots crunched into the gravel, inches from his face.

They would only have to turn around to see him there, cruelly exposed. There was at least a foot of space between the undercarriage of the truck and the valley floor below, thanks to the enormous modified wheels.

Stealth wasn't an option, unfortunately.

King raised the Five-seven, acting out of impulse, and shot each man twice in the small of their backs. They seized up simultaneously, crippled by the horrific pain. Their legs gave out in unison and the pair dropped onto the loose rocks, all tension gone from their limbs.

King had a better aim now. He adjusted the sights and fired two final shots, treating each thug's forehead as a bullseye target on the range. Their necks snapped back, one after the other, and they lay still.

Blood started to pool from the grisly exit wounds in the backs of their skulls.

As the reports of the gunshots echoed off the

surrounding hillsides and faded quickly into silence, King rolled onto his back and let out the breath that had seized in his throat.

# 22

It had been the most precarious conflict of his short but storied career. Four men were dead, and he was unhurt. Now that he had time to think back on what had unfolded, it surprised him just how long the ordeal had felt. It couldn't have taken more than a minute from the time he was forced off the road for the battle to reach its violent resolution.

In the heat of the moment, it had seemed like an eternity.

He stayed underneath the truck, listening out for any sign of reinforcements. He doubted that Ramos had any more men in the area — it seemed that the man had known where his truck-from-hell was stationed in Tijuana and had lured King into the mountains under the guise of fleeing in a random direction.

King didn't expect any more resistance.

Yet, he didn't want to take any chances. He rolled onto his stomach and shimmied himself out from underneath the truck, darting his gaze left and right in search of anything out of the ordinary.

The valley was dead quiet.

A droplet of blood ran down through his brow, blurring his vision. He lifted the sleeve of his shirt and wiped his face clean, wincing as the material dragged against the open cuts. He didn't imagine he would look pretty tomorrow. Staring wide-eyed at the crumpled Chevy and the now-dormant dump truck, he shook his head in disbelief. He slotted the safety lever on the side of the Five-seven into the "on" position and tucked the gun into the rear of his waistband.

He was alive.

But Ramos had escaped.

He peered up at the twisting mountain road halfway up the hillside, where occasional bursts of traffic were the only sign of civilisation for miles around. He crossed the valley floor to where the Chevy lay and ducked back into the wreckage. Locating the duffel bag, he swung it over one shoulder, then checked the interior of the car for anything he might have left behind. Satisfied, he began the ascent, trudging delicately up the slope, the ground under his feet dotted with loose pebbles.

As he walked, he considered his situation. Any contact with Lars would spell disaster. He would be forced to reveal that Ramos had identified him as an imposter and made it out of harm's way. Lars — or whoever was in charge of this black operation — would almost certainly call him back across the border. He didn't think that four dead henchmen and two beat-up enforcers would provide the results that his superiors had been searching for.

They wanted Ramos' head on a platter.

King decided to make one last attempt at finding the cartel leader. It would be nigh-on impossible, given the fact that he knew King's face. He also knew that there was an elite operative searching for him, and when news spread that the occupants of the dump truck had been brutally gunned down in their vehicle, he would high-tail it out of Mexico before King could act.

King remembered what Lars had said about the cryptocurrency wallet they had briefly located — apparently Ramos was sitting on fifty million USD in assets. That was enough to provide him with a life of luxury for the rest of his days.

He didn't need Tijuana.

If he thought his life was in danger, he would disappear.

*Or would he?*

King wasn't certain. The young psychopath had sported all the characteristics of a committed leader, cutting a wave of bloodshed through the ranks of Tijuana's authorities in an attempt to seize the upper hand. Perhaps Ramos wouldn't be fazed by King coming after him.

Maybe he was enough of a lunatic to welcome it.

As King stepped out onto the mountain road and stuck out his thumb to wave down a passing car, he found himself plagued by the hunch that Ramos wouldn't leave so soon.

King hoped that the man stayed.

It would be a foolish decision, but Ramos clearly hadn't ascended to the position of power he currently held by playing it safe.

That would give King a chance. A slim one, but a chance nonetheless.

It also meant that he would have to go on the offensive if he wanted to ascertain the location of Ramos' hideout.

His palms tingled in anticipation.

He realised that he had no hope of voluntarily hitching a ride in his current state. His face was covered in dried blood, which had seeped into the collar of his shirt. Dust and dirt from the valley floor coated his exposed forearms. The Five-seven was tucked away in his waistband, but that didn't make him any more visually appealing to passing cars.

He would have to do things the old-fashioned way.

A rust-coated minivan came into view further down the road, heading back into Tijuana. It would pass him by in a few seconds.

King stepped out into the middle of the road.

The minivan screeched to a halt, slowing from sixty miles per hour to zero in the space of a few seconds. He expected a torrent of abuse from the driver, but when he looked through the windscreen he saw a Latino woman in her fifties staring at him like she'd seen a ghost.

He crossed slowly to the driver's window — rolled all the way down to cool the interior — with both hands raised and spread wide in an attempt to defuse the tension. The driver didn't budge. King stared over her shoulder to see two young dark-skinned boys in the back seats, both clutching small figurines of famous soccer players.

He smiled warmly to them, aware that his teeth were likely blood-stained.

'Hello,' he said simply, unsure if he was going to have to try to surpass the language barrier.

'I speak English,' the woman said.

'Oh. Great.'

'Please don't hurt us. I'm bringing them home from their match.'

King glanced at the two boys again. 'Soccer?'

The woman nodded, still looking petrified.

'This isn't what you think,' King said. 'I'm an American tourist. I fell down that slope back there. No funny business.'

'Uh-huh.'

'I promise.'

'Uh-huh.'

He wasn't sure if she believed him — likely not. 'Look, I just need a ride back into town. You can drop me at the first street corner you see. I'll sit in the passenger seat and I won't say a word the whole time. I don't want to cause any trouble. I just need to get out of here.'

'Call an ambulance.'

'I don't have travel insurance. And I'm almost broke as it is.'

He laced his tone with desperation, and it seemed as if something in his voice caused the woman to reconsider. She reacted to the revelation that King had money troubles.

He wondered if she could relate...

'Get in,' she said.

He nodded his thanks and jogged around the hood, taking care not to let the FN Five-seven's grip sticking out the back of his pants show. He opened the passenger-side door and clambered into the seat, trying to mask the adrenalin still flooding through his body. His attempts to still his shaking nerves could only go so far. He had been in a life-or-death situation just minutes previously.

The woman accelerated wordlessly, peeling off the shoulder and heading back onto the mountain trail. King hoped that she didn't take a look down the hillside and see the dead bodies sprawled around the armoured truck at the bottom of the valley.

Thankfully, she was too occupied with the road ahead. As the sun dipped in the sky, heading fast for the opposite skyline, they roared down the road toward Tijuana.

# 23

Dusk had settled over Tijuana by the time the minivan made it back inside the city limits.

King stayed silent throughout the journey, electing to bother the woman across from him as little as possible. She was doing him an enormous courtesy by lending a helping hand — even though he imagined she hadn't wanted to risk it with two young boys in the car. He wondered if they were both hers, or rather she was shepherding her son and a friend back and forth from their game.

He didn't bother to try and find out. Their personal business was their own. He had his own problems to mull over.

Namely, the fact that he had nowhere to be, and nothing to do. Aside from being murdered by Ramos' thugs, the day could not have unfolded worse. The lone man he was responsible for eliminating had gotten away, and he was left grasping at straws in order to find him.

There was a surefire way to increase his chances. That would be to trawl the streets of Tijuana, showing his face to every gangster in the city until one of them recognised him as the man after Ramos' and they attempted to kidnap him.

Highly dangerous.

Almost sure to get him killed.

But his only feasible option.

The minivan pulled to the side of the road as they reached the city centre and the woman nodded a half-hearted farewell. She probably wanted nothing to do with him. He glanced around at the sidewalk he would be exiting onto. The coast seemed clear — a handful of tourist couples strolled tentatively from their hotels into the nightlife district, but otherwise there was no sign of hostile activity.

King nodded back to the woman, and waved politely to the two little boys in the back seat. They ignored him.

Unsurprised, he pushed the door open and stepped out into the orange-tinged evening.

The sunset melted piece-by-piece into the horizon, rapidly accentuating the shadows. The minivan peeled away and King focused on putting one foot in front of the other, trying not to draw attention to himself just yet. He wanted to get his bearings, and make sure that he would be prepared in the event that he was spotted by one of Ramos' goons.

Quickly, reality set in. Tijuana was enormous and gravely dangerous at this point in time. As he strolled slowly through the largely-deserted streets of the inner city, he realised just how unlikely running into one of Ramos' men would be. Like Lars had said, the man barely focused on maintaining a street presence, due to the majority of his business being conducted online.

In the end, King had more of a chance of being stabbed by one of the Draco cartel's thugs before the night had drawn to a close.

Nevertheless, he decided to persevere. He had little

other options — yet now it began to set in that the freedom this operation provided was also a disadvantage. He had no clear idea of where to go next, and at twenty-two years of age he found himself second-guessing his every move.

*Break it down piece by piece,* he thought.

First — cleaning up.

He found a public restroom after several minutes of searching and took a deep breath before heading into the men's section. Sure enough, the entire place was absolutely putrid, the floor littered with syringes and excrement and the walls scrawled with obscene graffiti. He crossed to one of the dirty, broken sinks and ran cold water from the tap. He splashed it over his face, taking care not to touch the sink itself at the risk of contracting a cocktail of diseases.

When his face was clean, he rinsed the dirt and gravel off his forearms and shook himself dry. He studied his reflection in the cracked, fingerprint-stained mirror.

*Good enough.*

He looked relatively presentable, albeit with a handful of long slashing cuts across his cheeks and forehead. A nasty purple bruise had started to form on his right arm, but otherwise he looked okay. He could easily have been mistaken for a young, seedy U.S. tourist in search of cheap thrills in Tijuana's world-renowned pleasure district.

He didn't care what people thought of him — as long as their judgment didn't get him arrested before he could accomplish the task at hand.

The sudden solitude gave him time to ponder the mistakes he had already made. Back in the apartment complex, he hadn't expected Ramos to move so fast. The man had exploded into action like a bat out of hell when the fighting broke out. King had figured he could take out the two bodyguards before dealing with Ramos, because they were armed and ready to shoot him dead.

By doing so, he'd let Ramos escape.

On top of that, he'd failed to frisk search any of the four bodies in the valley. They might have been carrying vital information that would lead him to the whereabouts of Ramos, although he doubted it. The man seemed to run a tight ship. He would be impossible to find. King could already tell.

Despite his shortcomings, King experienced a strange sense of gratitude for being in the position he was in. There were no military officials twenty years his senior waiting to chew him out, driving home all the mistakes he had made in an attempt to rattle him. He wasn't operating alongside fellow soldiers, all at least a decade older than him, silently judging him for his youth. He used to find it incredulous when — at the age of twenty — he had made it into the Delta Force while still not being able to legally purchase a beer in the United States. He couldn't imagine how the other operatives would have felt, when they themselves all had to spend years and years making their way up through the ranks in gruelling fashion.

Natural talent had its disadvantages, at least in a social setting.

That thought stirred something in him. Alcohol made conversation flow. It led to mistakes. He decided his first port of call would be to trawl the dozens of bars in the multi-block strip dedicated to Tijuana's pleasure playground. He recalled a visit to the Avenida Revolución the last time he had visited Tijuana. It had ended in a hangover still yet to be rivalled.

He would have to be a little more responsible this time.

He composed himself, splashing a final handful of water

across his face, and headed back out into the streets. By now, the sun had fully set. The deep neon lights of Tijuana's nightlife flickered into existence. It was a warm night — just as all the nights were in this arid portion of the continent.

The first bar he visited proved unsuccessful. It was a wood-panelled room set underneath a bright green neon sign, low-ceilinged and stretching deep into the building. King bought a glass of tequila on the rocks and sipped periodically at the beverage, letting the sharp tang snake its way down his throat and settle his racing heart. He tried in vain to strike up a conversation with a collection of locals around the bar, but they shunned him off.

Dejected, he drained the glass and headed back out onto the Avenida Revolución.

The street was filthy — it seemed that any attempt to keep it respectable in appearance had dismally failed. King eyed two long rows of brothels and strip clubs, their entrances dark and shadowy and drenched in the glow of neon. The bustle of tourist life picked up. He merged into the crowd, many of whom were heading straight into the various sex shops dotted along the avenue. King kept his chin up, scouring the crowd for any sign of hostility. He wasn't hiding from anyone.

He wanted to be found.

After ten minutes of inactivity, he spotted a cantina set between a pair of seedy-looking brothels and glanced in through the open storefront. A fair crowd had gathered within, many lining the artificially-backlit oak bar running the length of the far wall.

*Good enough.*

He took his chances and stepped inside.

## 24

Upon entering the bar, King found himself fed up with how the operation had stalled. He elected to be brash, taking a few chances to try and find someone who could connect him to the elusive cartel leader.

He ordered a second tequila from a disinterested bartender and rested his elbows on the countertop, stationing himself next to a pair of mean-looking young Spanish men. They were deep in conversation, talking in low voices. King received his polished glass of tequila, downed the shot, and noted the scorpion tattoos snaking their way up the forearms of the pair.

He didn't know what that meant, but he could hazard a guess.

He hoped they were affiliated with a gang that knew of Ramos.

'Joaquín Ramos,' he said quietly, barely audible over the loud cantina music drifting through the room.

They completely ignored him. Unsure of whether they had heard him or not, he leant a little closer.

'Joaquín Ramos,' he repeated.

One of the men stared up at him, scowling. 'What?'

'You heard me.'

'You want something?' the second guy said. He seemed to have a shorter fuse. King got the sense that the man would make a lunge at him in any moment.

'Have either of you heard that name?'

'Who said you could talk to us, gringo?' the first man said.

'I just want to find my friend.'

'Your friend?' the second guy cackled. 'Esé, he ain't your friend.'

'So you know who he is,' King said.

'Everyone in Mexico knows who he is. Doesn't mean you go throwing his name around. That could get you killed.'

'Good,' King said. 'Get me killed. Point me in the direction of someone who could take me to him.'

'You think we're fuckin' stupid?' the first guy said. 'You think Joaquín Ramos is fuckin' stupid, too?'

'If you can take me to him,' King said, 'I might think otherwise.'

The first guy let out a laugh that resembled a hyena's cackle, loud enough to attract the attention of every patron in the bar. 'You're out of your depth, esé. Get the fuck out of here.'

King shifted a little closer. 'Tell me anything about him.'

The second guy shoved King hard in the chest, almost knocking him off his feet with the force of the push. He had put everything into it. King stumbled, righted himself, then took a deep breath.

'Look...' he started.

By that point, the second guy was manic. His eyes had widened considerably. He looked ready for a fight to the death. King tensed his body like a coiled spring in anticipation, but the preparation for a brawl was cut short by a firm hand clamping down on his shoulder from behind.

'Come with me,' a deep older voice said. 'Right now.'

King turned on his heel to meet the furious gaze of an elderly Latino man wearing an oversized floral shirt and a pair of brown corduroys. He had lost almost all of his hair and sported the expression of a man who life had simply passed by. Deep wrinkles were set into his cheeks and his brow looked to permanently furrowed. His hazelnut eyes bored into King, analysing him, sizing him up.

'Did I bump into you?' King said. 'Sorry about that.'

'No. Come with me.'

The guy turned on his heel and strode off purposefully. King hesitated, then moved to follow him deeper into the bar. The hyena cackle from the first thug repeated itself, slicing through the quietened bar like a knife through butter.

'Go with your daddy, gringo,' he called.

King didn't react. He suppressed his emotions and continued after the older man. He was led to a dimly-lit two-seater table in the far corner, surrounded by a maze of similar set-ups. He guessed the tables were meant for facilitating conversation. Many of them were occupied by couples from out-of-country, and a few were home to locals. Everyone was sipping on their drinks. King felt the warm buzz of the two tequila shots in his stomach as the elderly man gestured for him to sit in the spacious leather chair opposite him.

King sat.

'The fuck are you doing throwing that name around, huh?' the man growled, seemingly infuriated by King's brash decision.

'I didn't realise it was such a sensitive subject,' King said. 'Who are you?'

'My name is Juan,' the man said. 'But that means absolutely nothing to you, eh?'

King shrugged. 'Always nice to get someone's name.'

'And yours?'

'Jason.'

'That's a nice name. Now — what the fuck were you thinking?'

King hesitated. Juan seemed deeply maddened by the way King had brazenly demanded answers from the two thugs. He decided to try and alleviate the aggravation. 'I didn't mean to cause any offence.'

Juan smirked. 'You didn't cause me offence. But you are a very stupid man.'

'Thank you.'

'I mean it.'

'I'm flattered.'

'Do you know who that man is?'

'Yes.'

'What do you intend to get from him?'

'I just want him to answer a few questions for me.'

Juan scoffed and sipped at the long-necked bottle of beer in his palm. 'You do not know who he is then, my friend.'

'I know exactly who he is,' King said, running his hands through his long hair to slick it back off his forehead. 'In fact, I'm here specifically for him.'

Juan paused, raising an eyebrow. 'What business do you have here?'

'I'd rather not discuss it. Actually — I wouldn't mind telling you. But I'm not legally allowed to.'

'You some type of hitman?'

'No.'

'Then what?'

'I just want to speak with him.'

'You want to work with him?'

'I can't say. No matter how badly you want to know. What do you know about it, anyway?'

Juan smirked again. 'I can tell you're from out of town, boy.'

'My accent?'

'No,' Juan said. 'Because of how casually you are treating this. Ramos will gut you like a pig.'

'I'm fully aware of the consequences.'

'I don't know if you are.'

'Trust me.'

'No,' Juan said. 'Trust *me.* Do you know what is happening in this city because of him?'

'I've heard rumours.'

'The rumours are watered down, my friend. I've seen the bodies of little six-year-old kids lying in the streets, riddled with bullets. Little pre-schoolers. Innocent people murdered. The deaths are becoming more and more frequent, you see. No-one can go outside anymore without fearing being caught in the crossfire of a cartel shootout.'

'Is that because no-one has challenged the existing cartel before?'

'Draco has a monopoly, yes,' the man admitted. 'But no-one has tried it in this way. No-one has been so reckless.'

'You think Ramos would run for the hills if he thought his life was on the line?' King said.

Maybe Juan would have the answer to the question that had been plaguing him since the mountain chase.

The man simply laughed. 'You definitely do not know

Joaquín Ramos. He lives and breathes confrontation. It would only encourage him to work harder.'

'I see.'

'You know — people should hate the cartels, eh?' Juan said, as if he finally had the chance to voice all the thoughts that had built up in his head. 'Everyone should despise them. But it's like magic, my friend. They do a few good deeds here, they help out a few poor people there. Suddenly, everyone loves the Draco cartel. They don't see all the killings. They hate who they're told to hate. Ramos is just as bad, but both sides are pure evil. Fuckin' thugs, man...'

'How do you know so much about Ramos?'

Juan lifted his gaze off the floor to meet King's, and King saw genuine sadness in the man's eyes. 'I don't want to discuss it with you. Just like you don't want to discuss your business with Ramos.'

King furrowed his brow, contemplating what would come next. He believed that Juan had nothing to do with Ramos, evident from his clear hatred of the man. He decided he could trust him. 'Tell me, and I'll tell you why I'm here.'

Juan shrugged. 'My two young boys ... twins ... they ...'

He trailed off, blinking back tears. King thought it wise not to open his mouth. He sensed intense raw emotion in the elderly man's tone. He blinked hard, making sure that his gaze stayed unwavering, more for moral support than anything else.

'My boys,' Juan continued. 'They needed the money. I'm not well-off, you see. I guess I wasn't really ... there for them. They both went out to work for Mr. Joaquín Ramos. Two months ago. There were rumours, you see, that he could provide a life of luxury with little downside risk. Because he was doing things differently. Because he wasn't on the streets, so there was no risk of being killed in a gang war — of course, how could there be any risk at all?'

'What happened?'

Juan stayed completely silent, letting the tears finally flow. He clenched the neck of the beer bottle hard enough to turn his knuckles white, clearly dealing with a wave of raw emotions. King said nothing. Beads of condensation on the bottle ran down over his shaking fingers.

Finally, Juan spoke.

'I'll never know exactly,' he said. 'They must have done something wrong, eh? Must not have been very good at their jobs. The police found both of them dismembered in a ditch between two maquiladora factories. You never know — maybe they were good people in the end? Maybe they decided to go to the authorities about Ramos' brutality. I'll never know. I like to think they died trying to do the right thing. I'll ... I'll never know...'

King had no idea what to say. He couldn't imagine the sheer grief, the trauma, the emotional weight of such a horrific burden weighing down on the old man. He tightened his mouth into a hard line to stifle emotions of his own. Then he began to speak.

'I'm here to kill Ramos,' he said, leaning forward so that he could lower the volume of his voice. 'I'm a government agent. You might not believe that, but it's the truth. You give me anything — any goddamn thing — to lead me to him and I'll make sure he pays for what he did to your sons. Okay?'

A wry smile spread across Juan's face. He wiped his eyes dry with the sleeve of his floral shirt — which suddenly looked completely ridiculous in contrast with his harrowing tale — and shook his head slowly from side to side.

'I don't know a thing about him,' he admitted. 'I got

angry at you because I thought you might want to go working for him. You seemed young and impressionable. You might have been drawn to making a quick peso. I thought ... maybe I could be there for you like I wasn't for my kids.'

King grimaced. Genuine sadness needled deep into the pit of his stomach, making him gulp back emotion. 'There's nothing you can give me?'

'I'm afraid not...' Juan said, suddenly pitiful. 'I ... I'm sorry about that. I don't know what came over me. I don't usually pour my sob story out to the nearest tourist. I apologise. This isn't your responsibility.'

King got the idea that Juan felt suddenly uncomfortable about what he had told him. He figured that the best option would be not to intrude on the man's time any longer.

Slowly, he got to his feet. He touched a hand to the man's shoulder. 'I'll find him, don't worry. When it comes out in the news that Joaquín Ramos died a grisly death, you'll know who to think of.'

Juan smiled, a hollow, empty gesture. 'I hope you do. Good luck. Don't get yourself killed.'

'I'll try not to. I'll leave you to it, Juan.'

'Goodbye.'

King turned and didn't look back, heading for the avenue. Absent-mindedly trawling the streets of Tijuana over the last half-hour had subtly broken down his confidence, causing him to doubt the future of the operation. Now, he made a silent promise to himself not to leave the city limits until he'd put Ramos in a bodybag. Silent fury coursed through him at a deeper level. He recognised the foolishness of letting emotions affect him while on the job, but he couldn't help himself.

He would take Ramos down, or make a trip to the city morgue in a bodybag.

There were no other options.

On the way out, he passed the two thugs, both of them still sitting at the bar. He barely even registered them in his peripheral vision, focusing intently on the path outside. He needed to breathe fresh air after the shocking story Juan had told him. He barely paid them any attention.

The guy with the hyena laugh cackled again as King walked by. 'You touching that old man's shoulder, esé? Very cute. How much is he paying you for a quick fuck?'

The pair of them roared with laughter in a deliberate attempt to attract as much attention as possible.

They weren't anticipating what came next.

King burst sideways, darting laterally into range before either of the two had a chance to react. He seized the first man's head on either side of his skull, gripping the guy's scalp like a bowling ball. He drove it down into the oak countertop with enough force to rattle the entire bar, accompanied by an ear-splitting impact. The guy went instantly limp, smashed into unconsciousness in a heartbeat.

Before the other guy could react, King spun on his heel and delivered a straight left punch into the man's stomach. He put his entire bodyweight behind the strike, sinking his fist so hard into the guy's soft mid-section that he felt his knuckles crack through two or three ribs.

The guy vomited a full stomach worth of alcohol and greasy fast-food onto the floor, then collapsed into the puddle in grotesque fashion.

King left them to their own devices and exited the cantina with a spring in his step.

# 25

It turned out that King needn't have bothered attempting to hunt down any of Ramos' friends.

They came to him.

He stepped back out into the balmy night air, slinging the duffel bag over both his shoulders and securing the straps tight to prevent anyone running off with his personal belongings. There was sensitive information within, including forged identification documents. If it came to light that a member of the U.S. government had knowingly impersonated another citizen, King imagined he would have the book thrown at him in a court of law. He was the scapegoat for this new division — he was sure of it. That's why they had sent him into Tijuana with such a barebones plan of attack.

As a test subject.

There was a certain indecency in the air tonight. The people swarming all around him were either drunk, high, or both — they stumbled around the Avenida Revolución, heading from thrill to thrill. This was the pleasure district, and the tourists in the area were making full use of its vices.

Music swelled in every direction, pouring out of jukeboxes in open bars and blending together into a deafening amalgamation of noise.

King made the decision to keep floating from bar to bar when the cold steel of a gun barrel jammed into the small of his back, bringing with it a wave of heightened emotions. He felt each individual aspect of the change in his demeanour, from the adrenalin flooding his veins to the quickening of his pulse to the sudden clarity of his vision.

It was like the murky haze of everyday consciousness had been stripped away.

His primal instincts kicked in, activating in the event of a threat on his life.

Slowly, he turned his head to get a look at whoever was threatening it.

Three men total. One had a firm grip on the pistol — a Sig-Sauer P226. Its unsuppressed barrel needled further into the sensitive area just above King's hip. He stifled a wince. The guy had narrow beady eyes and long thinning hair hanging in wild strands over his forehead. He had the distinct appearance of a man who enjoyed getting high on his own supply. The two thugs behind him were of similar build — broad-shouldered, dressed in casual attire, putting on a terrible acting performance in an attempt to blend into the crowd.

It might be good enough to pass off to the swarms of drunk tourists flooding around them.

It didn't convince him.

He recognised that they were operating as a trio, and planned accordingly.

'Heard you been talkin' to some people, esé,' the guy with the gun snarled.

'You going to shoot me here?' King said, keeping his

voice low despite the din of the jam-packed avenue. 'That'll be loud. It'll cause commotion.'

'You think we care?'

'If you were going to shoot me you would have done it already.'

'Boss wants you alive.'

'I see.'

'Let's take a walk.'

'What if I don't want to take a walk?'

'Then I have permission to shoot you down like a dog right now. You want to go that way?'

'I'm good.'

'Thought so. Fuckin' walk. Slowly.'

King shifted uncomfortably. If he had tucked the FN Five-seven into the front of his waistband back on the mountain road, he would have easy access to the weapon without the three thugs knowing any better. But — as fate would have it — the weapon rested directly above his rear. He couldn't reach back and extract it. The guy with the gun simply had to pump the trigger once, and that would be that.

The first bullet would likely paralyse him, given the position of the barrel against his upper hip. There were all kinds of sensitive nerves bunched up in that area.

King gulped as he realised his options were slim, and elected to follow the man's demands.

He started to stride forward, slowly, just as the guy had instructed.

It didn't take long for the man to see the gun in his waistband.

'Stop walking,' the man hissed in his ear.

King pulled to a halt, disrupting a tourist couple attempting to cross the avenue. The man — a college frat boy in his early twenties — bumped into his shoulder. King had two options — roll with the impact, or hold his ground and send the guy stumbling away. He decided on the option that was least likely to cause the P226 against his back to go off.

He held his ground.

The college kid went flying, almost tumbling off his feet due to the awkward clash.

King grimaced.

The kid's eyes were glazed over from either drink or drugs, and he looked ready for an altercation with anyone. He squared up to King, eyes wide, brows flaring. King sensed the trio of cartel gangsters behind him visibly stiffen, all of them wondering what the hell was going on.

'Hey, man,' the college kid said. 'You got a fuckin'...?'

'Keep walking if you want to live,' King hissed with reckless intensity.

The frat boy must have noticed the unhinged look in King's eyes, because his gaze wandered over to the trio of thugs standing ominously close to King, all their eyes fixed on him.

The guy dropped his head and hurried away as fast as his feet would allow.

## 26

King breathed a sigh of relief. Minimising civilian casualties was of the utmost priority. The last thing he wanted was for a college kid to get murdered for a drunken mistake. Briefly, he considered the fact that he was probably close to the same age as the man who confronted him.

*What could have been,* he thought.

Sometimes he weighed up the possibility of living a relatively normal life. Going to college, getting a degree, settling into a nine-to-five and squirrelling away ten percent of his paycheque until he enjoyed a short-lived retirement and fell into a grave at the age of eighty.

Only sometimes.

The cartel thug behind him wrenched the Five-seven out of King's waistband and tucked it into his own pocket, stripping King's only chance of survival away.

'Now you walk,' the guy spat.

The three thugs directed King to a quieter section of the multi-block pleasure district. The guy with the gun instructed him on the directions, tugging the back of his shirt viciously in one direction after the next. Finally, King felt the guy's free hand shove him in the back, and he stumbled forward into a dark alleyway between two bars.

With the number of witnesses minimised, the other two thugs built up the nerve to pull out their guns.

Three identical P226s aimed at King's head. He flicked his concentration from one barrel to the next, sizing up the distance between the three of them, analysing and assessing until he ultimately concluded that there was no chance he could mount any kind of offence.

Not yet.

The guy who seemed to be in charge gestured down the alley with the barrel of his P226, shaking the gun for a moment. 'There's a car waiting at the other end. Let's go.'

King nodded, turned on his heel, and started walking. The alleyway smelt of puke and urine and dried puddles of liquor. Trash lined each side. The only light came from pinpoints of luminescent LEDs positioned above the exit doorways to the buildings lining the length of the alley.

Back exits to dispose of the trash.

There were no dumpsters in sight — it seemed that any waste was dumped on the putrid ground and left to rot. King held his breath as he trudged slowly through the muck, trying to make out the path ahead in the sheer darkness.

At the other end of the alley, he spotted his worst nightmare.

By all appearances, the panel van seemed unassuming, but King recognised its true intentions. It had been reversed up to the lip of the alley and its rear doors hung wide open, inviting the four of them into its darkened interior. Even from this distance, King eyed the steel cage that had been outfitted inside the body of the van.

Genuine fear arced through him. His hands turned

clammy, his pulse reached its maximum capacity, and his imagination started to run wild. He pictured all the horrors that a drug cartel could enact on him. As a SEAL, he'd gone through intense resistance training, designed to ensure that he didn't share a word if he was ever captured or interrogated. He had faith in his ability to keep his mouth shut. He wouldn't share any details of what he was doing in Tijuana.

But that wouldn't make the pain any less real.

He pictured them melting his skin off with a flamethrower, yanking out all his toenails, waterboarding him, electrocuting him, slicing his fingers and toes off one by one, cutting out his tongue.

He had killed four of their men.

He didn't think they would take it easy on him.

It provided him with the adrenalin dump necessary to spur him into action. He needed to make a move within the next twenty feet, before he was forced inside the panel van and all his freedom vanished into thin air.

In the darkest section of the alley, he froze.

'The driver's telling me to drop my bag,' he said, gesturing to the duffel strapped across both shoulders.

The three men pulled to a stop behind him. 'What?'

'The driver.'

'What fucking driver?'

'He's gesturing at me to put my bag down.'

'Where?'

'Right *there!*' King said, lacing his tone with sheer confusion, like he could see something in the shadows ahead that they couldn't.

'Keep walk—' the guy started, but King had already reached for the straps over his shoulders.

He slid one arm out of the duffel and slowly lowered it to the ground. He dropped the bag into the dirt, relieving fifteen pounds of weight off his back, and held up his hands to feign innocence. 'Just following orders, man.'

Visibly frustrated, the first man stepped forward — into range. 'I dunno what the fuck you think you're doing, gringo, but...'

Mid-sentence, the guy reached down to angrily snatch the duffel bag off the filthy ground and shove it back into King's hands.

As he did so, King burst off the mark like a defensive end charging at the quarterback.

# 27

Bedlam broke out.

King's first move was to control the wrist of the hand that was clutching the Sig-Sauer. He clamped down both hands on the guy's meaty forearm and squeezed with every ounce of pressure his fingers would allow. The guy wasn't budging, no matter how hard he tried.

With the chance of catching a bullet from the first man eliminated, King avoided a desperate punch from the guy's free hand and tugged him into range. He pressed his body against the guy, awkwardly pinning him in place. Then he braced himself.

His instincts paid off.

After the sudden barrage of motion, the other two trigger-happy thugs panicked. Their pulses would be rising. The terror involved with their target fighting back would be kicking in. King didn't imagine they would handle the situation rationally.

They didn't.

Both men fired, once, twice, three times each. By the time they realised their mistake and let their fingers out of the trigger guards, their friend had been pumped full of lead. King felt each impact resonate through his hands as the thug's body jerked unnaturally, still pinned in front of him.

A human shield.

When he slid his hands down the guy's wrist to strip him of the P226, he was met with no resistance.

The man had lost consciousness already.

King wrenched the pistol out of his limp hands and let the body fall to the alley floor. It hit the ground with a wet slap, but King saw nothing. His vision had laser-focused on the two murky silhouettes across from him.

They hesitated, staring in abject horror at their dead comrade. The comrade they had stripped of a life.

Before they had a chance to recover their wits, King shot them both down.

The muzzle flares lit up the shadows like a flashing strobe light, briefly illuminating the arterial blood that arced from each man's chest. They had opted not to wear any form of body protection, instead choosing to blend into the crowd back on the Avenida Revolución.

Loose singlets did little to stop steel core rounds.

The alley went dark again. Over the ringing in his ears from the close-range gunshots, King heard the van's engine cough to life behind him. He turned to see the vehicle roaring away from the sidewalk, fleeing the confrontation as the driver recognised that his friends had been incapacitated.

Then silence.

Then, only just audible in the unnerving quiet of the alley, a wet gargle.

One of the men had survived his wounds.

King dropped instinctively onto his stomach, landing

hard enough amongst the filth to knock the breath out of himself. He didn't want to take any chances. If the guy still had his hand on his weapon, it would only take one shot to shut the lights off upstairs.

In the field, luck played a significant part.

In the end, he shouldn't have worried. He scurried over to the pair of thugs in a military-style crawl, staying low, staying quiet. He reached the source of the pathetic noise and frisk-searched the man, feeling for any sign of a handgun in his palms.

Nothing.

King's eyes began to adjust to the lowlight. He made out the shape of the trio, their incapacitated forms arranged in a rudimentary triangle formation. The other two guys were entirely motionless, already dead.

The guy he'd just frisk-searched was close to it.

King spotted one of the alleyway exit doors just up ahead, set underneath another weak, flickering LED tube. The pale glow that it cast over the entrance would be useful for one thing.

Hammering home the extent of the man's injuries.

King bent down and snatched the wounded man by the collar, dragging him through the muck. He strode into the radius of the harsh light and dumped the guy back-first against the lone concrete step below the locked door.

In the light, he could see where the man had taken the bullets.

He couldn't have been far over twenty years old. High on something — crack or heroin, more than likely. But the bullets had stripped him of his thuggish demeanour. Now, he simply came off as a wounded, whimpering youth. Which was exactly what he was, once you were able to tear through the drug-crazed, violent exterior.

A pang of unease speared King in the chest. He realised how vulnerable people were so close to death, and momentarily regretted having to shoot the three of them.

*Are you insane?* he thought. *They were about to hand-deliver you to Ramos to be tortured and maimed.*

He hardened his nerves. There was no time for hesitation in this god-forsaken city. He squatted down by the young man and assessed the guy's wounds.

The kid had taken a bullet through the collar bone, bleeding profusely across his thin singlet. Another round had sliced through his upper arm, and a third had punched straight through his stomach.

The stomach wound was the fatal one. He would die from blood loss within minutes.

King grabbed him by the chin and pointed his pale, gasping face in his direction.

'Look at me,' he said.

The guy drew in rattling breaths. He didn't have much time left.

'You speak English?' King said.

'Little... little bit.'

'You want to live?'

'Yes.'

'You ever had anything like this happen to you before?'

'No.'

'Then think very hard about this. You need to give me information. That's what I'm here for. You help me, and I'll get you to a hospital.'

The guy managed a wry smile through bloody teeth. 'I talk. I die.'

'You die either way. I'm giving you the opportunity for a chance.'

'No.'

'Are you really ready to die?'

He kept quiet, letting the words sink in. The warm silence of the alley settled over them. The only audible sound was the young guy's throaty rasps as he struggled to suck air into his lungs.

King saw cold fear spread across the man's face.

'Where's Ramos?' he said.

'I don't know.'

King believed it.

'Where had you been told to deliver me?'

'We...' the guy said, trailing off. Then he thought better of keeping his mouth shut. Maybe reality was setting in. 'We hold you overnight. In an apartment. Then we take you to factory in the morning.'

'Which factory?'

'Packaging ... packaging plant. That's where we work. Ramos collect you.'

'Where?'

'Over the river from the bus terminal. Where all the maquiladora factories are. Ours says *Importaciones Perez.*'

'Thank you,' King said.

'Hospital, please.'

'Yes,' King said, nodding. 'Close your eyes.'

The man complied.

King shot him through the forehead.

# 28

King felt nothing as he tucked the Five-seven and the P226 into his waistband, collected the duffel bag, and hurried toward the lip of the alley.

It had been a mercy killing. Even if King rushed him to a hospital, there was a ninety-five percent chance the boy would have died a slow, painful death from his wounds. On the off chance that he survived, Ramos' cartel would have exacted crippling torture upon the boy for the information he had provided King with.

It was a lose-lose situation.

Best to end it quick. He never would have realised what was coming. It would have been a quick trip into the great beyond.

*Shouldn't have joined a cartel*, King thought. *And you definitely shouldn't have fucked with me.*

Nevertheless, he pitied the young guy.

They were probably close to the same age. Same as the college frat boy out on the main road.

*Different paths*, King thought.

Three vastly different lives.

As he stepped out of the lip of the alley, leaving the three dead men lying in great pools of their own blood, he checked the coast for any sign of reinforcements. Finding no sign of hostile intention, he began the slow trek to one of Tijuana's many cheap motels — something told him that he would need rest for what was to come.

He walked aimlessly, stabilising his breathing and returning his nerves to a normal state. In the moment, the battle felt like nothing, but in the silent aftermath of conflict King had time to reflect on just how brutally the violence had unfolded. More than that, he had time to consider just how little room for error there was at this level. One well-placed bullet from his adversaries, or one ill-timed move on his part, and he wouldn't even know that he had met his end.

A switch would simply be flipped.

And out he would go.

He also had time to consider the path that he had taken, the path that had led him to the slums of Tijuana on a balmy July night. He didn't shy away from the strange nature of the decisions that had led him to this point. Most young soldiers joined the Armed Forces due to a broken home life, or a devout, unwavering duty to serve one's country.

King had experienced neither of those when he'd first signed up.

He'd simply been attracted to the thrill.

Sure, his old life back in the outskirts of Green Bay, Wisconsin, hadn't been ideal. The grief that had fallen over his father in the aftermath of his mother's unsuccessful battle with cancer had cast a shadow over the family home. King had barely communicated with his dad for the year prior to joining the military.

They'd never been talkers, the Kings.

So it had certainly come as no surprise to Ray King when his son announced his decision to join the military. To King, it always felt like his father preferred solitude. He considered himself a burden on the peace and quiet that Ray seemingly wanted to live out the rest of his days in.

He remembered it vividly. Striding into the recruiting office in Green Bay with a small collection of personal belongings and nothing else to his name.

Aged eighteen.

Ready for anything.

From there, he had embraced every new challenge — and excelled. He'd risen to the occasion. He'd been drawn to the thrills, the uncertainty, the achievements. He'd been informed time and time again that the opportunities he was being gifted with were far from normal.

One of the youngest SEALs in military history, surpassed only by a seventeen-year-old prodigy born in 1965.

The youngest Delta Force operator in military history, by three years.

He had never protested the promotions. He'd welcomed them with a stern nod and a determination to press onto the next objective.

He couldn't pinpoint one all-encompassing thing that drove him.

He simply got up every day, and got to work.

For the past four years, life had been moving too fast to process anything else.

Now, he found a single-storey motel on a darkened street corner, with paint flaking off the exterior walls and a small car lot out front. The lot was entirely empty. A fluorescent bulb over the door to reception shone bright amidst the darkness, inviting him in. King glanced at his surroundings, noted how quiet the area was, and nodded approvingly.

He headed into the motel's reception.

He had the money to book a room in any of the five-star resorts or hotels scattered around Tijuana's tourist district, yet he considered such a move entirely unnecessary. He needed a bed, and a few hours of sleep. Anything else was inessential.

Besides, he had no time to waste deciding on an adequate room.

He needed somewhere quiet and small, to think about what lay ahead and plan his next move.

This place was perfect.

'Just yourself, sir?' the chubby man behind the desk said, deliberately ignoring the cuts and bruises dotting King's complexion.

King guessed that his appearance was a relatively normal occurrence around these parts. There were fetish clubs in this district, after all.

'Yeah,' he said. 'Thank you. Can I pay cash?'

'Of course.'

'Do we need to bother with ID?'

'Four hundred pesos extra. I will also ignore anyone who comes searching for you. I'll tell them I saw you head past hours ago. Might that be something you'd be interested in, sir?'

'That'll work.'

King unzipped one of the duffel bag's pockets and came out with a thick wad of pesos, held together by a heavy-duty rubber band. He slid the band off and counted out one thousand pesos in bills, roughly the equivalent of ninety American dollars. The room fee, plus extra.

A small price to pay for full discretion.

He handed over the money, which the receptionist accepted with a warm smile and exchanged for a single room key.

'You've got the room right next to this one. Largest room in the motel.'

'Thank you.' King made for the door, then hesitated, turning back around. 'Any other customers tonight?'

'None so far, sir.'

King nodded and continued outside. Immediately, he spotted a group of shadowy figures across the street, laughing harshly and waltzing along the sidewalk.

They looked like trouble.

He kept his head down and unlocked the door to the adjacent room, stepping into a glum space with a low ceiling and a sagging double bed in the corner. It was a pitiful sight — if this was the best place in the motel, King didn't want to imagine what the other rooms looked like.

He dropped the duffel bag to the floor and shut the door behind him. As the latch clicked closed, a switch in his head activated, flooding his brain with fatigue. His arms were intensely heavy all of a sudden. The tranquil, steady hum of a small air-conditioner set into the opposite wall only seemed to add to his exhaustion.

It was the first respite he had received since crossing the border.

The motel room turned into a safe house, an area where he could relax and let all the worries of the past twelve hours melt away — of which there had been plenty.

At least ... temporarily.

He wrenched the P226 and Five-seven out of his waistband one by one, checking the capacity of each magazine in turn. Then he made sure that both weapons were ready to fire before placing them on the small nightstand next to the bed.

He dropped onto the mattress. A handful of broken springs pressed into his back, but they barely fazed him. With the dim light overhead still shining, he closed his eyes and began to drift into a much-needed sleep.

His adrenalin reserves had been entirely depleted.

And they would need recharging for tomorrow.

As he dropped off, he thought of *Importaciones Perez*. No doubt a front for one of Ramos' packaging facilities, where thousands of pounds of coca leaves were converted into pure cocaine powder by a small army of sweatshop workers.

He wondered if Ramos would be there to collect King tomorrow. He wondered if the three thugs who had tried to kidnap him were meant to check-in with Ramos later tonight.

*Will he have his guard down? Will he be expecting me in chains?*

King doubted it. Ramos was cunning. There would be safety measures in place, detailed check-in times to ensure that King had been apprehended successfully. There was no chance the trio would meet them, all of them marbleised as corpses in the back-alleys of the grimy pleasure district.

They'd got what they deserved.

Junkies looking for a quick payday, giving no regard for King's wellbeing.

But it meant that Ramos would likely be anticipating King to come in guns blazing.

Good.

*I like a challenge.*

He began to drift away.

He had never dreamed, never been haunted by the deeds he had committed in the field.

Not yet.

As he dropped off, he pondered whether they would start after he was done in Mexico.

# 29

King woke up to eight missed calls on the satellite phone that he fished out of the duffel bag.

They were all from the same number.

Lars.

He stared at the screen for a full minute, weighing up the pros and cons of returning the man's call.

Lars had explicitly told him that he could do as he pleased. The task of dispatching Ramos rested squarely on his shoulders, and he had been granted permission to operate regardless of any outside interference. There were no reinforcements waiting for his call. No superiors — aside from Lars — to report his every move back to.

Full discretion.

Exactly why he had accepted the job in the first place.

He decided not to return the calls just yet.

He didn't want Lars breathing down his neck for the course of his time in Tijuana. He was hesitant to divulge the fact that he had failed to pin Ramos down the first time. Determined to complete the task on his second attempt, he shoved the satellite phone back into the duffel bag and tucked the entire thing under his bed.

There was nothing in it that he needed — just identification documents, a wad of cash, and a few changes of clothes.

The rising sun filtered in through the cheap blinds, spilling a warm orange glow through the room. King showered fast, realised that he hadn't eaten in over twenty-four hours, and headed out to find some sustenance. Before he left, he tucked the two pistols into the rear of his waistband and dropped his shirt down over them.

Violence always dulled his appetite.

He still wasn't hungry, despite his last meal having been consumed back in the United States, but he would force the food down.

He'd need it for the day ahead.

He locked the motel door behind him and sauntered across the street to a twenty-four-seven diner. The clock on the wall behind the counter informed him that it was six-thirty in the morning. He ordered a large pot of black coffee and a plate heaped high with chilli tomato stew and eggs wrapped in corn tortillas.

A plastic corner booth in the corner had just been wiped clean by a young waitress with heavy bags under her eyes. King slotted into the booth and drained a cardboard cup of the coffee, letting the warm liquid snake its way down his throat. The caffeine kickstarted his heart rate, bringing his senses up. It had taken considerably longer than usual to shake free the symptoms of lethargy.

He needed more sleep.

He helped himself to another cup of the bitter brew and dove into the tortillas, wolfing them down in the space of a few minutes. The first bite activated his hunger, and before he knew it he'd paid for the meal, gulped down a third cup of coffee, and stepped back out into the Tijuana sunshine twelve minutes after entering the diner.

He had a Sig-Sauer P226 and a FN Five-Seven at the ready.

That was all he needed.

He set off for the so-called "city of factories" that was sure to house one of Ramos' facilities.

The multi-block district running around the perimeter of the Avenida Revolución wouldn't appear on any of the Tijuana tourist brochures. It was a rundown, degraded strip — exactly why King had selected it as a place to stay the night. No-one wanted to be here, which he had hoped would allow him to keep a low profile.

He was still breathing — so, evidently, it had paid off.

He strode fast down streets that seemed abandoned, like the aftermath of a nuclear war. He couldn't tell whether that was due to the early hour of the morning, where the junkies and the seedy tourists were still sleeping off the sins of the night before — or whether it was due to the drug war that had escalated over the course of the last few months, forcing good men and women to stay indoors and prevent getting caught in the crossfire.

The further King headed into the district, the more he thought it was the latter.

The apartment complexes and suburban developments in this area were all walled-off, as if they were hiding away from the open air. Havens of sorts, there to protect locals and tourists alike from the inherent dangers of the streets.

He suddenly felt strangely exposed.

He pressed on, asking the odd passer-by for directions to the maquiladoras. He imagined it would become clear when he had ventured into the city of factories, as his surroundings would be replaced by towering warehouses and the early-morning bustle of determined shift workers heading in for a long day of packaging and processing.

Some legal, some illegal.

Eventually, he was pointed roughly in the right direction by an elderly woman from California who had spent over three weeks here. Her directions had racist undertones, but King ignored them. She referred to the maquiladoras as "monkey factories", an area quietly forbidden to tourists. King nodded his thanks and moved on, letting her go about her business without kicking up a fuss about her poor choice of language.

He had enough problems of his own to deal with.

He skirted along the edge of the Avenida, through a collection of shops and bars that sported a similar theme — that of the ancient Mayans. The buildings were complete with artificial bamboo banisters and over-the-top plastic stone blocks. Fake theme park architecture at its finest. Sure enough, the street was completely deserted.

King chalked it up to the early hour and continued on.

Slowly, his surroundings started to morph and shift. The wider lots became more and more prevalent, with the claustrophobic, overbearing nature of the residential sector melting away. Factories began to dot the sidewalks, enormous warehouses painted all-white, fenced off from the streets.

King played the part of a curious tourist taking an early-morning stroll and continued to waltz further into the district.

The foot traffic shifted from half-tourist, half-local to one-hundred-percent workers. King tried his best to blend in, but it was next to impossible. At six-foot-three he stuck out like a sore thumb amongst the tight clusters of shift workers hurrying through open gates, their heads down, dressed head to toe in cheap and dirty clothing. The atmosphere had an air of determination. He figured that few of the maquiladora workers were permanent, instead opting to make a temporary living for themselves while they searched for a new life.

Tijuana had that air about it.

The whole city seemed like a grey-zone, home to no-one but occupied by everyone. There was clearly a strong population of migrants battling to make ends meet while they waited for their opportunity to cross the border into the States. King didn't want to generalise — he figured that there were broad swathes of the city populated entirely by permanent residents. But the only districts he had spent time in so far felt like giant waiting rooms.

It would be an effective breeding ground for the types of workers that Ramos would look for.

The desperate.

The easily exploited.

A worker with a dirty face and a rucksack over one shoulder shoved King hard in the chest as he walked by. He let out a string of obscenities in Spanish, gesturing for King to fuck off back to the tourist precinct he'd come from.

King clearly didn't belong here.

He ignored the man, trying not to draw attention to himself. He shoved past the guy and powered on, scanning each building he passed for any sign of the "*Importaciones Perez*" logo that the young guy had mentioned the previous night.

Ten minutes into the walk, he found it.

# 30

He pulled to a tentative halt on the other side of the street, already sweating as the sun beat down directly opposite. Still rising, with dawn only having just broken, the harsh light blocked his vision. He held a hand to his brows to act as a temporary visor and peered across the street at the enormous facility, also fenced off from the main street.

It looked literally identical to the dozens of factories King had already passed, which made him wonder how many businesses in this district were simply a front for cartel operations. The warehouse stretched out on either side, covering at least five thousand square feet. It was surrounded on all sides by the everyday hustle of factory life — lorries reversing into loading docks, small huts that acted as makeshift guard booths.

The only difference King could spot between this place and all the others he'd observed was the heightened security.

Three mean-looking thugs patrolled the front of the property, protecting the thin gap in the wire fence that shift workers were allowed to squeeze through in order to access the factory. They openly wielded Kalashnikov rifles, clearly not concerned with legal trouble. The trio scowled at every passer-by, of which there were few. No-one came to this district without a purpose — King included.

It didn't take long for them to notice him loitering on the other side of the street.

'Keep walking, gringo,' one of them called.

The man's voice echoed across the street, ringing off the nearby buildings.

King nodded, smiled warmly, and kept slowly strolling along the sidewalk. He stared down at his feet, rapidly trying to piece a plan together. He couldn't do anything to draw attention to himself — it would be a simple matter to gun down the three guards out front, but there was likely a small army waiting for him inside.

He had severely underestimated the extent of Ramos' operation.

Lars' information had painted the picture of a man who had haphazardly thrown a plan together and executed it in relentless fashion. What King saw now was an airtight setup, which he should have expected in the first place. He didn't know what the point of the walk into the maquiladora city had been. Perhaps subconsciously he'd imagined strolling through the open gate and finding Ramos sitting in his office with his back turned.

That would never have been the case.

King spent so long focusing on his shortcomings that he failed to pay attention to his surroundings. The first indication that all was not right came from an ominous growling in his ears. He had almost reached the far edge of the street and left Ramos' facility behind when he turned to identify the source of the noise.

When he did, his eyes boggled involuntarily.

A convoy of armoured vehicles had materialised on the horizon, their engines screaming as they tore towards King's end of the street. He tensed up, terrified that Ramos had located him and brought a small army of thugs with him to finish the job.

Maybe he wasn't underestimating King any longer.

Then King realised that he had nothing to do with what was about to unfold.

Factory workers ducked and ran, most of them screaming and flailing. King sensed the raw, abject terror in the air, and he held his breath for imminent chaos.

He was right to expect it.

The trio of guards out the front of Ramos' facility noticed the long line of armoured dump trucks, Ford pick-up trucks, and modified wagons heading straight for them. They brought their Kalashnikovs up to shoulder-height, all in unison, and unloaded their magazines at the approaching convoy.

The deafening rattle of automatic gunfire ripped through the otherwise-quiet factory district. Screams rose in a horrifying chorus from nearby buildings — like people knew what the gunshots signified.

The convoy had been prepared for an attack. The bullets bounced harmlessly off their steel-plated hulls. King heard the metallic clang of ricochets and dropped instinctively, praying that he didn't get hit by a stray round.

The lead vehicle in the convoy — a massive semi-truck that had been modified specifically for war — veered off the empty road, mounting the opposite sidewalk. Two of the perimeter guards dived out of the way, but the third man was too distracted, busy unloading his rifle at the bullet-proof windshield of the truck.

He realised his mistake far too late.

The semi-truck mowed him down, simply pulverising him underneath its giant hood. It carried on, tearing through the flimsy wire fence. The sound of twisting steel screeched through the district. The truck bounced down onto the opposite driveway, its suspension handling the off-road trip effortlessly, and it barrelled into the complex at a blistering rate.

Capitalising on the opening, the rest of the vehicles sped through the opening. Two, then three, then four, then five.

Within the facility, gunshots cracked and bedlam erupted.

King couldn't believe his eyes. He'd stumbled into a full-scale gang war — his best guess was that the Draco cartel had reached their wits' end and mounted a staggering retaliation against Ramos' provocation.

He paused for a single moment, eyeing the gaping hole in the front of the property and the steel-plated vehicles screeching to a halt out the front of the massive roller doors.

Then he shed his hesitation, ripped the P226 and the Five-seven free from his waistband, and sprinted across the road toward the site.

Heading into a war zone.

# 31

It would more than likely get him killed, but he couldn't comprehend a better chance to capitalise than right now.

He pumped his arms and legs like pistons, racing across the smooth asphalt and mounting the opposite sidewalk. The two perimeter guards who had dived for cover noticed him barrelling towards them. They scrambled for their dropped firearms simultaneously, desperate to arm themselves. Their expressions had twisted into determined scowls.

King knew they would gun him down without mercy if he hesitated.

He raised the P226, preferring to use a single weapon instead of attempting to dual-wield, and pumped the trigger twice, sending a round through each man's upper back.

*Maximise the target area,* he thought.

Both men slumped forward, abandoning their attempts to snatch at their guns. They started to bleed profusely, crippled by the wounds. A shot through the upper torso spelled disaster no matter where the bullet struck. There were all kinds of juicy, vulnerable organs up there. King let the pair deal with the consequences of their actions and sprinted straight past them, heading into the facility.

The hundred-foot stretch of flat driveway between the perimeter and the main warehouse left no cover whatsoever. King recognised how vulnerable he was as he raced across the concrete. He abandoned any attempt to minimise his potential to get shot. If someone fired at him from here, he would be helpless to stop it. Instead he concentrated on speed.

By the time he reached the towering roller doors at the front of the warehouse and vaulted inside, his lungs had started to burn. They screamed for oxygen, but he shut out the sensation, focusing entirely on what lay ahead.

It was difficult to choose what to concentrate on first.

A skirmish had broken out inside the facility, waged between the army of gangsters that had just invaded the property and the factory guards already stationed here. Screaming, howling workers cowered underneath long rows of workstations, trying to avoid the crossfire as best they could.

*Find Ramos,* King thought. *Just fucking find Ramos.*

He brought his adrenalin back under control, just as a volley of rifle fire blasted chunks of concrete into shreds right near his face. He ducked back under the lip of the warehouse entrance, taking cover momentarily.

*Three.*

Streams of Spanish curses ripped through the warehouse.

*Two.*

Gunshots cracked and popped.

*One.*

Screams emanated from the factory floor.

*Go.*

He waited for the gunfire to settle as gangsters on both sides ran out of ammunition and paused to reload. There was still the odd staccato of a three-round burst, but the initial adrenalin dump seemed to have passed.

King took that opportunity to vault up onto the warehouse floor, landing awkwardly on the dusty concrete. He hurried over to the nearest available cover — a chunky steel workstation covered in half-full wooden crates, each crammed with airtight packages. All the crates had permanent marker scrawled on their sides, labelling them: C17H21NO4.

If he wasn't mistaken, that was the formula for pure cocaine powder.

Unsuppressed gunshots roared close by, coming from the other side of the workstation. King rose into view and let loose with the Five-seven, firing four shots into a pair of singlet-clad, heavily-tattooed thugs that he assumed worked for the Draco cartel.

They dropped amidst flying droplets of blood exiting from the bullet wounds.

Instantly, a cluster of Ramos' men halfway inside the facility fired their AK-47s, littering King's surroundings with the metallic clang of ricocheting rounds.

He ducked back behind the workstation, but the brief reprieve from getting fired upon had allowed him a better look at the layout of the facility.

He'd glimpsed a row of smaller offices at the back of the warehouse, on the other side of all the production equipment. Between them was a literal maze of workstations, giant industrial ovens, hundred-gallon barrels of unknown product, and at least twenty gangsters from opposing cartels. The infighting had reached boiling point — the invading Draco thugs had pressed further into the facility, turning the gunfight into a close-quarters riot.

If Ramos was on the premises, he would be in the offices.

That's where the Draco thugs were headed.

That's where King would head.

Satisfied that Ramos' goons and the Draco henchmen were preoccupied trying to kill each other, he skirted around the side of the workstation and hurried over to a vast wall of barrels, arranged by forklifts into neat stacked rows for ease of access. He took cover behind the closest forklift and glanced inside the contents of the first row.

They were filled at random, with no pre-determined pattern — some contained wet cement that had just been produced for the day's work, others were full to the brim with gasoline, and a last batch contained some kind of dry fertiliser that gave off a horrid stench.

King posited that the foul ingredients were used during the process of converting coca leaves into the pure cocaine he'd glimpsed at the first workstation, probably combined into a brew to draw the necessary ingredients out of the leaves themselves.

He didn't get the chance to finish that thought.

A six-foot-five giant of a man rounded the side of the forklift, spotted King cowering behind the vehicle, and raised his pistol. The man bared his teeth as he aimed, milliseconds from having a lock on King.

King dotted his bare pectorals with a triangle of expertly-placed bullets from the Five-seven. Each steel-core round tore through muscle and bone, like heat-seeking missiles locked onto vital organs. The giant man jerked unnaturally with each impact and collapsed in a sweaty heap, knocking over one of the open-topped barrels in the process.

It had been filled with gasoline.

King sensed an opportunity. He darted over to the closest fertiliser barrel and fired the last two bullets in the Five-seven's twenty-round magazine into the dry heap of mulch. Then he tossed the empty firearm away. The heat of the rounds singed a small patch of the fertiliser. King reached in, snatched a handful of the burnt gunk, and tossed it over to the expanding puddle of foul-smelling fuel.

Flames powered out in all directions from the impact point, spreading fast. They snaked their way up the nearest workstation and set the coca leaves atop its surface ablaze. The leaves cracked and popped under the heat, drawing enough attention for King to slip behind the wall of barrels and sprint for the other side of the warehouse, still clutching the Sig-Sauer P226 in his right hand.

He couldn't suppress the panic much longer. The warehouse was a ticking time bomb, packed full of high-testosterone cartel-employed killers intent on causing as much chaos as humanly possible. He was relying on the distraction of the inferno near the entrance in a desperate bid to buy himself some time. With each passing second, he realised the unlikelihood of finding and eliminating Ramos. There was no guarantee that the man was even here in the first place.

If he was, he almost certainly would have fled the premises by now.

But King wasn't a quitter.

He pushed himself faster, racing down the empty stretch of concrete floor, shielded by the wall of barrels to his right and the corrugated iron wall to his left.

Suddenly, a group of four cartel thugs appeared at the

end of the corridor. All of them were in the process of backing into cover, avoiding a sudden burst of fire from the opposing party. King couldn't tell whether they were members of the Draco cartel or Ramos' men — every thug in the building was dressed in loose casual clothing.

They saw him, though.

And they seemed to know exactly who he was.

King's heart spiked into his throat as he saw four assault rifle barrels swinging in his direction. There was nowhere to take cover, no viable alternative to getting his torso shredded to pieces.

Then he saw an exit door set into the wall to his left. It was firmly shut, probably locked. Acting with animalistic intensity, he powered off one leg and threw himself into the door, lacking the time it would take to reach for the handle. A handful of initial gunshots sounded from the other end of the corridor, just as he went airborne.

If the door didn't give, he would very likely knock himself unconscious from the impact, rendered helpless to stop the cartel thugs gunning his limp body into a bloody pulp.

He forced the thought out of his mind and hoped for the best.

He crashed shoulder-first into the door, hitting it with an almighty *thud.* His brain rattled inside his skull, dazing him, but he was brought back to the realm of the living by bright sunlight flooding his senses.

The door had burst outward from the impact.

King sprawled awkwardly across the parking lot outside the building, slapping the smooth concrete with his hands first. He rolled in ungainly fashion onto his back, keeping an iron grip on the P226. It was his only lifeline.

He brought his aim around to lock onto the open

doorway he had just burst through. It wouldn't take much effort for the four thugs to follow him out of the building. King didn't fancy his chances against the group.

One sidearm against four heavily-armed adrenalin-fuelled gangsters weren't the best odds.

At some point, sheer firepower overwhelmed even the most acutely refined reflexes.

He spent so long fixated on the dark space in the side of the warehouse that he tuned out everything happening behind him. He didn't hear the howling sirens — they were drowned out by his heartbeat pounding in his ears.

As he vaulted to his feet, he didn't sense the movement behind him, approaching fast.

He heard the yelling, the frantic authoritative commands blurted out in Spanish, but didn't turn in time. He kept his vision tunnelled onto the open doorway, expecting the four cartel thugs to come barrelling into view at any moment.

He realised his mistake far too late.

The police officers closed in on him and tackled him to the concrete.

# 32

He squirmed and bucked and writhed, with no success. The pair of bodies outweighed him heavily, and he found himself unable to resist arrest.

Firm hands yanked his arms behind his back and the cold bite of steel sunk into his wrists. The cuffs were wrenched tight, pinning his arms against the small of his back. Someone tore the P226 out of his grip, disarming him in the space of a second.

He struggled to get his vision under control, head swimming from where it had smacked face-first against the concrete. He tasted rivulets of blood in his mouth — he'd bitten his tongue in several different places. A couple of the cuts from the previous day had re-opened, sending crimson rivers dripping off his chin into his lap.

The two police officers sat him up and one of them trained their rifle on him.

King gulped back apprehension.

Unless something changed, he was going to jail for a long time.

Or worse.

As he sat on the scorching ground underneath the intense glare of the sun beating down overhead, he narrowed his vision in an attempt to make out what was going on. Everything was unfolding too quickly.

An officer stood on either side of him, both dressed in plain olive uniforms and communicating back and forth in Spanish. He had no idea what was being said. He waited to see what would happen next.

Then the four cartel henchmen materialised in the open doorway, just as King let his head droop onto his chest from fatigue.

He bolted upright, suddenly terrified.

As far as he could tell, he was about to be caught in the no-man's-land of a devastating shootout. Cartels and law enforcement spelled nothing but disaster.

But nothing happened.

King sat helplessly on the ground between the two parties, wincing involuntarily, ducking his head in a feeble attempt to protect himself. No gunshots followed. There was no panicked screaming, no rapid outbursts of commands.

Just silence.

One of the policemen piped up. 'Draco?'

The four-man team of cartel thugs nodded simultaneously.

'*Go!*' the policeman yelled to his colleagues.

A cluster of law enforcement officers hurried inside the building, letting the Draco thugs lead them to their predetermined destination. King couldn't believe his eyes. One of the officers stayed back to watch over King, keeping the barrel of his sidearm trained on the top of his head at all times.

King realised he shouldn't have been surprised.

Lars had explicitly told him that local law enforcement was on the payroll of the Draco cartel. That had been the main obstacle in Ramos attempting to seize control of Tijuana. It seemed that once the Draco cartel had located one of Ramos' facilities, they had stormed the place themselves, but called in bribed officials as reinforcements in the event that their attack didn't go as planned.

The police would move in to clean up the rest.

King stared at the ground, riding out the pounding headache that had flared to life behind his eyeballs. He contemplated just how far the influence of the cartels reached. In the end, he was out of his depth. His initial questions to Lars had been spot-on.

*What can one man do against this system?*

He had entered this dark city with a single goal — eliminate Joaquín Ramos. When that hadn't unfolded according to plan, he'd foolishly allowed himself to get wrapped up in the quagmire of the cartel wars.

Now, he would pay the price.

With gunshots echoing off the walls inside the building, accompanied by ear-piercing screams, he considered the ramifications of his actions. He would no doubt be treated as a member of Ramos' cartel, seeing that he had been apprehended outside one of the man's facilities. That would lead to a back-alley firing squad, or an unobstructed trial and a life sentence in one of Mexico's toughest prisons.

Neither option appealed to him all that much.

*Why would Ramos have been here?* he thought.

Realisation dawned on him. He had been acting on a wild hunch, based on the idea that Ramos would be foolish enough to hang around one of his packaging facilities and risk arrest or murder. The man was smarter than that.

Evidently, King was not.

He tuned out the distant din of gunfire, detaching himself from the war taking place within the warehouse. He never should have let himself get involved with it. He should have accepted defeat when Ramos first escaped from the apartment complex and retreated back over the border with his tail between his legs.

Instead, he had only worsened the situation. Lars would no doubt be vilified for believing in an inexperienced, twenty-two year old prodigy with no extensive training in solo operations. He had worked off his impulses, having bought into Lars' belief that the tunnel vision he experienced in the heat of battle would be enough to pull him through death-defying situations.

It had been.

But the only result of those actions were a few dead gangsters.

He was no closer to the people in charge.

And he was headed for a corrupt police station next.

King barely noticed the conflict reach its conclusion. Policemen emerged from the side exits to the warehouse, dragging their wounded comrades with them, bloodied and bruised. A pair of the hard-faced officers hauled King to his feet, ignoring his questions.

'What did I do?' he said as they dragged him toward one of the sedans that had pulled into the otherwise-empty parking lot. Its lights were still flashing.

The policeman to his left backhanded him across the face. King spat blood onto the hot concrete.

'I'm not involved with this,' he said. 'I'm not with them.'

No-one cared.

They were on the Draco payroll.

They would do as their financiers requested.

Which clearly meant delivering King and anyone else who had lived through the shootout into their open arms.

He forced all thoughts of what they might do to him out of his mind.

How long would it take them to realise he knew nothing about Ramos' operation?

How damaged would he be by that point?

Another police officer caught up to the pair hauling King, and the trio began to babble back and forth in Spanish, gesticulating wildly as they did so. They were in the midst of debating what to do with him. King kept his mouth shut and let them figure it out amongst themselves.

Maybe one of them was feeling merciful.

When they reached the police cruiser, fat fingers pressed into the back of his neck and forced him into the vehicle. A thin sheet of wire mesh separated the rear compartment from the driver and passenger's seat. With his hands still crushed behind him, King found himself helpless to resist. One of the officers piled in on either side of him, pinning him into the middle seat. They kept their weapons trained on him.

*They think you're dangerous,* he thought.

Their caution meant there was nothing he could do. The third guy skirted around to the driver's side and slipped into the car. He placed a hand on the wheel and fired the sedan to life.

They squealed out of the lot, rubber burning against the asphalt as the driver hurried away from the scene. King got the sense that they wanted to hide the fact that they had him in their possession. A broad-shouldered American male would be noticeable, an odd sight amidst the army of Latino thugs and maquiladora factory-workers occupying the warehouse.

Maybe they thought he was in charge of the facility.

Maybe they were going to hand-deliver him to the Draco cartel as fast as possible.

And Draco wouldn't know any different.

The thought made him squirm slightly in his seat, causing the police officer on the left to jam the barrel of his sidearm into King's ribs. He froze in an attempt to calm the situation. The last thing he wanted was a trigger-happy cop ending his life before he had the chance to try and flee.

The possibility of escape began to grow less likely with each passing second. Their sedan mounted a curving single-lane path that ran around to the front of the complex. King peered through the open roller doors as they passed the warehouse entrance. He spotted corpses everywhere — some were clearly wearing the cheap, baggy clothes of factory workers.

Maquiladora workers who didn't know any better, trying to make a hard-earned peso and caught in the crossfire.

*Ruthless bastards,* King thought.

Already, commotion had unfolded around the entrance to the property. The scene had been cordoned off by a makeshift barricade of similar-looking police sedans. Local law enforcement, out in full force at the request of the Draco cartel.

They weren't here to keep the peace.

They were here to hinder Ramos' operation.

King didn't condone what Ramos was doing, but the Draco cartel were no better.

*The enemy of my enemy is my friend...*

Not in this case.

Two of the sedans in the barricade reversed away from each other to let the cruiser through. King glanced out the windows on either side of him, making eye contact with a handful of local police officers standing guard out the front of the warehouse. They all gave him the evil eye as the sedan he sat in roared out onto the open road.

The driver stamped on the accelerator and gunned it away from the warehouse.

King bowed his head, struggling to control his nerves. It was the first time he'd found himself in a truly dangerous situation, helpless to the decisions of a corrupt handful of police officers in a foreign country.

The drug war was not a safe place to make mistakes.

Suddenly, King realised that also applied to the corrupt policemen all around him.

It began with the man in the passenger seat arching forward in his seat, peering out the windscreen at an odd angle. King saw the guy's eyes widen significantly. As they reached the T-junction at the end of the long, factory-lined street, the man started to babble incoherently in Spanish. He gesticulated ahead, turning to the driver, his voice rising in volume with each passing moment.

'*Federales!*' the man screamed.

The driver cursed and yanked on the handbrake...

... just as an armoured police cruiser cut them off, crushing into the sedan's bonnet with enough force to send the car squealing into an uncontrollable centrifugal spin.

# 33

No-one had bothered to put on their seat belts, let alone secure their prisoner.

King went airborne, crushing the officer to his left. He smacked his head against the roof and suppressed a grunt of agony. At the same time, the officer he'd thrust into the door accidentally fell against the handle, releasing the mechanism. The door swung outward.

With the sedan still fishtailing wildly across the intersection, King and the policeman were helpless to resist the laws of physics. The officer tumbled out of the moving vehicle, and with no handhold to snatch at, King tipped across one shoulder and sprawled out of the open doorway.

He saw nothing but a blur of motion before the hot asphalt rushed up to meet him. He rolled as best he could, his hands still secured behind his back by the cuffs. He was still largely inexperienced in volatile situations like these, but he used the massive dose of adrenalin to full effect, ignoring the bumps and bruises that were smashed into existence as he slapped the hard road in the middle of the intersection.

He rolled to his feet in one smooth motion and sprung out of the path of an oncoming pick-up truck. The driver shook his fist at King out the open window, infuriated by the commotion. Then he noticed what was unfolding in front of him and carried straight on, accelerating away from the madness.

King struggled to comprehend what was going on.

The armoured truck that had destroyed the front half of their sedan wasn't haphazardly thrown together like Ramos' monster truck in the mountains. This was a legitimate, official vehicle, stamped with the insignia of a law enforcement division.

Which division that was, King had no idea.

*Federales,* the local officer had said.

*Federal police.*

Traffic screeched to a standstill as the altercation played out in the middle of the intersection. Federal police in riot gear spilled out of the back of the truck — at least four men, maybe more. King couldn't focus on one aspect for long enough to get an accurate estimate. But the masked, heavily-armed policemen made straight for the destroyed sedan. King watched as they methodically swept the barrels of their automatic rifles from window to window, checking for signs of movement.

One of the federal officers noticed the man in the driver's seat of the sedan sitting up, blood dripping onto his uniform from his injured mouth.

The federal officer fired a three-round burst through the shattered passenger window.

The uniform got a whole lot bloodier.

King froze in his tracks, suddenly acutely aware of how vulnerable he was. There was no available cover nearby, and his hands were locked behind his back. Without making a wild, awkward break for the nearest alley, he wasn't sure what his options were.

One of the federal officers saw King standing there, and held up a gloved hand, palm facing towards him.

*Stay right there,* the gesture commanded.

King complied.

There was little else he could do.

He watched the four-man riot squad clear the local police sedan in clinical fashion. The other officer in the back seat caught a round through the forehead, killing him instantly. Then the only man left was the guy who had spilled out of the car alongside King.

King glanced over at the man — a young guy, his uniform a size too large, probably ambitious that he would pack on some muscle throughout the years and grow into his gangly frame. The man was on Draco's payroll, clearly, but King got the sense — as he had a few times in Tijuana — that there was little other choice for men like them.

Work for us, take a bribe, or meet your demise in a shallow ditch for daring to defy us.

'*Run*,' King mouthed.

The guy had seized up in terror, caught in the no man's land between the row of traffic that had banked up at the mouth of the intersection and the sinister-looking team of law enforcement hitmen in the middle.

He flapped his lips like a dying fish, confused, unsure.

'*Run!*' King screamed.

The guy turned his back and took off.

He made it three steps.

King watched the rounds punch through the back of his thin shirt. The shirt had been recently ironed — maybe the guy wanted to look good for his new job. King grimaced as blood fountained from the wounds and the man face-planted the asphalt, coming to an unceremonious halt just a few feet from where he had first taken off.

He never stood a hope.

King had known that.

But it was either stay on the spot and see the barrel aiming in your direction, or make a run for it and never see the end coming.

King wished that the man had been holding onto some semblance of hope when he died.

It might have made it easier.

He turned to face the squad of federal policemen. There was no point shying away from his own death. With his hands useless and his position vulnerable, he knew that he was at the mercy of the approaching federal policemen.

In the midst of the adrenalin dump, he had no time to think about why the different police divisions had attacked each other.

It didn't cross his mind until the barrels of the assault rifles dropped to point at the ground.

They weren't going to kill him.

At least, not yet.

King registered the confusion of the situation, and decided to use it to full advantage.

One of the federal officers stepped forward from the rest of the pack, brandishing a set of keys that he had fished out of the half-demolished sedan. King nodded his satisfaction and turned on the spot, indicating that he wanted to be freed as fast as possible. The officer complied, unlocking his cuffs and tossing them onto the asphalt by their feet.

King spun back to face the man, secretly astonished as to what was unfolding.

The federal officer said something in Spanish.

'I'm American,' King said, rubbing his wrists in an attempt to soothe them.

'Oh,' the man said.

'Thanks for getting me out of there.'

The man paused, studying King's accent, analysing his demeanour. 'In what capacity do you work for Ramos?'

*So that's what this is,* King realised.

These men were on Ramos' payroll. Evidently, Ramos had sensed that existing local law enforcement wouldn't budge if he attempted to sway them over to his side. They were already firmly in the clutches of the Draco cartel. But Mexico had a complex web of authorities, separate divisions that had no loyalty to Tijuana but operated in the same territory.

He'd bought certain members of the federal police.

And in the confusion of responding to the warehouse attack, these men had set about freeing anyone who had been apprehended by the Draco-bought police.

A complex web, indeed.

King would use it.

'In no capacity whatsoever,' he said. 'But thanks for the help.'

He reached down and wrenched the Colt 9mm sub-machine-gun out of the man's gloved hands with enough force to throw the policeman off-balance. The guy's fingers stayed wrapped around the grip, with one slotted into the trigger guard, but King tugged harder, breaking the man's finger with a gut-wrenching crack.

The guy slackened his grip, and King tore the weapon free.

He had a gun.

# 34

King knew he needed to act fast.

There were three armed federal officers ahead, all having already killed fellow law enforcement comrades. They clearly cared little about murder, and would happily gun King down if they recognised that he wasn't part of Ramos' operation. They were protected by anonymity, their features concealed by riot masks.

They wouldn't hesitate to add another body to their kill count.

But neither would King.

This was a reckless city, and he would have to compensate to survive.

He noted the model of the Colt SMG in his hands — a RO639. The selective fire had been set to three-round-burst. Three bullets expended for every pull of the trigger.

King darted sideways, stepping out of the way of the man he had stripped the weapon off, opening up the space in front of him. He raised the Colt SMG to his shoulder and squeezed the trigger three times.

Nine rounds total.

The federal officers were suitably geared up for the occasion, clad from head-to-toe in body armour. King targeted the narrow slit between their chest plates and their riot masks with each three-round-burst, working his aim like he was back on the shooting range. Before he fired, he allowed his nerves to calm, turning his trembling hands into stone. He narrowed in on his targets and let all other thoughts flow out of his mind.

It paid off.

The three officers dropped one after the other, arterial blood spilling from the bare skin below their riot masks. They went limp in unison, offering no resistance to King's attack.

When the trio had collapsed to the road, King sliced the barrel back around to lock onto the man he had disarmed seconds earlier.

'Fuck,' the guy said, a single syllable that spelled out every thought in the man's head.

'Yeah,' King said.

The officers had taken an unnecessary risk. They'd mercilessly gunned down an entire squad of local police officers just to appease their unofficial boss.

It hadn't worked out for them.

King killed the fourth federal officer with the same tactic, sending three Parabellum rounds through his throat. He didn't have a shred of remorse while doing so.

Out here, it was kill or be killed.

With eight law enforcement officers dead on the scene, King knew he couldn't waste a second. He sprinted over to the three dead federal police near the sedan and swapped his near-empty Colt SMG for two of their fully-loaded ones. Then he continued his pace across the street, darting between two long, low buildings and vanishing out of sight of the civilians who had witnessed the carnage.

Alone in a filthy alleyway, he was able to let out the breath that had stalled in his throat since Ramos' warehouse had been invaded.

It had been a chaotic chain of events. At any point he could have caught a stray bullet or disappeared into the bowels of the corrupt police system. As he made it through to the next street and shoved the two sub-machine-guns underneath his shirt to prevent any unwanted attention, the shock began to set in.

He had come horrendously close to death time and time again, with nothing to show for it. A handful of cartel thugs and police officers were dead — little else had been achieved.

He was no closer to Ramos.

He hurried through the Eastern La Mesa district, home to a sprawling network of rundown offices, warehouses, and industrial complexes. The sun beat down overhead. King wiped his shirt-sleeve across his forehead, which came away stained with a mixture of sweat and blood.

He must have hit his head against the asphalt while falling out of the police sedan.

He shook off a brief spell of dizziness and continued through the narrow streets. Traffic ran thick in these parts of Tijuana, with thousands of battered vehicles resting almost bumper-to-bumper. The daily rush of mid-morning, as workers headed for their shifts.

He kept up an awkward gait, half-shielding the bulky sub-machine-guns with his shirt. To a keen eye, what he was concealing would be obvious. But he had no intention of hiding it completely. He simply wanted to avoid arrest until he made it back to his motel room.

The time passed slowly. It couldn't have been more than a fifteen-minute-walk back to the motel, but his limbs seemed to drag as he started to overheat. The flood of neurochemicals to his brain that had allowed him to operate at peak capacity during the conflict was beginning to disperse. His hands and feet were heavy. It took great effort to put one foot in front of the other.

And — at all times — the fear never left.

He imagined running into Ramos' men, or members of the Draco cartel, or any of the multitude of police divisions operating in Tijuana who had been bought off by gangsters.

He wanted peace.

He wanted quiet.

But he hadn't achieved anything yet, so he would press on.

When he reached the motel complex and eased back into his room, he made the decision to call Lars.

It was now ten in the morning in Tijuana. He'd delayed getting in touch with his handler for long enough. Lars was probably close to abandoning all hope of King's return.

Maybe the U.S. thought he was dead.

Would they send a squad of elite operatives to retrieve him?

*Of course not.*

He would be chalked up as another statistic of the war on drugs, and the new division that Lars had pioneered would be swept back under the rug.

A colossal failure, in all regards.

*Not just yet,* King thought.

He dumped the two Colt SMGs on the mattress and pulled the duffel bag out from underneath the bed frame. He fished the military satellite phone out of the top of the duffel and dialled the single contact number in the phone.

'Where the hell have you been?' a voice barked barely a second after the call went through.

# 35

'Lars,' King said.

'So you are alive.'

'Unfortunately,' he quipped.

'Do you have results?'

'I wish I did.'

'Tell me everything that's happened so far.'

'It's complicated.'

'You've done something right,' Lars said.

'Oh?' King said. 'Please enlighten me. Because it feels like I've fucked everything up completely.'

'Whatever happened... it sure scared Ramos off.'

'How do you know?'

'He's not in the country.'

'How do you know any of this?'

'I've been trying to get in contact with you all night,' Lars hissed. 'Why the hell didn't you answer your phone?'

'I was avoiding this very conversation. Thought I might have something to show for my work this morning.'

'And?'

'Still got nothing.'

'What did you do this morning?'

'I thought I'd pay one of Ramos' facilities a visit. I was supposed to be delivered there by a trio of kidnappers last night. Thought Ramos might be there.'

'Like I said, he's not in the country.'

'How the hell do you know where he is?'

'The TOR encryption that he's using for all of his operations,' Lars said. 'We made a breakthrough. With his tech team gone, he's had to try and handle the digital workload himself. And, frankly, he has no idea what he's doing. He's left a trail of breadcrumbs through his encryption. He isn't coding things correctly.'

'And you can capitalise on that?'

'We invented TOR,' Lars said. 'The US Naval Research Laboratory actually developed the technology that the encryption is based on.'

'You've lost me entirely,' King said.

'Basically, we know the encryption very, very well. Any slip-up is something we can take advantage of. His previous team were bulletproof — they didn't make a single error the entire time we were keeping tabs on them. But Ramos has made plenty. He's been trying to anonymously communicate with his men back in Tijuana. He left his location wide open.'

'Where is he?'

'Northern Guatemala.'

King glanced at his watch. 'Already? Jesus Christ. That's a few thousand miles from here.'

'It's obvious that he's retreated to somewhere familiar,' Lars said. 'From what we can guess, Ramos has processing facilities out there. It's cheap labour, and all the cartels seem to be doing it these days. The Mexico-Guatemala border is effectively lawless. Ramos can take advantage of the hordes of locals looking for work, then smuggle his product through to Chiapas and up to Tijuana.'

'Is this all just a guess?'

'There's no other reason for him to be there. He's in the middle of the jungle. Near an ancient Mayan city by the name of Piedras Negras. Unless he's decided to revert to living as a caveman, then he has important facilities out that way. He's gone into hiding.'

'I can't imagine why,' King said. 'He almost killed me over and over again yesterday.'

'Well, what happened this morning?' Lars said. 'This situation is multi-faceted. There could be any number of reasons why he decided to flee.'

King recalled the convoy of Draco vehicles storming into Ramos' warehouse. 'One of the rival cartels hit him hard this morning. Maybe he was expecting it.'

'Maybe. It seems like everything unfolded all at once. He's in panic mode.'

'You think he's growing his product out that way?' King said.

'No. Cartels rarely grow their own product. It's packaging — I'm sure of it. A number of different gangs fight for power out there. All the coca is grown in either Bolivia, Colombia, or Peru. Cartels are like supermarket chains. They buy from the farmers, process the drugs themselves, then sell onto dealers. At least — that's what Ramos is doing.'

'So he really has fallen back to his last resort?' King said. 'Where will he go from Guatemala?'

'Our guess is that he'll stay there as long as he needs to,' Lars said. 'We can put a team together to take him out. Look, King, you did your job. You funnelled him into a corner. SEALs or Delta can do the rest of the work. Well done.'

'It wasn't me,' King said. 'It was the Draco cartel. I'm just a slight grievance to these massive organisations.'

'I realise that,' Lars said. 'But it doesn't look that way. I can spin this to look like we achieved our plan flawlessly.'

'But we didn't.'

'That doesn't matter. Don't you get it?'

'Oh, I get it,' King said. 'But I'm not happy about it.'

'There's not much time to be happy in this business.'

'I'm going to Guatemala.'

'You're ... what?!' Lars yelled, suddenly infuriated. 'No, you're fucking not.'

'We can spin this however we want,' King said. 'But in the end, the truth will come out. I did nothing but exacerbate the problem. You want something to show your superiors? Let me go into the jungle. I'll come out with Ramos' head.'

'You won't come out at all. You know how that corner of the world works? It's madness.'

'I like madness.'

'There's nothing left for me to do here,' King said. 'It took what happened this morning to make me realise the extent of the drug war that's gripping this city. Nothing I do will change that. The corruption runs deep. There'll always be people to replace the ones I kill.'

'You were never there to do anything else,' Lars said. 'You were there to kill Ramos.'

'Then let me do what I came here to do.'

'I've been informed that we have other operatives who can deal with that.'

'Then send me back to Delta.'

'You'll be a useful solo operative,' Lars said. 'You've proven that you can be sent in to stir things up. That'll be seen in a positive light.'

'I don't want to exist solely to stir things up. I want to exist to get the job done.'

'King...'

'I'm going to Guatemala,' he said. 'You can discharge me from the military if you want. Arrest me, for all I care. I'll kill Ramos if it's the last thing I do. You sent me into Mexico with a task, and I know I can complete it.'

'You sure?'

'I'm sure.'

'If I give you permission to head in there, and you don't succeed...' Lars said. 'You know what's at stake here.'

'I'm not asking for permission. I'm going to do it. I have a personal grudge against the man.'

Lars drew air in sharply.

'You don't let anyone hear that apart from me, okay?' he hissed. 'What on earth are you thinking? You think we have time for personal vendettas in this business?'

'If it didn't involve the job, I'd abandon it,' King said. 'Luckily, it involves the job.'

'How do you propose you're going to storm a heavily-protected processing facility?' Lars said, his tone sardonic. 'Not to mention the other cartels that operate out of that area. You'll run into a war zone. There's ten or more entities fighting for territory out there, and a small army of hired guns to protect each camp. You understand that, right?'

'I understand.'

'You're more than likely going to get yourself killed.'

'What do you care?' King snapped. 'You barely know me. Don't let your heart get in the way of your head, Lars. We don't know each other well enough yet. You shouldn't care if I die out there. Just another deceased operative. Move on to the next.'

'I think I have something with you,' Lars said. 'Your reflexes. They're not like anything I've ever seen before.'

'Then you should have faith that I'll get the job done. Imagine what we can do with this division if I bring Ramos' head back over the border. One man. Against a drug cartel. Let me do it.'

'Fine.'

'That's it?'

'That's it. You were going to do it anyway.'

'I know. But I wanted your approval.'

'How's working alone?' Lars said, diverting from the main topic of conversation for the first time. 'Everything you were expecting it to be?'

King parted the curtains and gazed out the window at the stuffy urban sprawl of downtown Tijuana. The room was humid, soaking his shirt through with sweat. He felt cramped, boxed in, choking on the fumes of an industrial grid.

'Not yet,' he said. 'But I don't think I work well in tight spaces.'

'Tijuana's too cramped?'

'Maybe. Let's see what I can do in Guatemala.'

'Do you need anything?' Lars said. 'I can have supplies sent across the border within hours.'

King glanced at the Colt SMGs on the bed next to him. 'I've got guns. That's all I need. Anything overly complicated will just weigh me down.'

'I don't know if you fully realise what you're getting yourself into.'

'I realise.'

'That part of Guatemala is a nightmare,' Lars said, hammering the point home. 'Their armed forces are down to roughly ten thousand men. They used to have thirty thousand. You know what that means?'

'Tens of thousands of soldiers looking for employment by any means necessary?'

'Spot on.'

'He'll have an army,' King said. 'I'm aware of that. That's why this is going to work. I can settle a personal score, and do it quietly in the process. You can prove to your superiors that sending a SEAL team up against an army of hired guns would only have made the situation worse. I'll be in and out without anyone knowing.'

'I didn't know stealth was your forte,' Lars said.

'It's not,' King said. 'Violence is. Send me the co-ordinates of Ramos' last known location. Give me two days.'

He ended the call.

# 36

King understood that twelve hours ago things would have unfolded very differently.

The failure to achieve anything at Ramos' packaging facility would have demoralised him. More than likely, he would have abandoned all hope of success and followed Lars' first orders to return to the United States, satisfied with the meagre progress that he'd made.

But, deep down, he found himself fuelled by an animalistic desire to kill Joaquín Ramos.

His encounter with Juan the night before had changed something in him. With no surrounding soldiers or operatives to sway him in one direction, he had been left alone with his thoughts. It had given him time to mull over what Juan had told him. He couldn't force the mental image of the two dismembered brothers out of his mind.

Ramos had to die.

There were — no doubt — countless other atrocities being committed by all members of the drug cartels across the country, but King had found himself personally involved in this instance. It went against all his training, everything that had been drilled into him since the first day he had stepped foot in a military recruiting office at eighteen years of age. If he found himself personally swayed by an operation, he should detach himself from it immediately.

This time, there was no-one around to tell him what to do.

And — thankfully — the operation aligned with his personal intentions.

But he knew that, even if it didn't, he would have followed his heart. In any other situation it would have got him dishonourably discharged from the military.

Or worse.

He would need to learn to bring that under control.

Just, not yet.

He made a quick mental calculation as to how long it would take to reach Guatemala. The border was way down south, thousands of miles away. How Ramos had reached the country overnight was lost on King. Briefly, he considered stealing a car and making the journey via land. That way, he could keep the two Colt SMGs.

But it would take too long.

Two full days of non-stop driving, plus whatever time King needed to take to rest.

By that point, Ramos could have fortified his encampment with hundreds of hired guns. Or, worse — he could have taken his profits and fled, starting a new life with a new identity somewhere more tropical. He would get away with everything he had done, with enough blood money to live out a life of luxury for the rest of his days.

The sheer thought made King's blood boil.

No — he would have to get there as fast as humanly possible.

By air.

It would mean ditching the guns.

He could find weapons when he touched down in Guatemala.

Now, he was just an ordinary civilian booking a last-minute flight to a neighbouring country. Interested in exploring the ancient Mayan ruins.

Nothing more than that.

He left the guns on the bed, first wiping them down with a sterilised cloth he fished out of the bottom of the duffel bag. He wiped the fingerprints off everything he thought he'd touched in the motel room — there was little that he had. Then he combed through the bedsheets for any kind of hair follicles he could find. He didn't bother spending much more time on the room, satisfied with a rudimentary sweep.

He slung the duffel bag over one shoulder and stepped out into the Mexican heat.

There was no sign of the motel owner. King elected to let the man discover that he was no longer residing at the room on his own — he had paid cash, and left no valuables at reception. He strode out onto the busy main road and peered up and down the length of cars to try and find a cab that could take him to Tijuana International Airport.

It only took a couple of minutes of waiting for trouble to arise.

King sensed the guy approaching, but thought nothing off it. There were plenty of pedestrians on these sidewalks, and not all of them were out to murder him. He expected the shadow to pass him by on the left-hand-side, but the man stopped right alongside King, stepping straight into his personal space.

Uncomfortably close.

King turned to look at him, regretting the fact that he'd left all his guns back in the motel room.

But it wasn't anyone who was after him specifically.

It was a common, low-level street thug.

The guy was bald, with an oversized white singlet hanging down to his nipples and oversized baggy cargo shorts that almost reached his ankles. He wore unlaced, filthy sneakers and stared King up and down like a meth junkie proudly protecting his territory. He was certainly high on something — King noticed his dilated pupils and the slight twitch in one corner of his mouth.

'What's up?' King said softly.

'You in the wrong place,' the dealer said, remaining less than a foot away from King. 'You get fuckin' moving.'

'Just trying to get a cab,' King said, gesturing to the traffic flying past just in front of them.

'Get it somewhere else.'

'I'm good here.'

'You don't got a choice.'

'Just let me get my cab, man,' King said. 'I'm not causing you any trouble. Leave me alone.'

The dealer took that as the most reprehensible comment in the history of man. His eyes widened even further and he mocked a reach for his belt, where a distinct bulge signified that he was carrying a piece. 'Who you fuckin' telling to leave you alone? You keep movi—'

He didn't make it through the rest of the sentence, because King threw a twisting elbow at close-range into the point of the man's jaw. The resulting *thump* of bone against bone resonated down the street, loud enough to make King wince. The guy stumbled back a step, stunned by the sheer force behind the blow. It looked as if he had been hit by a freight train. Sheer shock registered on his face.

When there was enough space between them for King to stretch out, he threw a teep-kick into the guy's solar plexus.

Kinetic energy transferred straight through into the man's torso, sending him stumbling back off his feet. He dropped onto his rear, hard enough to rattle his brain inside his skull.

He froze, sitting on the hot pavement like a stunned animal.

King pointed a finger at the man's belt. 'Don't reach for that.'

The guy complied.

He hadn't been hit like that before.

'Put your hands on the ground,' King said. 'So I know you won't try anything.'

The dealer — still turned to stone before King's eyes — stared vacantly down at the pavement. 'Ground's hot, man.'

'That's your only option.'

The elbow to the jaw had knocked the guy into a different demeanour. The thuggish bravado had vanished. He nodded solemnly and placed his palms on the concrete.

'Keep them there,' King said.

Another nod.

'Do you know who I work for?'

'No,' the guy said.

'Best to keep it that way. If you make a move, you'll catch a bullet in the forehead. Got it?'

'Yeah. I ain't movin'.'

The guy slumped forward, dejected, defeated.

'Smart man,' King said.

He set off across the street, refusing to look back, exerting unbridled confidence with every step. He needed the man convinced that if he even thought about pulling his gun and shooting King in the back, the consequences would be grave. If the man realised that King was on his own, he would take advantage of it.

All the reflexes and fighting capabilities in the world were no use against a close-range bullet.

King hailed an approaching cab as soon as he reached the other side of the two-lane road. The flaking sedan coasted to a stop by the sidewalk. He threw open the rear door and ducked into the middle seat.

'Where to, my friend?' the driver said, fiddling with the meter.

'Airport,' King said, keeping his eyes fixed on the thug across the road. The man was refusing to look up from the pavement, intimidated into sitting on his rear and staring hard at the ground between his legs. Beaten into submission with two well-placed, well-timed strikes.

'Heading back home?' the driver said as he peeled away from the sidewalk.

King shook his head. 'On to Guatemala.'

'What's in Guatemala?'

'A bit of business.'

The driver flashed a quizzical glance over his shoulder. 'There's not much business in Guatemala, my friend.'

'Just a quick thing I have to take care of.'

'What do you do?'

King stared out the window, watching the overbearing sprawl of Tijuana flash by. It might be the last glimpse he had of the city for quite some time. He wouldn't look back on his time here fondly. It had been a confused, fast-paced blur of a trip.

Something told him it was only going to get worse.

'I fix things,' he said.

'Like repairs?'

'Yeah,' King said. 'Something like that.'

# 37

*Mundo Maya International Airport*
*Flores*
*Guatemala*

The small plane hovered low over the thick canopy of rainforest as it descended towards a narrow runway in the distance. The atmosphere surrounding the craft was oppressive — it was intensely hot. The air ran thick with humidity, choking the fluids out of anything it came into contact with.

King had spent little time in tropical climate zones, and as he stared out the small circular window at the shimmering jungle below, he realised it would take some getting used to.

The view out the plane's window spelled trouble. It was still afternoon, but the roiling storm clouds masked all sunlight from spilling through. They hung in the air like grey wraiths, bearing down on the jungle below in ominous fashion. King grimaced as he studied the darkness above. It looked like the mother of all tropical storms was set to break out in Flores.

Hopefully, his forthcoming journey to the western border of the country would take him out of the perimeter of the storm.

Something made him doubt that it would.

The plane touched down with an almighty thump, rattling against the uneven tarmac below its wheels. King rode out the bumps and jolts, gripping the arm of his seat with white knuckles. Small planes still terrified him, despite his best efforts to shake their effects on his psyche. Time and time again he felt his heart leap into his throat whenever he was forced into one of the flimsy crafts.

Ironic, considering he had endured paratrooper drills as part of his SEAL training. With a parachute strapped to his back, he had no qualms over being thrust into a tiny, unstable aircraft. It didn't matter if the plane held together or not — whatever the case, he would be exiting with his lifeline attached to him.

Commercial flights provided no such relief.

Somehow, he couldn't see how flimsy oxygen masks and the standard brace position would protect him in the event that the engines stalled and they dropped at terminal velocity toward the rainforest canopy below.

But — as usual — his worst fears were left unrealised. The brakes kicked in and the plane slowed as it approached the tiny terminal. A broad sign above the building read "*Mundo Maya International Airport*".

King closed his eyes and soaked in the last few minutes of respite he would receive before heading straight into the madness.

There had been no trouble when heading through customs back in Tijuana. He was just an ordinary young

American backpacker, carrying little in the way of personal possessions. He had booked the next flight to Flores, a small city that lay in the centre of Northern Guatemala. From here, he would have to rent a car and make the journey west to Sierra del Lacandón National Park, the vast patch of rainforest that bordered Mexico.

Lars had warned him that all kinds of trouble lay within its limits.

King found himself jittery with anticipation.

He collected his duffel bag from the locker above his seat — it was small enough to be allowed as carry-on — and made his way to the front of the plane, following the three other passengers on the flight towards the exit. Having no luggage or belongings stored underneath meant that he could skip baggage claim altogether.

An open-framed transport buggy pulled up to the foot of the plane's exit stairs, ready to shepherd them to the terminal. King followed the people in front of him into the buggy. He took up a position at the back of the vehicle and snatched the military satellite phone out of the duffel bag.

He noted the proximity of the other passengers, and decided to hold off on making the call until he was well and truly alone.

The humid air whipped through the open frame and lashed against King's face as they sped towards the terminal entrance. He guessed that the driver and plane staff wanted the journey over as quickly as possible — there were more pressing matters at hand than dealing with an under-populated flight. Four passengers would be more of a burden to the airline than a potential full flight of people to impress.

King and the other three were just extra unwanted items to be discarded out into Guatemala.

He wouldn't have wanted it any other way.

It meant they weren't likely to look at him twice.

When the buggy reached a pair of motion-detecting entrance doors that seemed to be the only piece of technology in the airport, the driver barked a command in Spanish. King understood the message first, carrying his duffel in one hand and the satellite phone in the other as he departed the vehicle as fast as he could. He stepped into the terminal itself, feeling the artificial cool of the vast air-conditioning systems wash over him.

It took thirteen minutes to make it through customs.

He timed it in his head.

No problems.

No second looks.

Just another American lunatic to be thrown out to the wolves.

As he made it out onto the hot, cracked sidewalk running the length of the terminal's exterior, a man in a cheap button-up shirt approached him, holding a clipboard.

'Sir,' he said in an artificially-pleasant voice. 'You speak English?'

'I do.'

'Which agency did you book your tour with?'

'I'm not here for a tour.'

'I'm sorry, sir?'

'I'm doing my own thing.'

The man beamed, exposing teeth that were too white to be real. He nervously wiped a bead of sweat off his forehead. 'There must have been a mistake, sir.'

'No mistake,' King said.

He wondered how long it would take for the guy to leave him alone.

'You didn't book through a tour guide? Where are you staying?'

'Still haven't figured that out yet.'

The man's expression turned dark. He shook his head in disapproval. 'Guatemala is a dangerous place, sir. I wouldn't recommend going off on your own.'

'No?' King said. 'What's the risk?'

He wasn't sure whether the man's intentions were misplaced and he wanted to funnel King into the most lucrative tour guide package, or whether he truly was worried about a young foreigner attempting a solo expedition.

'The tours have armed security guards with them,' the man said. 'Unfortunately, that's something of a necessity out here.'

'I think I can manage.'

'Don't go west,' the man said. 'Okay? I'm not trying to sell you anything. Just avoid anywhere near the border. Telling you this isn't a good look for my country, but I'd rather you were safe.'

'I appreciate it,' King said. 'I'll be fine. Thank you.'

'I mean it.'

'I understand.'

The man adjusted the single sheet of paper in his clipboard — upon which a detailed itinerary had been printed — and nodded his satisfaction. King could see that he thought he'd done his good deed for the day. The guy shuffled off to the next unsuspecting tourist wandering out of the terminal.

King went west.

He made his way to the only rental car agency attached to the airport, which offered a range of vehicles for hire — all in similarly terrible condition.

First, he moved to the nearest ATM and withdrew a lump sum of Guatemalan quetzals from an off-the-record government bank account, the details of which had been provided to him by Lars to use at his discretion.

Then he strolled into the agency and worked out a deal with the dark-skinned man behind the counter, opting to pay the equivalent of a few hundred USD extra to avoid handing over a driver's license or passport. The man begrudgingly accepted, ultimately swayed by the large bribe. He chose the cheapest car in the lot to hand over.

King could tell he was a pessimist. The guy wasn't expecting the vehicle back.

Frankly, King wasn't expecting to return it in one piece.

He eyed the Toyota Hilux pick-up truck at the back of the lot with an inquisitive eye, noting the botched paint job and the way the vehicle sat at an odd angle on its wheels. He wondered if it would even be capable of making the journey into the jungle. It looked to be close to twenty years old.

The rental guy flashed a smile full of rotting, yellowing teeth at King and handed over the keys.

'Great,' King muttered, returning the smile with a hint of sarcasm.

It started up all the same.

*Reliable old bastard,* King thought.

He heard the engine cough and splutter into life. With a twist of the wheel, he turned out of the muddy parking space and gunned it away from Mundo Maya International Airport. As he scrutinised the rusting signs above the wide, potholed roads for any sense of direction, the satellite phone still gripped in his left hand vibrated harshly.

He received the call without even glancing at the screen.

It could only be one person.

'You made it?' Lars said.

'I made it.'

'You caught a flight?'

'Yeah.'

'Do you have a gun?'

'No.'

'King—' Lars started.

'Don't worry about it,' King said. 'I'll improvise.'

He spotted a main road, simply labelled "5", curving out of the city of Flores and into the rolling hills of rural Guatemala. It seemed to be pointing west. He twisted the wheel, turning onto what amounted to little more than a churned-up dirt track, and pressed on.

Almost instantly, the storm clouds seemed to grow thicker.

King let the chugging of the Hilux's engine settle over him, basically the only sound in these parts.

The calm before the storm.

# 38

'Can you track this phone?' King said into the receiver as the Toyota ploughed through a vast puddle of mud, kicking up geysers of brown gunk on either side of the pickup.

'Sure can,' Lars said. 'Keep doing what you're doing. Did you see a sign that said "5"?'

'Yeah.'

'Stay on this road until you bear right onto a road labelled "13". That'll take you all the way up to the very edge of the Sierra Del Lacandón National Park. From there, it's on you. I can get you to its perimeter, but the roads inside the National Park are pretty much uncharted.'

'It's not that archaic, is it?'

'You didn't understand what I was saying before, did you?' Lars said. 'That entire stretch of land is fair game for anything. Nearly half the murders in Guatemala are the work of the cartels. They do what they want out there. The few authorities that control Guatemala have basically given up trying to patrol the border. It's hopelessly unregulated.

No-one dares to go out there anymore. That's what you're heading into.'

'Perfect,' King muttered, his tone dripping with sarcasm.

'It's not too late to turn around and hand this over to a more experienced division.'

'What will that make me look like?'

'It's not all about image.'

'It is at this stage,' King said. 'You want to get this division up and running. You need results. You want me to succeed, don't you?'

'I want you to,' Lars admitted. 'But not if it gets you killed. Or worse.'

'Can't get much worse than dying.'

'Ramos could take you alive.'

'Touché. How far's the drive?'

'My program says just under three hours.'

'I'll aim for two. I want to make it there before it gets dark.'

'Do you have a flashlight?'

'No.'

'You're going to get yourself killed,' Lars stated.

It sounded like he was speaking what he believed to be a universal truth. Like King would achieve the impossible if the dawning altercation went any other way.

'I'll be fine,' he repeated, more to reassure himself than anything else.

He ended the call. There was nothing else that Lars could help him with. He had a set path in front of him.

All that was left was to see it through to its conclusion.

The sky growled ominously, threatening to crack and unleash a torrent of water across the state. King gave up on wrestling with the air conditioning, accepting that the Toyota's interior wouldn't cool. He rolled down the windows on either side of the vehicle, letting the hot, thick air swirl through the cabin.

He pressed the Hilux faster, throttling the engine. It made for a bumpy ride on the unkempt roads of rural Guatemala, but comfort was the last thing on his mind.

He was focused entirely on speed. In almost all aspects, he was at a disadvantage to Ramos. He was outmanned, outgunned, up against a trained killer and what would no doubt be an army of hired ex-soldiers.

Contract thugs. Mercenaries. Soldiers of fortune.

He had yet to experience the capabilities that ex-military had to offer. So far, his adversaries had been low-level street thugs and insurgents in the Middle East.

Both the setting and the enemies were unknown to him.

And this was the harshest learning grounds of them all.

But if he could keep surprise on his side, then maybe he had a chance. He reached up and drew a coarse sleeve across his forehead. It came away soaked through, coated in sweat. He blinked through the sheen of perspiration and concentrated on the uneven road ahead.

On either side of the Toyota, rugged terrain ran for as far as the eye could see, dense with vegetation and choked with overgrown weeds and bushes. King caught sight of a bare field dotted with dirty sheep. At random points through the rural landscape, rusting tin houses appeared, all on the verge of falling apart. There were no other vehicles on the road.

King had never been in a place quite like it.

He could sense the poverty from inside the car. It seemed to hang thick in the air, mixing with the humidity. It was an air of desperation, as if everyone in this part of the country was clinging to survival by a thread. He knew very little about Guatemala itself, but something told him that if he made it through the coming night, his best work would be done in settings like these.

Poverty-riddled, desolate locations, where good men and women could be exploited by anyone looking to earn blood money.

King found himself fuelled by the prospect of gunning down Ramos. Nothing would bring him greater personal satisfaction. He thought again of Juan, and how crippled the man had been by the emotions surrounding the death of his sons.

Fury swelled in his chest.

# 39

The hours passed slowly and quietly. The Hilux's radio had seemingly died years ago — in fact, most of the electronics on the dashboard had been stripped free. King got the sense that the rental car agency didn't ordinarily have this car available for hire. It was junk.

King shrugged to himself.

He was going to have to abandon it at some point anyway.

Just under two hours into the drive, the sun — barely visible behind the murky storm clouds above — drooped below the horizon. The dark grey clouds turned a shade of navy, trickling down into total darkness. The lack of light cast vast shadows across the rural plains, plunging the vegetation into night.

King reached out and switched on the headlights. Only one of them worked, cutting a lone path through the swirling darkness. Far above, thunder rumbled again. King cast his gaze skyward, but he couldn't see a thing.

If there was a downpour set to begin soon, he wanted to

cover as much ground as he could before the terrain turned to swamp.

In the distance, lightning flared, illuminating the scenic landscape in all its moody ambience.

'That's not good,' King whispered to himself.

The nerves began to set in, more from the theatricality of his surroundings than anything else. He didn't fear confrontation, or death, for that matter. If he died in service of his country, he would rest easy. He would know that he'd perished while trying to do some good.

But the approaching tropical storm, combined with the sickly warm air and the eerie silence of the unpopulated countryside, sent shivers down his spine.

He found himself more afraid of the unknown than anything else.

Sierra del Lacandón National Park presented itself moments later in terrifying fashion. King spotted the literal wall of trees looming on one side of the road. The thick, low wall of bushes that had flashed past for as long as he could remember shifted into jungle. The broad leaves of the rain-forest canopy hung over the road, like a natural ceiling for the twisting, turning path.

King followed the perimeter of the National Park for a couple of dozen miles, searching for an opening that would lead into the sprawling forest.

When the light vanished entirely from the sky and a nervous itch sprouted at the base of his neck, he tugged the satellite phone free from his belt and dialled Lars again.

'I see you,' was the first thing Lars said when he answered.

'Good,' King said. 'I'm lost as hell. Please tell me you've found something on this place. It's enormous.'

'I did some digging. There should be a long-abandoned

trail just a couple of miles ahead. It'll lead all the way through to the border, if it isn't overgrown by now. It passes Piedras Negras, which was where we last heard from Ramos.'

'Fill me in on that again.'

'It's a collection of ancient Mayan ruins that happens to rest right near the Mexico-Guatemala border. In the Usumacinta region. Archaeologists have been desperately trying to protect it, but it hasn't been much use. Rumours are that there's close to eight groups of drug-runners and gangsters occuyping that small stretch of land. The ping we received from Ramos' device showed him practically directly on top of the ruins. He has to have a facility right nearby.'

'Will you direct me to it?'

'I'll do my best. You have to understand — these are old maps. Times have changed.'

'I know.'

'This won't be easy. You'll either be caught in the middle of a territorial dispute, or you'll bump directly into one of the cartels. They all convert coca leaves into pure cocaine along the border. It's big business.'

'Don't worry,' King said, still guiding the Toyota through the humid night. 'I need to run into someone anyway.'

'W-why?'

'I'm still unarmed.'

'Oh, Jesus Christ...'

'Just tell me where to go. I'll take care of the rest.'

'Stop right there,' Lars commanded.

King stamped on the brakes, which took a few seconds to kick in given the ancient nature of the Toyota Hilux. The tyres bit into the mud, squelching to a halt in the middle of the road. It didn't cause any kind of traffic jam

— in fact, King hadn't seen another vehicle for over an hour.

'If the ping from your satellite phone's accurate,' Lars said. 'You should be right on top of the entrance to the trail. There won't be signage of any kind. All that would have been removed when the area became volatile. It's not a tourist destination anymore.'

King stared out the driver's window, peering at the literal wall of vegetation on the other side of the road. Between two towering trees, he thought he could make out a dangerously narrow mountain trail twisting away into the pitch-black night.

He gulped.

'Looks fucking sketchy, Lars.'

'You went into Guatemala's jungles thinking it was going to be anything other than sketchy?'

'I don't know if I can make it through. It's narrow.'

'Give it your best shot. We're fairly screwed otherwise. And — as much as I hate to admit it — you may have succeeded in what you were doing.'

'What do you mean?'

'I'm looking at the timeframe now. There's no way Ramos thinks you're in-country. It's only been half a day since he made it to his facility — and he was probably flown into one of the private airstrips along the border controlled by traffickers and illegal settlers. You would have had to drop everything and race cross-country to make it there so quickly — which was exactly what you did. He won't expect you to come so soon.'

'I still need a gun,' King said.

'You might be in luck. All the cartels use mobile laboratories to dry their coca leaves faster. They throw their gear onto the back of pick-up trucks and run it round the jungle all day and night. It's an important part of the process. See if you can intercept one of the trucks on the way. Act like a lost foreigner and then take them down.'

'You read my mind.'

'Good luck, King.'

King ended the call, stared at the dark hole in the rainforest in front of him, and took a deep breath.

It was time.

# 40

With a single, flickering bulb in a lone headlight paving the way for him, King entered a nightmare with a touch of the accelerator.

The Toyota Hilux rumbled over the pockmarked ground, its suspension groaning with each new obstacle it traversed. The driver's seat shuddered underneath him, threatening to collapse just seconds into the journey. King kept his foot down, pressing through the worst of it. The headlight bounced off the jungle ahead, cutting briefly through the wall of darkness to illuminate what lay ahead.

None of it was pretty.

The terrain wasn't going to smooth out for a long time. King kept a steady path, guiding the Toyota into the National Park. Lars had told him back in Tijuana that the park was large enough to consist of a number of different biomes. He hoped that the sub-tropical rainforest was the hardest of those biomes to venture through.

If the entire journey was like this, he didn't think the Toyota would make it to Ramos' complex.

Thankfully, the ground evened out roughly fifteen

minutes into the journey. King tried his best to stay on the path, but at times it was difficult to assess where the trail ended and the jungle floor began. There was barely any indication of where the boundaries were — at one point, he had to screech to a halt and throw the Toyota into reverse to compensate for a wrong turn.

Finally he made it onto a flatter stretch of land, still just as dense but with less dents in the trail than the previous section. King was able to shift in his seat and stretch out his aching muscles. The bones in his fingers and wrists ached sorely from riding out the rattling suspension, gripped tight around the wheel at all times to keep the Toyota on course.

Slowly, but surely, the tiredness began to set in.

At first when he entered the jungle his adrenalin had been through the roof, anticipating confrontation at every turn. But as the minutes turned to hours and the dusk turned to the blackest of night, his lids began to droop as the road smoothed out.

Then the Toyota hit a root on the side of the trail, throwing all loose objects around the interior.

King darted upright, suddenly awake and alert all at once. He squinted, narrowing his eyes in an attempt to make out what lay ahead.

He had lost all track of time. The moon — in fact, almost all of the night sky — had been masked throughout the journey by the canopy of leaves above his head. It could have been hours since he first set off. He had been in constant motion since early that morning, and almost died several times during the day itself.

He needed a rest.

It would come after his work was done here.

After a few more minutes of wrestling with the steering

wheel, he snatched the satellite phone off the passenger seat and called Lars.

'Where am I?' he said, his tone dejected.

'Everything okay?' Lars said, noting the intonation in his voice.

'Yeah. Long trip.'

'You've only been driving for thirty minutes.'

King sighed. His mind was playing tricks on him out here. 'That's just perfect...'

'Are you crashing?'

'What?'

'Energy tanks depleted?'

King paused. 'Somewhat. I feel heavy. Can barely keep my eyes open. I'm worried if I come face-to-face with Ramos, I might not be in the right state.'

'If you make it inside his facility,' Lars said. 'You could use some of his product.'

'Are you insane? You want me to die of a drug overdose out here?'

'Just a suggestion.'

'What if I'm tested en route back to the States?'

King could almost sense Lars smirking through the phone.

'If you knew what some of our guys were hopped up on, you wouldn't be making a word of protest.'

'I'm not protesting anything.'

'Then keep your options open. If it's between snorting coke and staying alive, I think you know what you should go with.'

'Once again,' King said, 'where am I?'

'You've made decent progress,' Lars said. 'You'll reach the border itself within the hour. Piedras Negras can't be more than twenty miles from you. How's your gas?'

King glanced at the fuel meter. 'I've got enough to get there.'

'And to get out?'

'Probably not.'

'You're not an extensive planner, are you, King?'

'Not exactly. I'll take one of their vehicles. They won't be needing it.'

'Found a weapon yet?'

'Not yet,' King said. 'But I'm keeping a lookout for—'

He dropped the phone into his lap out of sheer panic as a pickup truck's engine roared only a few feet ahead. Blinding floodlights seared up the trail. King brought a hand across his forehead to shield his eyes from the glare.

That way, he didn't see it coming.

The approaching vehicle elected to stop his Toyota in its tracks by ramming into its hood in a head-on collision. King couldn't have been travelling far over twenty miles an hour, but a direct hood-to-hood impact delivered a brutal shock-wave all the same.

He smashed chest-first into his steering wheel, inadvertently beeping the horn in the process. The harsh sound cut through the thick night air, discordant amidst the rainforest.

Frantic voices exploded out of the car ahead. King coughed up a warm liquid that felt very similar to blood. Realising that it would be suicide to stay in the driver's seat and allow himself to get surrounded on all sides by hostiles, he threw the door open and dropped into the mud, still stunned from the sudden confrontation.

As he rose to his feet, a hand wrapped around the back of his neck and forced him face-first into the puddle of gunk. He spat mud at his feet and scrambled for purchase on the slick ground.

Then a rifle barrel touched the back of his skull.

# 41

'*Hey!*' King cried, raising both hands far above his head, adopting the facade of an idiotic tourist.

He kept his fingers spread.

And his expression flabbergasted.

The oncoming headlights flickered off, allowing him a better look at who had ambushed him. The vehicle that had ploughed into his own was similar in both age and build. It was a rusty old pickup truck, same as King's Toyota. He got the feeling that old, reliable workhorses were popular in this region.

Because people were only out here for work, anyway.

There were four of them in total. All were bare-chested, their dark skin slick with sweat, their eyes rabid and crazed, their hands wrapped around four identical Kalashnikov AK-47s. King could barely tell one from the other — they were all munching on some kind of tobacco. He could smell the foul stench of their breath, even through the thick coat of mud dripping off his frame.

'What is this?' he panted. 'Who are you?'

The Kalashnikov barrel pressing against the back of his skull dug in a little deeper, maybe even drawing blood. King winced as the prodding motion forced him back into the mud. He picked himself up for a second time, breathing in rattling gasps.

One of the trio in front of him stepped forward. The guy's eyes were bloodshot as all hell. It seemed that he consistently committed the cardinal sin — *don't get high off your own supply.* He squatted down in the mud in front of King and snatched him by the chin, gripping hard.

'What you doin' out here, tourist boy?!' he screamed, loud enough to send a flock of nearby birds flapping out of their tree branches.

'Please,' King said softly. 'I'm lost.'

'*Lost?!*' the man roared. 'Do you know where you are?! This is jungle! You should not be here!'

'I know,' King said. 'I'm sorry.'

'Who you with?'

'No-one.'

'*Just you?!*'

'Yes.'

'*You sure?!*'

'I promise.'

The man slapped King across the cheek, hard enough to omit a resounding *crack* that echoed off the nearby trees. Hot liquid fire spread down King's neck. He rolled with the blow, but it still jarred him significantly. He crumpled harder onto his knees and tried not to let the heat of the moment affect him.

It wasn't time to retaliate.

He wanted them to let their guard down first.

Despite having to exacerbate the terror on his features, deep down he truly was frightened. In a situation as uncomfortable and volatile as this, it would only take one twitch from the man behind him to send his brains splattering across the puddle he knelt in.

He had training experience and cognitive abilities well beyond the external shell he was displaying, but that was nothing when up against four trigger-happy, drug-fuelled gangsters in the lawless jungles of Guatemala. If one of them decided to jump the gun — literally — and shoot him dead where he knelt, there wouldn't be a thing he could do to stop it.

They needed to grow careless.

They needed to turn their attention away from him.

Now that he had a proper view of the truck they'd leapt out of, King stared into the rear tray. Sure enough, Lars' information had been completely accurate. A giant, modified washing machine had been fixed into the floor of the tray. King could hear it working over the noise of the two running engines.

The plexiglass front of the machine was facing forward, allowing King to see inside. Massive hordes of coca leaves were churning within, dumping around and around in a centrifugal spin. He realised that these mobile laboratories were used to spread out the supply, wringing the cocaine out of the coca leaves while ensuring that there would be additional product spread throughout the jungle in vehicles such as these. It protected some of the stash in the event that the main complex was invaded by rival cartels or the authorities.

*Smart,* King thought.

He stared at the machine for a beat, before the barrel of the Kalashnikov ran down the base of his neck, coming to rest between the tightly-bunched muscles of his upper back.

He didn't know whether that spelled disaster, or whether he had been given longer to live.

The three men in front of him moved quietly over to his sad-looking Toyota Hilux. They swept the barrels of their guns over the interior, checking for any sign that King wasn't telling the truth. He noted their every move, registering the jumpy way in which they aimed with their weapons. They were almost certainly all high on cocaine. If King burst into action, he guessed that they would over-compensate, their heart rates skyrocketing as they aimed in his direction.

He hoped their first few shots would miss.

If they confirmed that he was alone, they would shoot him dead for even laying eyes on their operation.

There was no mercy out here.

Two men moved to the opposite side of the Toyota, creating a barrier between themselves and King. The third man continued trawling along this side of the vehicle, peering through each dirty window in turn. With King's sole headlight providing the only illumination on the narrow trail, it was hard to make out the shape of their silhouettes in the lowlight.

When gunfire broke out, it would be madness.

King tried not to give any visible sign that he was about to act. He kept himself composed on the inside, while continuing to pant with fear on the outside. When the guy on this side of the vehicle skirted around the rear tray to meet the pair on the other side, King realised he was alone with the man behind him.

He barked like a dog, just once, a sharp, strange outburst of noise that caused the thug to hesitate for a split second.

That was all the time King needed.

He capitalised on the confusion, twisting on one knee and slicing back with an open palm. As soon as his fingers touched the Kalashnikov pressing into his back, he pushed with all his might. The barrel speared away from his torso, now pointing into the jungle beyond.

The thug seized up in panic and locked his finger against the trigger.

Unsuppressed rifle fire flared, cracking through the oppressive rainforest, scattering all nearby wildlife.

King thundered a boot into the guy's groin, hard enough to feel phantom pain in his own nether region. A fight to the death had no rules, and he was fully prepared to take advantage of that. As the horrific pain of a close-range, unprotected front kick set in, the guy slackened his grip on the AK-47.

Big mistake.

King tore the gun out of the guy's hands, reversed his grip on it, and put three rounds through the man's tattered singlet.

The man dropped into the mud, coated in both blood and sweat.

King ducked low and pressed himself up against the side of the Toyota, shrinking away from any reactive gunfire, staying absolutely silent.

Like a patient hitman, he waited in the sudden quiet for one of the trio on the other side of the vehicle to make a move.

As he did so, he ran his hands over the grip of the Kalashnikov AK-47 and couldn't resist a brief smile.

Despite the odds, he'd acquired a rifle.

*Here we go,* he thought.

# 42

King let his breathing settle and kept both ends of the Toyota in his peripheral vision, waiting for any sign of human activity. He caught a glimpse of movement to his left — coming from the hood of the car — and let off a volley of shots in that direction. The guy ducked back instantly. King heard the scuffing of the man's trainers against the mud.

He swung the Kalashnikov in the other direction, and just as he suspected lined up on the other two men sprinting around the rear tray of his Toyota Hilux. He brought the sight of the AK-47 up to the empty space just underneath his eye and lined up a cluster of precise rounds. At such close range, the bullets had nowhere else to land.

The thugs jerked around like marionettes on strings as their chests were shredded by the Kalashnikov ammunition. King let go of the trigger, corrected his aim, and fired again as the two bodies were dropping — just to make sure that they were both dead once they hit the ground.

Nothing happened.

'Oh, fuck,' he whispered.

The magazine hadn't been full when he'd first pried the weapon out of its owner's hands. The guy must have spent the morning shooting at wild animals for leisure, or maybe they'd already run into a lost tourist just like the person King was portraying.

Whatever the case, the gun in his hands was now prematurely empty.

He took off for the other side of the trail, aware that there wasn't enough time to dive for one of the dead men's rifles. He would catch a bullet for his troubles if he did so. He smashed through the undergrowth and powered into the darkness just as a wild burst of Kalashnikov fire emanated from behind him, lighting up the jungle with its muzzle flares.

The last man standing, unloading his rifle in King's direction.

The guy was armed.

King was not.

King ducked behind one of the enormous trees, almost tripping head-over-heels on a gnarly root fixed into the sloping ground. He stumbled forward...

...just as a stray bullet whisked past his face, so close he could feel its path slice through the empty air.

He froze in terror and pressed himself against the trunk.

Breathing.

Waiting.

Staying calm.

He heard footsteps in the dirt nearby. The cocaine must have got the better of his adversary, for the man had abandoned all plans of standing still and waiting for King to come to him. He had sprinted full-pelt into the jungle after him.

King admired the man's nerve.

It would get him killed, though.

He ducked round the tree trunk, rounding it in a single step and slinking through the bushes, doubling back on the guy. In the near-darkness, he could only make out flashes of the man's movements amidst the undergrowth. Grimacing, he scurried back to the trail, abandoning all hope of confronting the man in the dense jungle. It would only increase the risk of death.

He broke out onto open ground and ran across the few feet of trail between the jungle and the two vehicles pressed head-to-head in the middle of the path.

He vaulted into the rear tray of the enemy vehicle.

The adapted washing machine was still running, trundling through its motions as it wrung the cocaine out of a mountain of coca leaves. King squinted in the lowlight, looking for the latches that fixed the massive cube to the vehicle underneath it. He located both of them, then flattened himself to the hot floor of the tray as he sensed the cartel thug re-appearing on the trail.

He stayed quiet, masking a grunt of pain as a loose piece of metal dug into his ribs. He allowed the thug to get closer and closer, letting the tension heighten. The man would be confused, wondering where King had ran off to, sweeping his gun barrel from left to right in an attempt to locate him.

King waited until it sounded like the man was directly on top of him. Then he flicked the latches open simultaneously, both of them clicking softly in the darkness. The thug audibly froze, his footsteps dying.

*What's going on?* the man was probably thinking.

King jumped into a crouch, wrapped two powerful arms around the enormous washing machine, and wrenched it off the tray bed with a primal roar of exertion. He estimated its weight at close to four hundred pounds, based on his prior powerlifting experience. Adrenalin and determination lent him an added boost in strength, and he used it to hurl the machine off the rear tray.

The industrial-sized cube barely covered a foot of distance through the air, but it was enough to reach the last thug left alive.

The corner of the machine crunched into the guy's upper back, dropping him like a deadweight. King saw the shock and pain register on his face as he was thrown off-balance by the weight of the object. It bounced away and thudded into the muddy trail floor with enough force to send reverberations down the path.

King leapt out of the rear tray and snatched up the AK-47 the man had dropped.

The guy's injuries were clearly horrific. Muscles had been torn in his back, and bones had been broken.

King put him out of his misery with a single bullet.

The relentless noise of a life-or-death battle faded into nothingness.

He took a deep breath, calmed his nerves, and let the resulting silence wash over him.

He'd done it.

# 43

In the moody darkness of the remote jungle trail, King collected the three AK-47s with ammunition left in their magazines and tossed them into the drug-runners' truck. It was a similar build to the Hilux, but the logo and paint had seemingly been stripped off — either deliberately, or due to the natural effects of the searing, suffocating humidity.

Before he left the area, he knelt down by the dented washing machine. Its plexiglass door had sprung open as it sunk into the damp ground, spilling dry coca leaves across the trail. The green leaves looked nothing out of the ordinary in the rainforest — a passer-by would never know that the cocaine contained within was the substance that propped up a billion-dollar worldwide drug industry.

King bent down, scooped up a handful of the leaves, and shoved them into his mouth.

He chewed vigorously.

The leaves themselves wouldn't get him high. At least, not in the same league as pure cocaine powder. Lars had told him that coca farmers in the Andes munched on the stuff all day. The leaves suppressed hunger, thirst, and fatigue — effects that he sorely needed in his current state. He crushed the leaves to pieces in his mouth, unsure if that was the correct way to go about it, or if the process would even have an effect on him. He was sure that there was more to it than that.

Unsatisfied, he spat the bitter tasting gunk into the mud and wiped his mouth with his shirt sleeve.

A bead of sweat ran off the bridge of his nose as he vaulted across the hoods of the two vehicles — crushed face-to-face in an awkward union — and crashed down on the other side of the trail. He grabbed his duffel bag out of the Toyota, checked the vehicle for any other belongings, then left the vehicle where it rested for good.

The thugs' truck had more gas.

The keys still rested in the vehicle, illuminated by the artificial ring of light around the ignition. King threw the truck into reverse and backed it along the trail. The front end separated from the Hilux with a groan of twisting metal. He backed right up to the wall of dense jungle, then turned around on the trail until was facing the way he had been headed in the first place.

He checked the rear view mirror once, observing the four dead bodies scattered across the mud...

... then he let all thoughts of the encounter drift from his mind and continued on toward Piedras Negras.

Now heavily armed.

He didn't know what he might find in the ruins. Had Ramos set up his facility directly on top of the Mayan site? King doubted it. In all likelihood the two sites rested alongside each other. The ruins would act as a beacon for all visitors to locate. If they saw the ancient site, they would know they had come to the right place.

King wondered what kind of business dealings took place in this lawless land.

He kept an eye out for any other mobile laboratories along the way. For all he knew, there could be a complex, intricate web of similar vehicles trundling through the empty National Park, searching for trouble at every corner.

He didn't want to get caught in the middle of a war zone.

It was a strange sensation rumbling along the abandoned trail, knowing that any human contact this far from normal civilisation could only spell disaster. There was no authority out here, no laws or rules or regulations, just a subhuman society of criminals looking to gain the edge over each other. The darkness weighed down on him. He couldn't shake off the urge that there was someone watching, peering at him through the shadows as he jolted and rattled the pick-up truck along the uneven trail.

Ten minutes later, the phone in the duffel bag barked.

King snatched it up and answered. 'Lars?'

'The one and only. You'd better have good news for me.'

'Such as?'

'Are you armed?'

'Yeah.'

A pause. 'How the hell did...'

'Maybe it's best you don't know.'

'Maybe so.'

'What's the update?'

'I'm ringing because you're just over a mile out. That's why I was praying that you'd found yourself a gun. You'll be on the site in minutes.'

'Piedras Negras?'

'Yes,' Lars said. He seemed hesitant, like he was selecting his words incredibly carefully.

'You think this is the last time we might talk?' King said.

'I don't know what to think.'

'You have little faith.'

'I'm just being realistic.'

'Don't be. We don't operate in a realistic field.'

'You think you can do it?'

'How the fuck am I supposed to know that?!' King barked, letting his emotions show for a brief moment. He brought himself back under control. 'Look, I'm hanging onto my sanity by a thread here. I have no idea what I'm going to find when I reach the facility. I have no idea if Ramos is even still there. I've been sweating my ass off for the last few hours and I'm probably on the verge of falling asleep on the spot. In all likelihood, he'll have a hundred ex-soldiers from the Guatemalan Army on his payroll and I'll be shot to pieces for a few hundred dollars each of blood money.'

'Why are you doing this?' Lars said. 'No-one's forcing you to. No-one even asked you to.'

'Because who the hell else is going to do it?' King said, suddenly riled up. 'If I retreat, what message does that send? Between you and me — I want this division to be a success. I would rather work alone any day of the year. So I'm doing everything I can to make sure I accomplish what I set out to do in the first place.'

'You're a good man.'

King shrugged, even though Lars would never see it. 'Look, that's debatable.'

'You're very close,' Lars said. 'I'd recommend covering the rest of the trail on foot.'

'On it. See you on the other side.'

'Poor choice of words,' Lars said.

King smirked and ended the call. He slowed the truck to a crawl in the middle of the trail and switched the headlights off with a flick of the lever next to the steering wheel. His surroundings were enveloped in sheer darkness, sending a tremor down his spine.

He stared at the three Kalashnikovs on the passenger seat. They had spent the journey clashing together, causing a ruckus inside the cabin. Quickly, he decided that carrying all three would act as more of a burden than an advantage. He grabbed one of the AK-47s, swung the door open, snatched up the satellite phone in the other hand and dropped into the mud outside the vehicle. As a final gesture, he fetched the wad of Guatemalan quetzals out of the centre console and shoved them into his rear pocket.

Just in case he needed to buy a ride out of the jungle...

He caught a glimpse of himself in the driver's side mirror, and his eyes widened at the sight. The mud that he'd fallen into an hour previously had caked dry across his features, turning his skin almost entirely black. He could barely see himself in the reflection. His clothes were tattered and a thin sheen of sweat had set his muscles glistening in the lowlight.

He left the pick-up truck where it was and set off down the trail.

One man, a gun, and a phone.

Heading into the unknown.

He wouldn't have wanted it any other way.

# 44

The first glimpse King received of the ancient city of Piedras Negras terrified him to the core.

He had been hiking through the jungle for the last ten minutes, avoiding the growls of nearby predators and the soft chirping of birds disturbed from their sleep. When he stepped through a collection of vast fern bushes and touched down on a flat expanse of grass and mud, he looked up to lock eyes with a towering, demonic face set into a cluster of stone rubble.

He jolted in surprise and touched a hand instinctively to the Kalashnikov hanging off his shoulder. It was an ancient *mascaron,* the type of ornament designed to ward off evil spirits. By that point his eyes had adjusted to the light, so he was able to stare into the twisted face's gaping maw.

In fact, he thought he could see something stirring in the shadows...

He had reached the perimeter of the city, which as far as he could tell stretched for a few hundred feet in all directions. Most of it was devoid of vegetation, aside from overgrown moss and weeds dotting the ancient sculptures.

There were plenty of them — King found himself taken aback by the sheer scale of the ancient ruins.

From the way Lars had described the Mayan site, he had expected little more than a small pile of decrepit rubble. What he laid eyes on was a sprawling ancient city, rundown and falling apart but still mostly intact. He saw remnants of a civilisation long extinct, and for a moment it made him pause. The setting stirred something in him — either a primal fear, or something much darker. He likened himself to an ancient warrior, clutching a modern weapon, heading through the madness to try and do some good.

Overhead, the canopy of trees had mostly cleared, revealing the dark sky above. King glanced up and saw the tropical storm set to unleash itself upon the jungle. The cumulonimbus clouds had swelled to a crescendo.

They were ready to release their payload.

King grimaced in the lowlight.

'Great,' he muttered. 'Just great.'

The distractions turned his mind away from the flicker of movement he'd noticed in the mouth of the *mascaron.* When he turned his attention back to the giant face, he squinted into the gloom. Even though his eyes had adjusted to the night, it was still hard to ascertain exactly what was happening in the shadows.

Then a flash of light emanated from inside the small enclosure. King shielded his vision from the brief spark, recognising it as a lighter flame flickering into life. The flame touched the foot of a thick cigar, which flared in turn. Its owner was momentarily backlit by the soft flame.

There was no doubt he was a soldier — or at least used to be. He looked like a native Guatemalan, with weathered skin and hard lines creased into his forehead. He wore a simple khaki uniform with no insignia in sight, with his trousers tucked into brand-new combat boots. There was some kind of weapon at his feet. Either a sub-machine-gun, or an assault rifle. Big, bulky, fearsome.

Then the lighter was shut off and the interior of the *mascaron*'s mouth plunged back into darkness. The only visible sight was the soft, muted glow coming from the foot of the guy's cigar.

A perimeter guard. Shielding himself from the approaching storm, lighting up a fat Cuban to calm his nerves. Maybe it was his first day on the job; an out-of-work soldier more than willing to serve Joaquín Ramos' needs in exchange for a hefty payday.

King imagined the man paid well, given that working for him required stripping away one's conscience.

King tried to stop thinking about the man in the alcove. He didn't want to personalise him too much, because it was entirely likely that he would have to kill him.

He didn't move a muscle, opting to blend into the jungle around him. He knew that the mud caked across his features would help to disguise his presence.

In the end, none of that mattered.

'*Hey!*' the guy suddenly screamed, fumbling for his rifle and letting the cigar drop into the floor of the *mascaron*'s mouth.

'Shit,' King muttered under his breath.

He had no other choice.

He raised the Kalashnikov up to rest against his shoulder, locked onto his target with the practiced motions of a trained professional, and pumped the trigger, holding it down for enough time to unleash a three-round burst out of the barrel.

In the otherwise-serene ambience of Piedras Negras, it sounded like three fireworks erupting simultaneously.

The perimeter guard died in a sudden blitz, jolted off his feet before he even had a chance to return fire, but the bedlam that erupted in the ancient city made King forget about the guard entirely.

He heard commotion far in the distance, panicked voices shouting at the top of their lungs. The racket drifted through the jungle. King could hear it clearly, despite the tinnitus setting in from the unsuppressed gunshots right near his head.

He stomached abject horror and sprinted across to the demonic face in the rubble, crouching in its lee while he rapidly assessed what to do.

There could be a hundred men headed for his position.

*Breathe,* he thought.

He inhaled a lungful of thick, rancid jungle air and let it sit in his lungs for a long three seconds. Then he exhaled slowly, drawing out the breath for an extended period of time.

It stilled his racing heart for a short while.

It gave him enough time to think.

He heard the footsteps heading through the ancient city. The ruins seemed to amplify the noise, turning the approaching paramilitary force into a distant rumble akin to a herd of sprinting buffalo.

*Here we go,* he thought again.

All the training. All the relentless hours in the gym. All the kickboxing and Muay Thai sparring and jiu-jitsu work and weapons training and time on the shooting range and physical fitness courses. All the mental discipline, pushing his body to its limits over and over again in an attempt to gain an edge on the battlefield.

It all came down to this.

All of his gruelling work would be rendered useless if he didn't make it through the coming firefight.

With that thought lodged firmly in his mind, he tightened his grip on the Kalashnikov and prepared for war.

His peripheral vision shrank away, narrowing in on what lay directly in front of him.

He set his expression to steel.

He rounded the corner, leaving the *mascaron* behind, freeing himself from its twisted glare.

He stalked through the ruins of Piedras Nagras without making the slightest noise.

Staring straight ahead.

Searching for any sign of movement.

Jason King, solo operative, ready for whatever lay ahead.

Doing what he was born to do.

# 45

King broke into a sprint down a mossy, narrow corridor between two of the decaying structures. He had heard someone approaching at the end of the path, and wanted to seize the upper hand before the man came into view.

He couldn't have timed it better.

The man who came stumbling into view had clearly been abusing human-growth-hormone or other testosterone-replacement-therapy products for the last decade, at least. It had clearly been black market synthetic stuff, unregulated and untested. He was Guatemalan too, with pockmarked cheeks from horrendous acne and skin that had turned burning red from excessive steroid abuse. His muscles bulged obscenely, complete with the perfectly-rounded shoulders and bulging trapezius muscles that lent him the appearance of a wild, rabid dog.

He clearly enjoyed his opiates, too.

His eyes were as dilated as the mobile drug-runner King had confronted back in the forest, amped up on cocaine and a cocktail of other stimulants. He was armed — wielding an identical Kalashnikov AK-47 — but King didn't think that would pose much of a problem.

He wondered how the ex-Army thug was conscious enough to even walk.

By the time the guy had stumbled into view, searching maniacally for a target, King's mad dash had allowed him to bear down on top of the man.

He thudded into the guy's chest, shoulder bone driving into sternum, sending the man flying back into the rubble behind him. King had less muscle than the guy, but the man's grotesque physique was clearly the result of artificial enhancement rather than sheer hard work.

The contrast was astounding.

King effectively manhandled the guy, bouncing him off the mossy stone wall and dropping him to the forest floor with a single right hook to the jaw. Nerve endings fired in his knuckles as they crunched against the lower half of the man's chin, rattling his brain hard enough to send him to his knees in a semi-conscious state.

The guy didn't even get a chance to fire his weapon.

King opted not to either. He didn't want to give away his position to whoever else was coming after him.

He planted a boot into the guy's face, applying just enough pressure to knock him unconscious and send him sprawling back into the undergrowth. King elected not to grab the second AK-47 the man had dropped.

Dual wielding rifles looked impressive in action movies, but in the real world it spelt disaster. He would rather wield a single firearm with greater accuracy than sprint around Piedras Negras unleashing a firestorm of bullets at no-one in particular.

He stepped over the thug he'd put to sleep and pressed on.

The path through the maze of ruins took a sharp turn up ahead, limiting King's view of what lay in front of him. It made him uncomfortable, coupled with the fat raindrops that began to fall from the heavens.

He glanced skyward and saw the rain intensifying with each passing second.

Soon enough, these paths would turn to canals.

Thunder flared overhead, resonating through the ruins. King continued down the path, thinking nothing of the booming noise. It blocked out all other sound...

...to his own detriment.

Muffled by the blast of relentless thunder, King didn't hear the man sprinting across the rubble at eye-level. With the crumbling city sprawling out in a tight grid of pathways, the trails between the ruined buildings acted as trenches of sorts. King didn't see the thug dive into his trench until it was too late. A rapid flurry of movement filled his vision, and a half-second later contact was made.

He had no time to react.

The boot planted square in the centre of his face, coming at the very end of a flying dropkick. King didn't hear the crack of snapping bone — instead, he felt it deep in his brain. His head exploded with liquid fire, thumping and roaring and tearing through his sinuses as his nerve endings dealt with his horrifically broken septum.

It was the first time his nose had ever been shattered in the heat of combat.

Deep down, he knew that if he survived this encounter, it certainly wouldn't be the last time.

He felt his legs go weak, which frustrated him no end. He grunted as the pain sent him down on his rear, thumping into the muddy trail with enough force to rattle his senses. His eyes began to water instinctively, blurring his vision. He blinked back excruciating pain, scrambled to his feet, and brought the Kalashnikov around to search for his target.

It was also the first time he had ever been put on the back foot in a live situation.

The true horror of grievous battlefield injuries hit him. He found himself unable to see, unable to hear, unable to think. Somewhere in front of him stood one of Ramos' henchmen, probably closing in, but King was oblivious to it. Rain began to fall in thick sheets, soaking through his hair, mixing with the blood pouring out of his nostrils.

He gasped, sucking in air.

Another blow drove into his stomach, rupturing something inside him. It proved that the first punch hadn't been a lucky shot. His assailant had years of training in striking — whether that be boxing or Muay Thai. He followed his punches through with a certain whip, a crack that added mountains of pressure to the blows. King doubled over as the knuckles crashed into his stomach, tearing muscle.

He switched gears.

Something activated inside him.

It was the knowledge that if he didn't respond to this relentless attack, he would succumb to the pain and find himself defenceless against a literal horde of trained killers.

He rolled away from the next blow, tearing moss out of the ground as he did so. The torrential rainfall dousing his face allowed him a brief reprieve from the horrendous pain, clearing his senses for just enough time.

He saw the guy advancing toward him for the first time.

He was enormous, at least six-foot-three, with roughly the same build as King. He had his fists balled determinedly. The man was of Asian descent, with the deep skin tone native to Thailand.

*Muay Thai,* King concluded.

A hired beatdown-artist, no doubt.

But he'd make the single mistake that would prove his demise.

He'd allowed King to make space.

King seized hold of the AK-47 he'd dropped a moment ago, swung the barrel up to meet the man's unprotected face at a blistering speed, and fired once.

The guy barely had time to widen his eyes. He took the bullet straight between his teeth. It was hard to make out in the darkness of the night-time storm, but King thought he saw brains and gore splatter out of the exit wound as the bullet punched through the back of the guy's mouth.

He twisted away, unquestionably dead, hitting the ground on his stomach and slumping to an early grave.

King let out a roar of pain, trying to release some of the vicious throbbing in his face. He could barely concentrate, but the massive spike in adrenalin levels was keeping him upright. He stumbled over the Asian man's dead body, cursing the guy's talents. His stomach burned and his nose had already swelled to a bloody, uncontrollable mess.

He pondered exactly how he was going to make it through what lay ahead.

# 46

The storm beat down, merciless in its intensity.

King made it to the edge of Piedras Negras, but the amount of time it took him to do so was lost on him. His consciousness had blurred into a single-handed attempt to mask the pain in his nose. He needed all his reflexes and senses ready to go for any potential confrontation, and that had been sorely impaired by the facial injury.

The rain washed the mud off his features in seconds.

He had never experienced weather quite like it. Sure, the United States had its fair share of storms — but he had never spent time in a region where the tropical storms sent rain down with such intensity that it was hard to breathe. For a moment, the panic of drowning seized King in its icy grasp. He shook it off and sucked in great, deep breaths through his mouth, inhaling the sheets of water as he did so.

As he accidentally swallowed a mouthful of rainwater, he coughed up the contents of his stomach, vomiting as the liquid triggered his gag reflex.

He wiped his mouth and pressed on to the outskirts of the city.

Above the din of the rainfall, commotion sounded from within the ruins. King could see flashlight beams flaring and darting around the maze of pathways. He kept low, allowing the agony of his broken nose to settle into a dull ache, and then turned away from the ancient city.

He had no business there.

They could spend as much time as they wanted looking for him.

It would only leave Ramos unprotected for longer.

The path ahead became clearer. Looking past the sheets of rainfall and the overbearing jungle canopy and the dense foliage covering every inch of available ground in sight, King could make out a man-made path that had been hacked into the perimeter of Piedras Negras, leading deep into the trees. The work had been done with machetes, creating enough space for vehicles to lumber through to an unknown destination.

It could only mean one thing.

The trail into Ramos' facility.

King hurried away from the ruins, staying low, shrinking into the foliage. It wasn't hard to remain unseen. The tropical storm had unleashed madness upon the Mexico-Guatemala border, strictly limiting visibility to a few feet and masking all noise other than the loudest of artificial sounds. It was all-encompassing, all-consuming.

King plunged back into the jungle.

The setting he found himself in was unlike anything he'd ever experienced. It took him a moment to process, especially due to the state of his nose. Already, the cheek area on either side of his nose had started to swell, puffing his skin up underneath his eyelids. It made it hard to see. He heard the thumping of liquid against the rainforest floor and looked up to assess what the hell was happening.

Big mistake.

A torrent of falling water splattered across his face hard enough to flare up his broken nose again. He winced and ducked his head, realising all at once where the deafening sound came from.

The jungle canopy had created an enormous makeshift canvas that collected rainwater across its broad fronds. The massive waterfalls came down sporadically as the fronds gave way under the weight of the liquid. King gazed out at the dark jungle before him, staring at the cascading streams of rainwater dotting the path ahead.

He kept striding along the path, thoroughly drenched and painfully sore.

Up ahead, he saw the facility.

It was effectively an enormous camp site, composed of a main, two-level warehouse surrounded by living quarters and a collection of small huts. Giant floodlights atop the warehouse pierced through the rain, flooding the encampment with fluorescent light.

Through the storm, it appeared as a blurry, heavenly glow.

King knew it was nothing of the sort.

He tightened his grip on the AK-47 and crossed the bare patch of land between the jungle and the facility's edge.

There appeared to be no-one home. They were all out in the ruins of Piedras Negras, searching for him. King wondered if Ramos was among them. If so, he would double back and mow through the enemy forces until he found his man.

He hadn't come this far for nothing.

Ramos had to answer for what he had done.

King burst into the warehouse with his adrenalin spiking through the roof. He experienced an overwhelming sense of deja vu — it was identical to the factory back in Tijuana, down to the finest details.

The floor stretched out for what felt like a mile, running all the way to a point in the distance. The workstations were aligned into neat, orderly rows, just as they had been back in the maquiladora factory.

The only difference between the factory in Tijuana and the one King had just stepped foot into was the complete lack of occupants.

It was a ghost town.

That was probably the way Ramos had intended it to be.

He thought he was safe out here.

He didn't think King would make it through his forces.

He was wrong.

With the rain pounding against the other side of the corrugated iron roof hard enough to block out all other noise, King slunk through the rows of machinery, passing barrels of hydrochloric acid and gasoline and other mixers that were used to filter the coca leaves into pure cocaine. He checked every shadowy corner for signs of life — the halogen bulbs dangling far above didn't provide much illumination.

It created something out of a horror movie.

The dim light cast long shadows over everything, exacerbating the tension and the uneasiness. King wrongly sensed movement in his peripheral vision every few seconds, twisting on the spot and aiming with the Kalashnikov to find nothing there.

*Where is everyone?* he thought.

They couldn't all have been sent out to look for him in Piedras Negras.

No-one would make such a foolish decision.

There had to be more forces here.

Somewhere...

King began to sweat uncontrollably in the intense humidity of the warehouse. Condensation clung to everything in sight, forming and evaporating before his very eyes.

He jolted on the spot, glimpsing movement in the distance. He narrowed his gaze and made out a similar row of elevated offices that he'd seen in the facility in Tijuana. They were slowly falling to pieces, rusting in the extreme conditions.

King didn't imagine the offices were used very often.

A flight of old metal stairs led up to the rooms, which were arranged in a long row of cubes. The movement he'd seen had come from the window to the main office. A shadow had passed across the dirty glass, backlit by a soft light that came from within.

King hurried across to the flight of stairs.

Everything about it felt like a trap. From the emptiness of the warehouse to the strategically-timed figure passing across the window above — all signs pointed to someone goading him up to the office. He knew exactly what was happening, but that didn't change a thing.

Subconsciously, something told him it was Ramos.

He was prepared to throw caution to the wind to capitalise on that hunch.

Despite his best intentions, he made a racket climbing the flight of stairs. They cracked and creaked and wobbled underneath his combat boots, struggling to support his weight.

He poked his head above the landing, staring up and down the shoddy stretch of flooring running along the front of the offices.

The coast seemed clear.

Gripping the Kalashnikov, unsure as to how many bullets he had left due to the adrenalin rush affecting his concentration, he stepped up onto the landing.

The room that contained the source of the movement lay dormant. There was no sign of life in the two windows, both fingerprint-stained and cloudy, making it hard to see what was going on inside. The door had been left ajar, with a single crack of light filtering through the gap.

King scurried over to the office's front wall and pressed his back against the warm steel, directly beside the doorway. He could see through the gap in the doorway through to the opposite wall.

It gave no answers.

'You don't quit.'

A voice resonated through the doorway, spilling out from the office. King recognised it immediately. It carried a flabbergasted tone, but it was still laced with icy determination.

Joaquín Ramos would not be going down without a fight.

# 47

'How did you know it was me?' King said, his mind racing as he weighed up the possibilities of what might happen next.

Ramos could bullrush him. There could be seven men crammed into the tiny office, all heavily armed, just waiting for him to make a move. The second he stepped into sight he would be met with a storm of gunfire, and that would be it for the short-lived career of solo operative Jason King.

'Who else would it be?' Ramos said. 'No-one has balls like that around here. No-one strolls into a tiny apartment pretending to be someone else when he's outnumbered three-to-one by me and my men.'

'I do.'

'Somehow, it seems to have worked out for you.'

'I have a question,' King said.

'I guess now's a better time than ever.'

'Did you retreat back to this facility because of the Draco cartel, or because of me?'

'Fuck Draco,' Ramos hissed. 'I wouldn't change my schedule for them if my life depended on it. Or almost anyone, for that matter. Don't think I was scared, either. I don't fear a soul on earth. But when someone as unpredictable as you shows up, I need to spend time assessing what the next move needs to be.'

'Now I'm here,' King said. 'You don't need to think any longer.'

'You step through this door and I'll put a bullet in your head.'

'You sure about that?'

'Try me.'

'I'm awfully accurate.'

'So am I.'

King listened to the way Ramos' voice carried itself across the room. From his rudimentary assessment, the tone seemed to fill the space rather easily. King guessed that other than perhaps a desk and a few chairs, the office was empty.

It didn't sound like there was a small force waiting for him.

But he couldn't be sure.

One on one, he liked his chances. It would come down to a matter of reflexes, a typical gunfight straight out of a Western. It would rely on who had the nerve and the calm focus in the heat of the moment to aim and fire accurately.

King liked his chances in that scenario.

But it wouldn't be as straightforward as that. He was sure of it.

'You're United States military?' Ramos said, his voice emanating from the same place. He hadn't moved from the same position. King pictured him with a barrel trained at the doorway, possibly crouching behind a desk. 'Special Forces?'

'Not really your concern right now,' King said.

'Of course you are. Only way you could have got to Bennett. He was intercepted at the border, right?'

King said nothing. He squatted down and pinched two fingers around a jagged piece of rust that had peeled away from the metal walkway. With a heave of exertion, he tore the palm-sized chunk free, cutting both his fingers in the process. Warm blood gushed out of the cuts, covering the piece of rust, but it didn't faze him in the slightest.

He hurled the thick sliver of rust and metal through the gap in the doorway like a fastball, turning his body as he did so. He put his entire bodyweight into the motion. It hit the opposite wall hard enough to sink into the plaster.

At the same time, King swung his boot around and kicked open the door with enough force to send it flying off its hinges. The rust embedding itself into the wall accompanied by the booming crash of the door landing on the office floor created a cacophony of noise.

Anyone inside couldn't help but react to it.

As soon as his boot met the door, King darted back out of sight and pressed himself against the wall. He hadn't caught a glimpse of the interior of the office, but he was certain of what was to come.

Sure enough, an automatic weapon roared and bullets shot past him out the doorway, carrying through to the main floor of the factory itself. Just as the gunfire started, it ceased a moment later. Ramos realised that the move had been a ploy to scare him into action.

Silence settled over the factory once again.

With his ears ringing, King couldn't be certain of what he'd heard, but he didn't think his mind was playing tricks on him.

It had almost definitely been a single stream of gunfire.

One man.

Ramos.

'Where's the rest of your men?' King said, still taking cover beside the doorway.

'Out looking for you.'

'Bullshit. You have more than that. I know it.'

'You think I'm going to tell you what I'm doing here just because you kicked a door open?'

'I thought you might be willing to help me out. If you're so certain that you'll make it out of here alive, then what's the harm?'

'I might not make it out of here alive,' Ramos said. 'But in the end, you—'

At that moment — just as Ramos had entered the middle portion of his speech — King rounded the corner and stepped into the open doorway.

He took in everything that lay in front of him in less than a heartbeat.

The room's sole purpose was to store unused furniture, judging by the straw-made wicker chairs piled high across the room. Stacks of flimsy furniture had been arranged in a rudimentary barricade, behind which Ramos stood cowering.

King had the Kalashnikov trained on the man's temple in the blink of an eye.

He felt the bullet slice through the skin on his shoulder as the muzzle flare registered before his eyes. Nerve endings screamed for relief, blood spurted from the thin line drawn across his sweaty, mud-coated skin, and he felt the fingers of his right hand against the AK-47's grip falter slightly.

He'd been hit — but beyond recognising that a bullet had struck him, he tuned everything else out. Adrenalin masked the pain.

Cortisol pumped through his veins, concentrating every

fibre of his being on the target directly in front of him. Most of Ramos' body was covered by the stacks of chairs, protecting his vital organs from a direct gunshot.

But not the top of his head.

King fired, rolling with the motion as the Kalashnikov kicked back against his shoulder, the barrel recoiling as it fired. He glimpsed a puff of fine red mist and Ramos went down behind the rudimentary barricade, collapsing unceremoniously to the floor.

The situation was still incredibly volatile.

King sprinted across the short stretch of space between them and leapt over the chairs with everything he had left in his body. He landed directly on top of Ramos, preventing the man from swinging his weapon around to fire off a last-ditch retaliation shot.

He crunched into the man's stomach, winding him. He heard the breath burst from Ramos' lungs, and felt his limbs squirming underneath his form.

He was still alive.

The headshot — miraculously — hadn't killed him.

King bared his teeth and spun on the spot, adopting the jiu-jitsu position known as "side-control". He lay on his stomach sideways across Ramos' chest, pinning the man helplessly to the ground underneath his own bodyweight.

He used the position to assess which hand Ramos was holding the gun in. When he located it, he snatched at the weapon and tore it free from the guy's grasp with animalistic determination. He hurled the gun away — where it bounced off the far wall and came to a standstill well out of reach — and seized Ramos by the throat, slamming him back down onto the wood-panelled floor when he tried to rise.

King breathed a sigh of relief.

*Victory.*

# 48

It was undeniable that Ramos was in horrendous shape.

The Kalashnikov bullet had sliced across the very top of his skull, carving a bloody path through his scalp. It had shot past him after that, embedding in the plaster wall instead of lodging in his brain and killing him. The hair in the centre of his head was gone, torn away by the Parabellum round.

Already, the wound had started to bleed profusely.

The blood drained from Ramos' cheeks, his eyes darting left and right with all the panicked intensity of a man who knew he was mortally wounded.

But he also knew that he had some time left.

'I can survive this if I get to a hospital, yes?' he said through a sweaty mask of terror.

King kept his hand pinned firmly across the guy's throat. In this position, he didn't look so intimidating. King thought of all the hundreds — if not thousands — of men and women that Ramos had slaughtered mercilessly in his quest for a dollar. He would never understand the psyche of men like the one underneath him.

He would kill them all the same, though.

'Probably,' King said. 'You'd better get there quick if you want to stop the bleeding.'

'You're going to take me there.'

'Somehow I doubt that.'

Ramos coughed pathetically, regurgitating a vile concoction of blood and vomit. 'You don't ever back a desperate man into a corner. You don't think I would have prepared for this after what you did to my men back in Tijuana?'

'Prepared for what?'

'You are a noble man, yes?'

King said nothing.

'You serve your country?' Ramos said.

Silence.

'You try to do good?' Ramos said.

King tightened his grip on the man's throat.

Ramos smirked through bloody teeth. 'That's what I thought. You can't let any of your precious innocents get killed. That won't do you any good in this world.'

'The fuck are you talking about?' King snarled.

'You will take me to a hospital, and then you will do exactly what I say from that point onward. Because I have the manpower and the contacts to cause massacres across Mexico. One phone call and I can gun down a hundred innocents. You want that blood on your hands, American?'

'You're not exactly in the position to be able to do that, Ramos.'

'Prepare for the worst,' the man wheezed, winking. 'That's how I got all this. That's how I built this fucking empire with my own two hands. Because I don't underestimate people like you.'

King stayed quiet, but he couldn't hide a slight tremor that ran its way down his arm, ending in his fingertips that were curled around Ramos' throat. The man sensed it, and sneered.

King shifted uncomfortably. He didn't know what to think. Nothing felt right about the deserted warehouse, and the mood exacerbated his uneasiness. From the rain slamming against the roof above his head to the unbearable humidity leeching sweat from his pores to the foul stench of the warehouse floor, jam-packed with vile and rancid processing ingredients.

Everything about it set him on edge.

'Spit it out,' he snarled, putting enough pressure on Ramos' larynx to cut off the man's airflow.

Blood rushed to Ramos' cheeks as he went red in an attempt to breathe. The crimson stuff continued to pour out of the top of his head, an event that would prove fatal unless the wound was tended to soon.

'There's a small village,' Ramos gasped as King released the pressure. 'Couple of miles from here. I sent my men there.'

'Bullshit.'

Ramos smirked again. For some reason it infuriated King. He smashed the back of the man's head against the floor.

'You'd better have more info than that,' he snarled.

'I saw this coming. Sent them off early.'

'You didn't think to keep them here to protect you?'

'You would have killed them. Just like you killed my bodyguards in the apartment, and my men in the armoured truck, and my men in Piedras Negras. You're like the fucking Terminator.'

'So you waved the white flag?'

'Far from it, bitch,' Ramos spat. 'If I don't contact them within the next five minutes, they're going to mow through every person in that village. Men, women, children. All dead. And it'll be your fault — unless you get me to a hospital and let me get in touch with them.'

Internally, King locked up, frozen in confusion. He had never been forced to make decisions like this on the fly, decisions with enough magnitude to change dozens of lives.

What he did next would either save innocent lives, or let them be massacred.

Ramos had him in a highly uncomfortable position, but he wasn't about to let it show.

He decided to play the idiot in order to squeeze more information out of the man.

'I already came from the village,' he said. 'There's no-one living there. You're lying.'

Ramos narrowed his eyes, as if he knew King was testing him. Then desperation got the better with him. King could see him visibly crumble under the pain racking his body. He broke, and spilled out information.

'That's not a village, you moron,' he spat. 'Those are ruins. They're headed closer to the border. West of this location. A small encampment of workers that live near a remote airstrip. They make an honest living, but they won't be alive to spend it if you don't let me go right fucking now.'

'Thanks for the heads up,' King said. 'Now I know where to find them.'

'You won't get there in time.'

'I'll take my chances,' King said. 'You just gave me everything I needed.'

Ramos went pale. It was dawning on him that if King was mad enough to trek solo into the jungle, into vicious cartel-occupied no-man's-land, then just maybe he was foolish enough to try and catch the party of thugs before they made it to the village.

'No,' he muttered. 'Please.'

King leant down to whisper in the man's ear. 'You shouldn't have tried to play games with someone like me. That shit doesn't cut it.'

Then he took his hand off Joaquín Ramos' throat, brought the Kalashnikov around to touch the cold flesh of the man's forehead, and sent a round through his skull at point-blank range.

# 49

Clutching the Colt AR-15 that Ramos had been carrying — the weapon that he'd used to slice King open across the deltoid with a well-placed bullet — King discarded the near-empty AK-47 he'd been using and ran for the flight of stairs outside the office.

The clock was ticking.

A multitude of doubts swirled through his head. He had no idea what the village looked like, he wasn't sure whether the path to it would be accessible by vehicle, he wouldn't be able to tell the difference between Ramos' forces and an ordinary militia, and finally the storm would make a gunfight near-impossible. Accuracy and ability would be thrown out the window in favour of whoever got luckiest.

Despite that, King surged forward, ignoring his broken nose and the blood pouring out of his shoulder and the pain searing through his ribs.

No-one else was going to do it.

So he would make sure he got it done.

With that mindset firmly entrenched, he took the stairs three at a time, landing on the dusty concrete floor of the warehouse less than ten seconds after leaving the office. He remembered seeing a set of double doors leading through to the other side of the warehouse, positioned underneath the raised offices.

He made for them, praying that they would be unlocked.

Even better, one of them seemed to be hanging open.

He thundered a boot square into the centre of the door and it shot around on its hinges, instantly soaked by the rain beating down. King followed the door out into the storm. The raging downpour drenched him once again, masking his vision as water poured down his face and through his hair.

Through the gloom, he spotted a military-style jeep parked in the gravel lot on this side of the facility. Both its rear doors and the driver's side door were hanging open, and a detachable leather top protected the interior from the elements. The whole vehicle was painted dark khaki, possibly purchased straight from the Guatemalan Army surplus.

*That's where all these hired paramilitary soldiers are from, too,* King guessed.

He ducked into the driver's door, sinking into a large puddle of water that had accumulated on the driver's seat from the doors being left open. The warm tropical rain sloshed into the footwell as he swung the door closed. Ignoring the hot, damp interior of the vehicle, he fired up the engine, using the keys that had been left in the ignition.

The last owners must have been in a rush to exit the vehicle.

He wondered if it was the same men he had killed in the ancient ruins minutes earlier.

The pain drilling through his face coupled with the solid

wall of water pounding against the windshield made it practically impossible to see.

He slammed the car into drive, set the wiper blades to their maximum output, and spun the tyres in the soaking gravel in an attempt to accelerate off the mark.

He quickly found that driving in such conditions was akin to yanking a blindfold over his eyes and putting the pedal to the floor.

Aside from the fact that he couldn't see a thing, he grimaced as the tyres fought for purchase on the jungle floor. Already the ground had flooded with rainwater, sending the rear wheels fish-tailing across the gravel lot with every touch of the accelerator. He twisted the wheel left, then right, overcompensating dangerously in an inexperienced attempt to drive through a tropical storm.

*You twenty-two-year-old baby,* he cursed at himself.

But he quickly learned that not even a Formula-1 driver could handle these conditions.

Lightning flared overhead, revealing the path through the jungle. Sure enough, there was another narrow trail leading into the darkness. He had no idea where it went, but his best guess was that it connected the facility to the nearby village. There had to be some way for Ramos to cart supplies to his encampment.

King pointed the hood of the jeep in the direction of the trail, hit the gas, and hoped for the best.

It was the only thing he could do anyway.

He plunged into the jungle, tree trunks flashing by on either side in a dizzying blur. Roadblocks presented themselves at the last second, only visible from a few feet away through the relentless bombardment of rain on the windshield. He couldn't hear a thing — the AR-15 could have gone off in the passenger seat and he would have barely been able to hear it over the deafening roar of the storm. The same waterfalls that had hit him before now smashed against the temporary canvas roof of the jeep, threatening to buckle the loose material under their weight.

He drove for what felt like an hour, but in reality couldn't have been more than five minutes. When the trail began to widen and a long row of huts materialised up ahead, King narrowed his vision. He leant as far forward as possible, controlling the steering wheel while pressing his face right up to the glass in an attempt to make out what lay ahead.

He saw shapes, ghosting through the darkness, shrouded by rain and night. The sharp crack of thunder tore across the sky above, scaring him enough to rattle his grip on the wheel. He brought the jeep back under control and studied the tiny village right near the Mexico-Guatemala border.

The residential sector was composed of a few parallel streets of identical huts, with wooden walls and thatched roofs. The small buildings had obviously been designed with sturdiness in mind, for it seemed that all of them were withstanding the brunt of the tropical storm.

*This kind of weather must be common in these parts,* King thought.

There were no civilians in sight. The menacing silhouettes that King saw slinking through the small yards were no innocent men. He could tell by the way they composed themselves, the way they ignored the rain and other exterior circumstances, moving as if the weather was perfect.

They were clinical in their approach to the huts.

Measured.

*And armed,* he realised.

He thought there were three in total. A pair were moving

in on one of the huts, both wielding sizeable firearms like they knew how to use them. There was no possibility of King recognising the make of the guns from this distance — all he could see were the sinister outlines.

The other man was further up the road, heading for one of the distant buildings. King couldn't be sure, but it seemed like he was carrying an enormous machete, designed for hacking man-made paths through the jungle, cutting down vegetation.

*Or slaughtering innocent natives.*

He saw the vehicles that the men had abandoned in their blood-lust. Two identical khaki-painted jeeps, parked in the middle of the road with their headlights cutting through the storm.

King wrenched the wheel to the right, mounting the row of well-kept yards.

He pointed his own vehicle in the direction of the armed pair.

They saw him coming.

Too late.

He picked up even more speed and crunched into the nearest two bodies at close to forty miles an hour.

# 50

One of the men spun away into oblivion like a ragdoll, his legs broken and his gun sent skittering away.

King forgot all about him, because the other guy rolled with the impact, jumping off both feet at the last minute so that the jeep's hood hit him in the legs. It spun him around in the air just the same as the other guy, but he came to rest on top of the hood, snatching for purchase on the slick surface.

King wrenched the wheel left and right in an attempt to throw him off.

It worked.

The man began to slide off one side of the hood.

Yet there was enough time for him to bring his massive assault rifle around and aim through the windshield.

King recognised instantly what was about to happen. He threw open the driver's door and launched himself out of the vehicle into the storm.

As he jumped, the windscreen shattered under a hail of gunfire. King ducked away from the volley of bullets in mid-air and then shoved his arms out to brace for landing.

He hit the ground hard enough to shock his system but with enough grace to minimise any serious injuries. The rainwater helped, acting as a shallow pool to land in and soften the impact. He rolled over one shoulder, sending geysers of water flying in all directions.

Blind, in pain, confused, he scrambled in the inch-thick layer of water, trying desperately to get to his feet.

A second later, he shot upright...

...to see the jeep finish its run by smashing through the front wall of the nearest hut.

Shredded wood flew in all directions and the off-road vehicle's suspension shuddered under the impact. Somehow, the man on the hood had managed to snatch a handhold at the last second. It ended up working out a hundred times worse for him. He was still perched on the front of the jeep when it crushed into the hut, spilling him head-over-heels into the midst of the wreckage.

King thought he saw the man's rifle still in his hands.

He had been forced to abandon his own gun in the passenger seat of the jeep.

He burst into motion, hurrying through the shallow water. He needed to make it to the hut before the guy came to his senses and shot him down in the middle of the street.

Or worse — turn the gun on the residents of the hut in a last-ditch effort to fulfil his leader's wishes.

King made it out of the newly-formed river in the road and vaulted into the front garden, tearing past plants and bushes, racing over a smooth patch of grass.

He skirted around the jeep wreckage, identified the man staggering to his feet just inside the demolished front wall of the hut, and launched himself into open space.

He crash-tackled the guy into the far wall of the hut, knocking the rifle out of his hands through sheer blunt trauma. The pair spilled to the ground. King came down on top of the man, driving the breath out of the guy's lungs. In his limited time in the field, King had come to learn that he excelled at one thing at close-range.

*Violence.*

Whether that was due to his natural athleticism or his ability to sense openings in his adversaries' guard, he didn't care. So long as he came out of these encounters in one piece, and his enemies didn't.

With water running off the damaged roof above and pouring down onto them, King dropped an elbow into the guy's throat, putting all his bodyweight behind the blow. The guy wheezed, his eyes widening, his features turning into a mask of terror. The strike had done serious damage.

The man scrambled for his nearby weapon — another Colt AR-15. It seemed that all of Ramos' forces were equipped with the same guns.

King let boiling rage take over his system. He had no illusions as to what the man had come here to do. This was the house that he had been headed for when King arrived.

King looked up to see a family of three cowering in the kitchen. They were natives of Guatemala, with skin the shade of caramel and simple, utilitarian clothing draped across their frames. Right now, they were looking on with horror at the scene of devastation before them. The front of their house had been obliterated by the jeep running straight through it.

King locked eyes with the child of the family — a small boy, no older than six.

He was terrified.

And this man would have gunned him down out of nothing but spite.

The anger swelled, rising in King's chest like a balled fist. He reached down and grabbed two handfuls of the thug's shirt, wrenching him off the ground. Keeping the family in mind, he carried the thug out of the house, shielding what would happen next from view of the young boy.

He slammed the guy down in the front yard, causing the man's head to whiplash against the soaked grass. The guy offered no resistance. The elbow to the throat had caused serious internal injuries, and King was manhandling him like a child, utilising his height and weight advantage coupled with the years of powerlifting experience.

King locked two hands around the man's throat and squeezed, staring into the guy's eyes as he died.

Nothing about the situation even registered on his mind. There was no pity in his soul for the guy below him, even when the man's eyes started to bulge in their sockets and the veins in his forehead started to protrude with alarming intensity. He died a slow, painful death, and King was glad.

The man deserved it...

...and much more.

When he was sure that the guy's pulse had stopped, King released his grip on the throat, which had already begun to bruise and turn purple from the strain that had been exerted upon it.

Then he heard a high-pitched squeal, up ahead.

A fresh wave of adrenalin punched through him as he remembered the man with the machete. He stared through the sheets of rain...

...and his heart bolted against the walls of his chest as he saw what was unfolding.

The machete-wielding psychopath — a beefy, six-foot-two Latino gangster with tattoos running up his arms — had a Guatemalan woman by the hair, dragging her out of the open doorway of one of the neighbouring huts. King watched him wrench her out into the middle of the street, sending water splashing over her chest and mouth as he hauled her through the river.

King took off, stamping on the dead body of the man in front of him in his haste. He had no time to go back into the hut and collect a weapon.

It was now or never.

He had his bare hands, and little else.

He would have to make do with that.

He narrowed in on the target.

There was twenty feet between him and the crazed thug. As he got closer he saw the dilated pupils and the rabid expression on the man's face. He was pumped full of cocaine, almost manic in his intensity. He saw King sprinting at him and smiled.

Fifteen feet.

Ten.

Not fast enough.

The guy slashed down with the machete, aiming for the woman cowering at his feet.

King was too far away to do anything about it.

# 51

King didn't slow down, even though his heart rate shot through the roof.

He saw the machete scything downward, horrifyingly fast. There was enough power behind the blow to decapitate anyone that met the blade head-on. The guy had his teeth mashed together and his face twisted into a contorted scowl as he threw everything he had into the machete swing.

But he missed.

The woman ducked away instinctively at the last second, plunging into the few inches of water in an attempt to get away from the man. His blade came within a hair's breadth of her scalp, cutting through the water and slamming into the road just below it.

He ripped the machete back out of the water and raised the blade above his head for another attempt. The woman came to a feeble halt in the water, dejected, defeated. She froze up in terror.

The next blow would take her head clean off.

King plunged forward with a staggering uppercut,

whistling his fist through the air like a heat-seeking missile, searching for the underside of the man's chin.

The guy was defenceless to resist the blow.

King hit the man in the jaw hard enough to smash half his teeth out of their gums, grinding the bones together and sending his head snapping back like a whip. He lost his footing and spilled backwards into the water, coming down on his rear in the shallow river that had formed in the wake of the tropical storm.

King pounced on the guy, clamping a hand around the wrist that held the machete, controlling the most dangerous factor in the fight.

When he had the giant blade under control, pinning it to the ground, he wrapped his free hand around the guy's throat and forced him underwater with the strength of a primal adrenalin rush juicing through his system.

The veins in his forearms bulged, protruding like a road map on the surface of his skin as he held the man's arm and head underwater.

Something close to an out-of-body experience unfolded. King's mind locked up like a steel trap, zoning in on the one thing that he needed to achieve — overpower the man underneath him.

He entered a different state, a long tunnel where normal reality melted away, replaced by something more animalistic and raw. He rode out each of the man's spasms as they came — the guy writhed under the surface of the rainwater like his life depended on it.

Which it did.

Air bubbles rose to the surface and popped, stamped out by the rain bombarding down from the sky. King narrowly avoided a boot to the jaw, as the guy lashed out in his final death throes, swinging blind in an attempt to make it out alive.

The world would be fading for him...

The guy's free arm shot out of the water all of a sudden, wrapping around King's throat in turn. He felt the cold fingers around his neck, strong and determined, fighting for life.

He didn't budge an inch.

He picked up the guy's head underwater and smashed it against the road — once, twice, three times, then four.

The last of the air spilled from the man's lungs and the fingers around King's throat went resolutely limp.

King slammed the back of the man's skull into the hard surface of the road three more times, even though the guy had already drowned. If he wasn't dead already, he would be shortly.

Even in the murky darkness, he saw a cloud of red spread out from the man's head. It hung in the rainwater for a second before the current washed it away, trickling downhill.

King released the corpse and slumped onto his rear in the newly-formed river.

The threat had dissipated.

He almost couldn't believe it.

He had succeeded.

He couldn't ascertain exactly how long he spent in the middle of the village, sitting immobile as the torrential downpour attacked him with sheet after sheet of intense rain. He let the storm wash away everything that had happened since he'd crossed the border from San Diego into Tijuana.

He couldn't comprehend the fact that it had all begun less than forty-eight hours earlier.

Two days of carnage. Two days of bloodshed. The bodies and the madness had all blurred together into a kaleidoscope of destruction. He couldn't ascribe an exact number to the amount of people he had killed. The whirlwind shocked him as he looked back on it. He could only realise the extent of what he had achieved when he reached the operation's conclusion.

And he had just reached it.

Sitting in the dark, up to his waist in rainwater, attacked by Mother Nature, breathing through his mouth out of necessity due to his swollen mess of a nose, he allowed himself a smile.

Over and over again for the past two days, he thought he'd drawn his final breath.

Each time, he'd proven himself wrong.

Somehow, he'd pushed through the adversity.

And he wouldn't have preferred it any other way.

He couldn't imagine conducting the same operation with a unit of fellow operatives. They would have weighed him down, questioned every decision, resisted heading directly into Guatemala and throwing themselves to the wolves.

Now, he realised that he could do what others dared not to.

And he was more than willing to.

As long as he did it alone.

Now that the major threat had vanished, and the heightened level of awareness that King had been running off for the last two days had begun to fade away, the pain began to take over.

His nose hurt like nothing he'd ever experienced. Coupled with the searing pain in his stomach and the needling fingers of ice in his shoulder, he slumped into a semi-conscious state, riding out the vicious waves of discomfort.

He barely even noticed the hands looping under his armpits and hauling him to his feet.

Eyes half-closed, he made out a shape that seemed vaguely familiar.

Whoever was helping him didn't seem to have hostile intentions.

He closed his eyes and let them guide him to destinations unknown.

# 52

King propped himself up on the thin straw mattress, allowing himself a better view outside. That came rather easily, as the entire front portion of the house he rested in was missing.

The husband and wife that he had saved earlier had scooped him up out of the elements, carting him back into their humble abode. The woman had sensed King overheating from his injuries and pressed a cool towel to his forehead, providing some relief from the overbearing humidity.

Then they let him be, wordlessly recognising that he still had a lot to process. The spare mattress they'd brought out into the kitchen provided a welcome respite from the storm, and it gave him a front-row view to the chaos outside.

An hour later, the storm passed. The deafening cacophony of falling rain faded into nothingness, replaced by the sound of the trickling streams of water running off the jungle canopies surrounding the village. King let the calm soothe his mind, ignoring the dead body still resting out the front of the property.

He would deal with that later.

Right now, he needed to recuperate.

Detox his brain from the horrors he'd experienced first-hand.

He hadn't spent long enough in the field to be affected by the post-traumatic stress disorder that wracked his nation's military, but something told him that what had unfolded in Tijuana and Guatemala would linger on his mind for years to come. It had been his first taste of madness, his first rush of unimaginable violence and raw instinct.

Something about it had also sucked him in.

He could feel the addiction taking hold. He was self-aware enough to recognise that he was blessed by unnatural reaction speed. Reflecting on all the violent encounters he'd been part of over the last two days, he understood that the level of clarity he experienced in the heat of the moment was a rare gift.

He felt *different* when it came down to life or death.

He felt like he could thrive.

He felt hooked on the process.

There was all the time in the world to assess whether that made him a psychopath at a later date. For now, he settled onto the mattress properly and closed his eyes, drifting into a restless sleep. Over and over again throughout the night he jolted awake, seized either by a fresh wave of pain from his nose or an uncomfortable dream in which he focused on the faces of the men he had killed.

Hours later, the hooting of tropical birds woke him at first light. He blinked once, rolled over, and came face-to-face with the man who had helped him inside the previous night.

King jolted upright, shocked by the man's silent presence. He looked to be in his early fifties, with a widow's peak hairline and rough skin coating his cheeks from years spent outdoors. His nails were cracked and his fingers hardened from manual labour work. Despite the gritty exterior, his eyes were kind, studying King more out of interest than anything malicious. He had been squatting bare-footed on the other side of the kitchen for what must have been some time, because King hadn't heard a peep from him since he'd stirred.

'Thank you for helping me,' King said, drawing out his words, unsure if he was falling on deaf ears.

The man smiled warmly and laughed. 'I speak English just fine. I was raised by parents fluent in the language, and they made sure to teach me to pass it onto my next of kin, too. You do not need to treat me like a fool.'

King nodded. 'Sorry.'

'That is not something to be sorry for,' the man said. 'What you should be sorry for is what you did to my house. That is a little worse, sir.'

King's gaze rolled across to the gaping hole in the front of the hut. 'Yeah. That's worse. Sorry about that, too.'

'It seems like you saved my life though,' the man said. 'And my wife's. And my young boy's. So this is a small price to pay. Were these men—?' He gestured outside, to the body on their lawn and to the other two dead men lying somewhere out of sight.

King nodded. 'They were going to kill you.'

'May I ask why? I can't think of what I have done to anger anyone.'

King shook his head, considering the horror of what Ramos had almost achieved. A senseless massacre would have unfolded, simply for the purpose of crushing his adversary's spirit. 'Let's not talk about that. It had nothing to do with you. The threat's gone.'

'Will there be more?'

'No,' King said.

He considered the handful of Ramos' men that he had left in the ruins the previous night. They had been combing through Piedras Negras when he'd abandoned them in pursuit of their boss.

He wondered if they would spell trouble...

He highly doubted it. There couldn't have been more than three men left alive in the ancient city. They were now leaderless, their ranks decimated by a single enemy. They would have returned to the warehouse to find it abandoned, their boss slaughtered in one of the offices and the rest of their force nowhere to be found.

They were ex-Army soldiers, the lot of them. Hired guns. In the game for a paycheque, a cheque signed on the dotted line with blood.

They would scatter at the first sign of adversity.

King guessed they were probably a dozen miles away from the Mexico-Guatemala border by now.

The war between the drug cartels would go on. That much was certain. King couldn't take down a multi-billion dollar industry on his own.

But he had single-handedly removed a radical new arm of the business.

There was satisfaction to be had in that accomplishment.

But not yet.

He needed to get the hell out of Guatemala first.

'And who are you?' the man said, staring at King with his head cocked to one side like a scientist observing a lab experiment.

'Just someone trying to lend a helping hand.'

'This is your job?'

King nodded.

'How long have you been doing this?'

'About two days.'

The man furrowed his brow, confused by the statement.

King didn't want to lie.

'You are a soldier?' the man said.

'Of sorts.'

'You like what you do?'

King flashed a glance across at the guy. 'Is this a counselling session?'

The man smiled again. 'I am always curious to hear from people with far different lives to mine. It's a valuable experience. Don't you agree?'

'I guess so.'

'So — do you enjoy it?'

'I don't get much time to think about that, man. Things happen too fast. It's not fun, if that's what you're asking me.'

'That is not what I'm asking you.'

King understood. Deep down in his core, did he feel like he had a purpose? Did he feel like he was doing good?

'Yeah,' he admitted. 'Yeah, I do like it. If I was doing anything else I'd feel like my time was being wasted.'

'I see.'

'What about you?' King said. 'What do you do?'

'I'm a gardener,' the man said. 'One of the airfields near here pays me to tend to their grounds. It is an honest job.'

'Who owns the airfields?'

'I prefer not to know,' the man said. 'The ownership changes with each passing week. Lots of conflict, lots of back-stabbing. Squatters, illegal settlers, drug runners. I mow the lawns and keep my head down. It is a simple existence.'

'Sounds pleasant,' King said.

'It is. I am trying to raise my boy to have better opportunities, though. The English my parents taught me did not go as far as I thought it would.'

'I'm going to wire you money to fix your house,' King said. 'It's the least I can do.'

'I would be humbled if you chose to do so.'

'You have a bank here?'

'There is a small branch in town. We have an account. There is not much in there, to be honest. We get by, though.'

'Make sure to get me your account details,' King said. 'I'll make sure you get taken care of.'

The man bowed his head. 'Thank you.'

'There's just one thing I need from you.'

'Oh?'

'A satellite phone.'

'I'm afraid…' the man began.

'Don't worry. I didn't think you would have one. But would there by anywhere in town that might be able to lend you one for twenty minutes? It's seriously important that I make a call.'

'I shall see what I can find, sir.'

The man rose to his feet and strode out the front of the hut, ignoring the bodies in the street. King imagined that either local or federal police would arrive in some capacity over the next few days. This section of Guatemala was barren in regards to law enforcement, but he couldn't imagine that such bloodshed could take place in plain view of a rural village and go unnoticed.

Two figures materialised in the bedroom doorway as soon as the man had left — the wife and child.

'Hello,' King said with a smile.

'Hello,' the woman said back. 'I'm going to cook something. Want a plate?'

'I'd like that very much.'

With the little boy trailing in tow, she set about preparing a dish made with sun-dried fish and a smattering of spices. King got to his feet and watched her cook with measured grace, silently pondering just how unbelievable his life had become in such a short period of time.

Two weeks ago, he'd woken up in Wyoming without a hint of knowledge as to who Lars Crawford was.

Now he was here.

# 53

The man returned less than half an hour later with a worn-out Garmin satellite phone, scratched and faded from years of use in the humid tropical conditions. King stared down at the device in disbelief, turning it over in his hand.

'It was that easy?' he said.

'There is no reception out here,' the man said. 'The grocery store needs one to communicate with their supplier and co-ordinate new deliveries. They are certainly expensive. I was told that I would be beaten to within an inch of my life if I did not return it promptly.'

'Understood,' King said.

He stepped out of the hut, noting the two bodies scattered across the lawn and the third man lying pale and motionless in the middle of the street. He watched locals emerging from their huts as daylight speared through the sky and the sun began to rise over the treetops, steaming and cooking the rainwater left over from the previous night.

To King's surprise, they barely looked twice at the dead men before going about their duties, heading off into the village centre or the neighbouring airfield without a shred of concern.

He wondered just how intense the cartel infighting was in this region to result in a response like that. The trio of corpses seemed like an inconvenience to the villagers, instead of something to raise an alarm about.

They ignored King similarly.

He dialled a number off the top of his head and waited a worryingly long amount of time for the call to be answered. He pictured Lars staring at his phone, confused as to why an unknown number was calling a top-secret military phone.

Finally, he answered.

He didn't say a word, patiently waiting for whoever was on the other end of the line to respond.

'Hey, buddy,' King said, his nose stuffy and sealed from the broken septum.

'Unbelievable…' Lars muttered.

'Where are you?'

'At a military base,' Lars said. 'Waiting for your call. If we didn't hear from you in the next eight hours, we were sending a SEAL team in.'

'Don't bother,' King said. 'But seeing that you're ready to go, I'd appreciate if you come pick me up.'

'Where are *you?*'

'Near Piedras Negras. There's an airfield near here, apparently. Occupied by illegal settlers. I'm sure you can find it if you look hard enough.'

'Any more detail than that?'

'No,' King said. 'That's on you. I got the job done.'

Lars stayed quiet for some time.

'What happened?' he finally said. 'If you did things that you don't want on the record, I suggest you keep your mouth shut about them. I'm required by contract to report everything you give me to my superiors.'

'Tell them everything,' King said. 'I killed Ramos, and over a dozen of his men. His organisation was already hurting, but that was the nail in the coffin. I imagine they would have fallen apart even without my involvement, but I made sure that whoever's left will go scurrying back to wherever they came from.'

'Was it a processing facility?'

'Yes.'

'Cocaine?'

'Yes.'

'Are you sure Ramos is dead, or is it speculation? Did you see the body?'

'I sent half his brains across the floor. He's as dead as dead can be.'

Lars exhaled loudly, letting out the breath that he'd been holding since he first answered the call. 'Do you have proof?'

'Send a team to the last location you found Ramos' ping. You'll find his corpse. And a few more to go with it.'

'All affiliated with Ramos?'

'Yes.'

'If we send a team in to verify, I don't want dead civilians turning up that can be traced back to you. You can promise me that no-one got caught in the crossfire?'

'Not by my hand. I worked clean. I only killed people who were coming after me in the first place.'

'Good fucking work, King. I'll find that airfield you spoke of — whatever it takes. I'll be in Guatemala mid-afternoon, as long as we get wheels up here in the next few minutes. You in any danger?'

'No,' King said. 'That's been dealt with.'

'I'll be honest, I doubted that I would be talking to you right now.'

'I know. I could tell from the way you signed off the last call. You thought you'd spoken your last words to a maniac.'

'I won't deny that...'

He trailed off, deep in thought about something.

'What is it?' King said after a few beats of silence.

'Do you realise what you've done?' Lars said. 'It's unbelievable. I don't want to jump the gun too early, but we might have something here. We might have a new division.'

'You thought of a name yet?'

'Not yet. Black ops don't worry too much about official procedures.'

'Call it Black Force.'

Lars paused. 'That sounds ridiculous.'

'If it's not official, then who cares what we call it,' King said, smirking. 'I feel like it'll stick.'

'Black Force...' Lars said. 'Not bad. Maybe.'

'Now stop masturbating over what we've achieved and get your ass to Guatemala,' King said. 'And bring a fucking doctor, if you can. My nose is a real mess.'

'Broken?'

'Badly.'

'Be there soon. Make sure you're at this airfield you're speaking about at two in the afternoon local time. We'll find it when we're in the air.'

'Got it.'

'And well done, you crazy bastard.'

King hung up, handing the phone back to the Guatemalan man who had emerged from his hut to inquire about the phone. The man nodded his respect and took the Garmin device back, sliding it into his pocket. He treated it like a precious artefact, to be protected at all costs.

'Was that the people you work for?' the man said.

King nodded. 'They'll be landing at the airfield you mentioned later this afternoon.'

The man sucked in air sharply through clenched teeth. 'I do not think that is a good idea, sir.'

'Why's that?'

'The settlers who currently own the airstrip will not appreciate an unannounced arrival.'

King raised an eyebrow. 'I'll make them listen.'

'I do not think this is smart, sir. They might retaliate against the villagers once you are gone.'

King nodded. 'Maybe the high road, then.'

'The high road sounds like a good idea.'

# 54

As the sun passed its peak in the sky and began to descend towards the opposite horizon, signalling that the time had ticked past midday, King gestured to the man — who had introduced himself as Oscar — that it was time to head to the airfield.

It was unfathomable that the region had been riddled by a storm less than twelve hours ago. Most of the rainwater had run down the sloping ground, trailing away into parts unknown. The rest had evaporated in the scorching heat. King winced with discomfort as his damp clothes were soaked with sweat almost immediately. Even moving in this climate spelled disaster for keeping clean.

Oscar had no car, so they set off on foot for the airfield. The man knew exactly where he was headed, nodding to passersby with warm smiles as they strode through the village to its outskirts. There was no sign of the bodies from the night before. King had spent the morning recuperating in Oscar's hut, and he hadn't seen what happened to them.

'Where are the dead?' he said softly as they reached the village limits and pressed into the jungle.

'Dragged away to somewhere unseen. The villagers will hand them over to the police when they decide to make their way over here. Who knows how long that will take...'

'They weren't shocked by what happened?'

Oscar shrugged. 'A side effect of living so close to the border. Drugs are everything out here. Death is not rare. We see it all the time. That said, it does not usually happen in the middle of our neighbourhood. Usually we just stumble across the bodies on the outskirts of our territory. And there are a lot of them.'

'Sounds grim.'

'That is the price we pay for living here.'

'You ever thought about moving? Your English is exceptional. I'm sure you have plenty of opportunities if you went looking.'

'The world is too scary,' Oscar said, smirking at the irony. 'I like my life. It's stable and simple. I like gardening. Maybe my boy will have more nerve than me.'

'I think you have a hell of a lot of nerve, Oscar.'

'Thank you, Mr...?'

'King.'

'Cool name.'

'I don't mind it myself, either.'

'Your nose looks horrendous,' Oscar noted, staring at King's face.

'I'm trying to keep my mind off it.'

'Of course you are. It looks like there's a balloon on your face!'

King grunted in frustration and kept his eyes squarely on the road ahead. He pressed down the waves of throbbing and mind-numbing pain that rolled over him as he inadvertently focused on the injury. 'How much further?'

'Not far.'

'What's the time?'

'Almost two.'

King nodded in satisfaction. If he and Lars' estimates were correct, the two should be reunited shortly.

'How are you going to handle the settlers?' Oscar said.

King tapped the back of his pants, checking that the bundle of rolled-up quetzals were still firmly in place. They were still probably soaking wet, but in the end cash was cash. 'I'll think of something.'

The settlers turned out to be two Latino-looking men covered in tattoos from head to toe, openly carrying Kalashnikov assault rifles and striding across the tarmac to meet the newcomers. They had exited a small bungalow on the other side of a cracked runway that had seemingly been dumped in the middle of the jungle, just large enough to allow a sizeable aircraft to land and take off.

Sparse, but efficient.

'Who is this, Oscar?' one of the men barked.

They were either affiliated with one of the cartels in the region, or they simply acted as a slave to the highest bidder, importing raw product from the Andes and distributing it to the production facilities out this way for a marked-up price.

Hopefully dollar signs would sway them either way.

If not, he would be more than ready to add another two tally marks to the total body count.

But he didn't imagine that would bode well for Oscar's wellbeing, so he kept his mouth shut and played along.

'A friend of mine,' Oscar said. 'He has a plane heading here to pick him up. I would like you to allow them to land on your runway.'

'And why the fuck would we do that?'

'As a professional courtesy, I would hope.'

'Fuck, no,' the second man said, spitting a glob of

chewing tobacco on the grass at their feet. 'This location is for business-only. We don't cut that shit. No favours. We pay you good money to keep the place clean, bitch.'

King reached behind him, searching for his back pocket in an attempt to calm the situation down.

He should have thought harder about what that might look like.

The two Kalashnikov barrels swung in his direction, and for a brief moment he looked death in the face.

'Easy, boys,' he said quietly. 'I'm getting you some money.'

The first man cackled, loud enough to echo off the surrounding trees. 'American! What are you doing out here, gringo?'

'I got lost,' King said. 'Now let me pay you and go about my business, okay?'

'How much?'

King handed over the entire wad of bills — enough money to keep the men going for a month, minimum. They tried not to let their excitement show, masking it with disinterest, but King could tell they were excited by the way they split the bills between them and tucked them into the deep pockets of their cargo shorts with shaking hands.

'Whatever, gringo,' the first guy said. 'Just make it quick. How long until your man's here?'

'Any moment now,' King said.

The second guy widened his eyes. 'Any moment?! The fuck would you have done if we said no? Landed anyway?'

'Let's not go there. Just be happy everything worked out this way.'

Neither of them knew how to react to the vaguely-disguised threat. Their pockets full of King's cash, they shifted uncomfortably and cast dark looks in his direction.

He didn't care.

Hateful glares hurt a whole lot less than a fistfight.

The rumbling of an approaching aircraft materialised only a few minutes later, time which King spent uncomfortably shifting from foot to foot in an awkward waiting game.

The private jet dipped below the tree line a moment after that.

It was a white Gulfstream G550, worth tens of millions of dollars and complete with potholed windows and close to a hundred-foot wingspan. Oscar and the two settlers stared with gaping mouths at the plane as it touched down on the uneven surface of the runway with pinpoint precision.

King imagined they had never seen anything like it. They were no doubt used to rattling single-seater biplanes touching down, unloading a mountain of bunched-up coca leaves, and taking off back into the scorching Guatemalan sky in a brazen attempt to avoid detection.

This was a different class of aircraft.

One of the settlers turned to King. 'Think I'm gonna need more money, gringo. You seem to have enough of it.'

King shot him a look that would have made anyone else weak at the knees. 'That's all you're getting. Shut up and know your place. One more word and I'll do something about it.'

The pair's confrontational nature flared up, then settled not long after that. One of the men abandoned the tough-guy demeanour, and his friend followed suit. King nodded to each of them in turn, as if to say *good call.*

He turned to Oscar. The man extended a hand, scarred and chipped from years of hard labour. King shook it.

'Thanks for pulling me out of the storm,' he said.

'Thank you for... you know,' Oscar said, his eyes filled with warmth.

King nodded.

He knew.

He turned away from the trio and hurried over to the Gulfstream, which had come to a halt at the very precipice of the runway's far edge. Another few hundred feet and the nose would have crushed against the tree line. It had been an uncomfortably tight landing.

The stairs were already descending towards the tarmac. King leapt up onto them, taking them three at a time. Before any of the passengers within had time to exit the aircraft and greet him on the tarmac, he had ducked into the luxurious interior and locked eyes with the two men inside the Gulfstream.

Lars Crawford. And an elderly man who appeared to be a doctor.

Before either of them had a chance to say anything, King said, 'Wheels up. Let's get the fuck out of Guatemala.'

# 55

The air-conditioned interior of the Gulfstream coupled with the supple leather of the rotating seat combined to form the most pleasurable experience of King's life.

For the first time in the last two days, he stopped sweating. He took a shower in the G550's private bathroom, washing away the dirt and grease and blood and perspiration caked thick over his skin. It seemed the rainwater from the previous night hadn't taken care of it after all. He scrubbed himself down with an exfoliating sponge, lathering it up with soap to work his body clean.

Feeling a hundred times better than when he'd first stepped foot on the aircraft, he stepped back out into the cabin dressed in a simple T-shirt and jeans that Lars had provided.

The doctor set to work on his nose, first dabbing it with antiseptic to prevent infection.

'This next part's going to hurt like hell,' the man said, wincing prematurely as he did so.

'Try me,' King said.

He shouldn't have said it. The doctor set his bones back into place in excruciating fashion. The pain wobbled his vision, threatening to force him down into the pit of unconsciousness. He gasped and gripped the corners of his seat with white knuckles.

'Ohhhh...' he muttered through clenched teeth as the elderly man finally forced the broken septum back to its natural alignment. He taped the nose into place with thick slivers of bandages that acted as pincers, holding the broken mess together until it naturally mended of its own accord.

Reeling from the agony but satisfied that the hardest part was in the past, King leant back against the soft headrest and stomached a wince.

Then he sat up to make eye contact with Lars.

'How do you feel?' the man said finally.

It was the first words they had spoken to each other since becoming re-acquainted. Before, King had wordlessly moved through to the bathroom. Lars had seemed to recognise his state and let him be. Now, as they reached cruising altitude above the jungle and levelled out in the air, they had a chance to reflect on what had happened.

'I've been better,' King said.

'I mean in terms of what happened down there.'

King shrugged. 'It went as well as it could have gone, given the circumstances. I'm alive. Ramos is dead. His men are dead. I'm going to pass you some account details when we get back to the States — I want a few grand wired across. It's the least we can do.'

'For who?'

'A guy who helped me when there was no need to do so. What's the Pentagon saying?'

Lars smirked, trying to hide his excitement but failing. 'They're mightily impressed with what you did. Of course, I told them it was my idea to head straight into Guatemala. You can't get all the credit, can you?'

King laughed. 'You're the tactical genius, after all.'

'I'm still learning how this new role will work,' Lars said. 'I want you to know I'm sorry if I made you second-guess yourself. You seemed to know what you're doing. Maybe the best approach is a hands-off one in future.'

'In future?'

'We've been fully green-lit. Black Force is operational. I don't think you could have had a more successful test run in terms of demonstrating your abilities.'

'Is any of it verified?'

'We've gathered reports of clusters of bodies turning up across Tijuana. They seem to align with your movements. So far, you're at a hundred-percent hit rate.'

'What's that mean?'

'All parties were involved with the cartels in some capacity.'

King furrowed his brow. 'Of course they were. You think I'd go around shooting up civilians?'

'In a world as muddied as the one we operate in, the government needs to be sure. You can't be left unchecked. Make sure your track record is clean for long enough and they'll let you do your own thing. The amount of discretion we receive needs its boundaries.'

'I'm not a psychopath,' King said.

'I know you're not. It's upper management that needs convincing. It's only procedure.'

King shrugged. 'Guess that's understandable.'

'You look like hell,' Lars observed.

'Everyone seems to be saying that lately.'

'Evidence of a job well done, I'd say.'

'And yet I can't help but feel like I achieved nothing.'

'What do you mean?'

'I got a sense of the sheer scale of the cartels. The drug industry — it's madness. I achieved everything I set out to do, eliminated Ramos and his thugs, and I feel like I didn't even make a dent in the Tijuana drug war, let alone the bigger picture.'

'That was never your goal,' Lars said. 'Did you honestly expect to solve all the world's problems in a single operation?'

'I guess not. I thought it would have more of an impact, though.'

'What you did will have an impact. Just not in the areas you can statistically measure. More young kids will make it home from school without getting killed in shootouts. The drug trade is a ruthless business, but Ramos' little push to take over Tijuana took it to new heights. You set the example of what happens to people who try and increase the bloodshed.'

'There's still bloodshed. So much of it that I can't comprehend it.'

'And there always will be. That war won't be won overnight. In fact, I don't know if it will ever be won. There'll always be sociopaths and greedy bastards out there willing to do whatever it takes to earn a dollar. The sooner you accept that, the happier you'll be.'

'So what happens now?' King said.

He realised that his entire future was riding on the answer. He had no home base, nowhere to settle down and start a family. Just the road and the military and the thrill of the fight. If he could do some good along the way, then so be it.

But more than anything, he wanted this rollercoaster to

keep chugging along. He loathed the idea of going back to Delta. Not after what he had just done.

It had been the most stressful, painful, uncomfortable two days of his life...

...and he wouldn't have traded it for anything.

He'd set a goal and destroyed it, eliminating scum of the earth in the process. He thought — perhaps misguidedly — that he'd made the world a slightly better place through his actions.

'Well, we have a unique opportunity here,' Lars said. 'You quietly eliminated an uncontrollable facet of the global drug industry. A single man achieved all that, in a situation that would have proved impossible for a team. If Ramos got the scent of an elite Special Forces *unit* heading for him, he would have disappeared off the face of the earth. He underestimated you, and that was his downfall. People in high places are talking about you already. There's enough interest mounting to keep us busy for the rest of our days. If you're onboard, and you liked the way things ran down there on the ground, then we can line up plenty more operations for you. You'll be compensated massively, as I'm sure you're aware.'

King paused. 'I had no idea about that.'

'Black operations have a staggering budget. If you're in, we'll funnel plenty of that into your personal accounts. For serving your country.'

'That's always a plus.'

'How'd you find working alone?'

'I was born to do it.'

'So you're in?'

'Of course.'

Lars smiled. 'Then let's get to work.'

JASON KING WILL RETURN.

## MORE BOOKS BY MATT ROGERS

### THE JASON KING SERIES

Isolated (Book 1)

Imprisoned (Book 2)

Reloaded (Book 3)

Betrayed (Book 4)

Corrupted (Book 5)

Hunted (Book 6)

### THE JASON KING FILES

Cartel (Book 1)

### THE WILL SLATER SERIES

The Wolf (Book 1) - Coming Soon.

Join the Reader's Group and get a free Jason King book!

Sign up for a free copy of '**HARD IMPACT**'.
Experience one of the most dangerous operations of King's violent career.
Over 150 pages of action-packed insanity in the heart of the Amazon Rainforest.

No spam guaranteed.

Just click here.

## ABOUT THE AUTHOR

Matt Rogers grew up in Melbourne, Australia as a voracious reader, relentlessly devouring thrillers and mysteries in his spare time. Now, he writes full-time. His novels are action-packed and fast-paced. Dive into the Jason King Series to get started with his collection.

Visit his website:

www.mattrogersbooks.com

Visit his Amazon page:

amazon.com/author/mattrogers23

74572425R00203

Made in the USA
Columbia, SC
01 August 2017